ACKNOWLEDGEMENTS

All of my 'First Readers' – A. Long, J Kitch, D Simmonds, J Brazier, D Church, 'flowerchamps',
V O'reilly, H Muir, S Allan, J Davies and RS the Author!
All friends and family for their encouragement
All college friends too numerous to name here!

One

It happens every day about the same time even if the alarm is shut off. Something is in-built in his body that cannot be removed. He wishes he could sidestep this event but it is impossible, he is stuck with it for the rest of his life and that was that.

It always starts when John Deverall wakes up.
No lie-in for a couple of hours or even just a few minutes. Staying asleep is something that you cannot *try* to do because when you are awake you are *awake*! The body is refreshed and ready for the day. The stomach is craving for the full English and the bowel is pressing to purge the remains of last night's curry. The mouth demands to be washed and the stubble spends its last moments connected to the face. But it is the brain – or more correctly the consciousness, the thoughts, memories and desires that cannot be controlled.

Waking up only starts them off.
In normal people the brain starts to plan the day, to organise the future. It makes deals, schemes and plots to get one-up on the office colleagues. It prepares little diversions to keep the staff in their place. It will select the colours and clothes for the day - the shirt, blouse, tie, trousers or skirt. It chooses the socks, stockings and shoes. It also takes care of the day to day ordinary things that the working man, or woman, is confronted with when *their* brain wakes up in the morning.

But not his.
His brain dispensed pain. Not physical - an aspirin wouldn't take that pain away. Once maybe, a few years ago, a whole bottle would dull the pain, but it could not take it away - it only made him more sick and confused because he couldn't sleep and that gave his brain more time to inject even more bad memories.

Stomach pumps and hospitals worried his family and his staff but they all understood. It made his wife leave and that caused more pain and more chapters of bad memories. During that time his brain had a field day. He lost his job and his home but something good came from it all. It was at that time, that he decided to get some measure of control on things. He was left with only his strength, mental and physical, to control this hell which was his life, awake and asleep. He was never going to get rid of the pain but he was not going to let others know that he had it.

This time in the morning always found him lying there and taking it. It was like a punishment that he must succumb to - like a man who knew he was guilty and wanted to be punished. There would be no flinching from the blows or squeals of pain in an attempt to appeal to his torturers sense of pity. There was no escape so he took it.
He lay there in the dark while the pain began to build.

It always started in the dark because he always woke in the dark - no matter what time of year, it was always dark when he woke. And he always took it.

Years ago, the pain was too much and he would cry in his pillow - scream in his pillow - and that was also too much for his wife. It was not a camel's back breaking type of too much, but after years of trying to take more than her share of their grief, she had to leave, so leave she did! Ask him and he would probably not be able to tell you how long she had been gone. Probably after the screaming and before his sobbing stages ended. It was about five years ago.

In the beginning they comforted each other but his pain made him twisted and soon, for her sake, he would grieve best by himself. He would shut her out. This was a time when she needed him the most, but he was out of control. His brain took over and gave him enough grief for the both of them.

The pain for him is still the same but now he can take it without making any noise. The tears, of course, still come every time but that is all you can see. He breathes a little shallower but an observer would only see the tears and not know about the raging sorrow, pain, hatred and loss inside of this man in the dark there in his bed.
It is too early to get up and do anything. His brain has woken him for his morning ritual and all he can do is lie there and take it. He looks at the ceiling there in the dark with tears in his eyes. He grips the bedclothes like he is clinging to a cliff - and he takes it.

His brain sets it up - sets it rolling. The scenes, the memories cannot be stopped. Getting up and pacing around the bedroom does not even make the pictures flicker. Squeezing his eyes as hard as he can, only makes everything sharper. The re-enactment of those terrible times is only slowed, if he tries to ignore it.

That day always starts with that knock.
It was an ordinary knock on the door. It was a sunny day. There was no need to rush because there was nothing out of the ordinary happening. The sounds in the house were normal. The radio and telly were both on - that was annoying sometimes but normal. The smells and aroma of food were good.

Would everything be different if he had not opened the door? If he had just shouted for them to go away, would he be in this pain now? Everything then was in colour. He was sure that he could remember colour then. His eyes should be greeted by the front garden - green - brick path - red – leading to the street – black, but his brain makes him see all of the details now in shades of grey, white and black.

The door was knocked by big men in suits - grey - uniformed police behind them - grey - neighbours on the footpath - grey - police cars with their grey flashing lights grey - grey - grey.

They were all looking down this huge funnel, everything widened out from him, he was at the base of the funnel and they were all looking so shocked. Hands to mouths, some crying and supporting others with weakening legs. There is no sound. There is only a tingling feeling on the face and the dry feeling in the mouth. His brain is very good at creating the feelings in these nightmares.

He cannot remember ever hearing that other people *feel* things in their dreams. His eyes dart here and there - cars - grass - people - windows - more people - more police - suited police - grave faces - policeman talking, asking his name - holding Helen's school bag - grey suited policeman's eyes - sorrow - terror - last grasp at possibility of mistake.

No mistake.
Life is over.

Everything from then on is grey and there is no light in his life anymore - only pain to be endured in the dark hours in bed before he goes to work.

Helen was their only child. Helen was their life - the little life that he shared with his wife Naomi. Helen was theirs and should have been their joy forever. They made her and she was the driving force in their lives. She also made them. She was the focus for the love they had for each other, she made them a family. These memories were supposed to be good and bring a smile to his face and a comfort to his soul but his brain is clever. It knows that memories of what you don't have, what you have lost and will never have again but you *could* have had, are painful - the most painful.

The school bag was empty. He remembered how concerned he was that her things were lost. What a foolish thought. They all greyly moved to the lounge and the telly was turned off. The radio was turned off. Officers everywhere and the outside world was shut out as the door closed - grey officer attending. Grey suited officer was speaking in low tones and every word was not real.

'Taken from school.'
'Body was found.'
'Woods. Hospital. Morgue.'
'Sorry for your loss.'

My loss? Our loss? The whole world is now at a loss. Helen was the sun, the moon, the stars, the very foundation of our earth and we won't to be able to live anymore. Hold on to something everybody because the tremors will be starting soon - but it's not like that. The grief-stricken parents stand alone at the end of that funnel - none of this is happening to anyone else. They have the chance to hold *their* children a little tighter because of this loss. There but for the grace of God, eh?
Grace of God - what God? This is where it all starts to come apart. You have to start with God because he is at the top. How can there be a God if he doesn't allow a little girl with such a shiny soul to reach the age of ten.

All of this is fast thinking - fast thought - the officer said something –
'murdered.'

Oh, there goes the breath, the stomach, the bowels and bladder. The visions that are conjured up, the grimy scenes and her little eyes and skin seeing and feeling it all until it is all too much and eternal sleep takes over.

John Deverall's ears prick up, he has a new hunger for details.
He has to know what happened. To the brain these are important. They need to be stored away for future reference. These little snippets of horror help to increase the pain level.

Helen was taken from outside her school by a young man. Within the space of one hour, he had taken her to nearby woods and killed her. That is the simple explanation. There was really no need for any more. One moment she was alive and had a future. She is now dead and her future is gone. Not on hold - just gone. Simple.

There was no need for a lengthy search. No need for an appeal to the media. No time. Helen had no more time. She was immediately identified and rushed to the hospital where she was pronounced dead on arrival only forty-five minutes ago. He remembers thinking - shit - I only missed her by less than an hour. What a short space of time. Like missing a bus. Coming in to the cinema late. Not being on time for dinner. Hey - another bus will be along shortly, you'll get where you are going, someone will let you know how the film started, you will get your meal. Forty-five minutes - shit - you are not going to *die*, like Helen.

But it is never that simple, is it? It all came out in the papers over the following weeks. No matter how much those good people around them tried they could not shield them from the gruesome details. Every inch of the murder was set before them in the press, on the telly, on the radio. It was everywhere. She was murdered - yes - but that was the *last* thing that happened to her.
She was raped, tortured, bitten, burned and then brutally murdered. Strangled to death.

Oh, his brain loved this. This did cause a great deal of pain and it made him grip the bedclothes even tighter. He would occasionally hold his breath and lets it go in huge gasps. This hurts but it is not over.

There is a slight hint of light behind the curtains and the alarm clock is nearing its programmed time. Like a seasoned performer the timing of the big scene is of the utmost importance. The time is now and his brain prepares the ground. He knows it is coming but there is nothing he can do about it. It comes every morning and a residue of it lingers throughout the day until he falls asleep again at night - when it is late and of course, dark.

Now John becomes the observer and because of all of the media coverage, he knows every inch of the scene in the woods.

Helen is thrown to the ground. In his dream, he is standing there, he screams for her to put up a struggle.
"Fight girl fight for your life!"
Stunned, she does not fight, her eyes are open wide in terror and she cries a pitiful cry. "Please" she says – "No" she says - but the young man is in a frenzy and he is ripping at her clothes.
There is a different cry from her when he rapes her.
A cry of pain. Until that moment the greatest pain she ever had was when she fell from her bike. A child should never know this pain.

Like Scrooge, John is powerless to intervene, nevertheless, there in the dark he holds out his hand to help.

The body of the young man arches and his whole attitude to the little girl changes. He tries to soothe her for a moment and for that moment it seems that he couldn't possibly hurt her any more. There is an air of compassion about him but Helen is weeping loudly and he cannot keep her quiet.
Here it comes, the brain is ready, every time this hurts more but he endures it every time.

Helen says just one word and it changes the entire course of events.
If she had just kept her mouth shut, she might be alive today.
There is a silence in the woods. The sort of silence that waits for the wrong word to be spoken, in a crowd, on a bus, you speak fractionally after this silence and everyone hears you.
Helen is sobbing and she calls out … "Daddy."

Everything changes.

The young man in a flash realises that he has gone too far and for him to survive, this girl must not be allowed to speak to anyone … ever! He uses a handkerchief to gag her and that gives him a feeling of power. He slaps her and he gains more power. He has to think about this and he pulls a packet of cigarettes from his pocket and lights one up. He slaps her again - more power. Now a punch and another. Somehow, he is thinking that if he does this enough the job might be done, but there is, at the back of his mind, the realisation that this will *not* be enough.

Helen is unconscious and hitting her gives him no more power. With his cigarette he burns her leg until she shrieks awake.

This is new. This is powerful. This continues.

John must stand there, powerless, until the young man makes his decision. This is the moment that John looks for. If he can get past this moment, he will survive another day. If he can watch his daughter die - he might live.

The young man takes both hands and grips Helen's neck and he squeezes. He squeezes so hard that her necklace is driven into her skin. Screams and shouts rise from her father, but no one hears. No real noise is made. Tears are streaming down his opened eyes as he wrenches the bedclothes. In reality all that could be heard at the killing ground was a shuffling of leaves as Helen convulsed towards her death. A passer-by would have thought it to be an animal, a bird, a blackbird or thrush. There were no animals in that vicinity.

Animals have a thing about death - they know when it is coming and they get the hell out of the way. They hide and stay silent.

The young man is gone now leaving the lifeless, crushed, abused and battered body of an angel. From his bed John Deverall looks down at his daughter in that grey wood, lying there in all shades of grey and he knows that her cry for him was never heard. Her cry for him was the cause of her death. He would never forgive himself for not being able to use his immense strength and bravery to save her.

His brain is finished now, at least for the moment. It has taken him to the edge of insanity and left him there on the brink. Too far and the torment would be useless. That is far enough for the moment. He uncurls his fingers from the tortured bedclothes. The alarm goes off and he shuts it down. Now he can think about the day, now he can have a shower and wash off the sweat and the tears.

Now John Deverall can go to work.

* * *

Drew Treevill was a tyre fitter. He tried very hard all day long to put his mind into his work but it was impossible. He was surrounded by four burly guys who constantly roughed around with each other and always made fun of him because *he* could not match their strength or stupidity. They were foul mouthed and they didn't care who heard them. They would leer at the women who brought their cars in for tyres, batteries and exhausts. It always amazed him how many times this sort of approach actually worked. One fitter had a tally sheet marked up on the wall in exhaust repair paint and his score was eight! They were disgusting, their women were disgusting, their lives were disgusting but he dare not let his disgust for them ever show.

Drew, like every down-trodden victim, kept himself down there for an easy life. If he could get through the day, put up with the name calling and the pranks he could skulk away and be rid of them. Then he could be by himself.
But sometimes there are little incidents which send us over the top. We act out of character. A man sees a drowning woman in an icy river and while everyone stands and stares, he plunges in and rescues her. Later we all find that he couldn't even swim. A boy is trapped in a burning building and his granddad defies the flames and rushes to his rescue. These are acts of extreme heroism. If they had not been successful, they would have been seen as stupidity.
Drew was guilty of one act of extreme stupidity.

It was a little thing really. Keith, the tallyman, had taken Drew's heavy leather welding gloves and glued them shut. Drew should have known that there was something amiss because they were all in the canteen after work. They should have been getting ready to go home but they sat there, quiet, waiting.

Drew walked in to a room full of expectation. When he picked up his gloves there was a joyous roar. Keith stood there half trying to hold back his laughter and asked if there was anything wrong. Drew stood there with his glued gloves and strangely he could hear nothing. He could not see the gloves in his hands but he *could* see the whole scene as if he were an outsider.

They were laughing at him not because the incident was funny but because he was pathetic. Their laughter was coming from way back in his life. It was a tip of the iceberg laughing. There was much more than this. They were laughing at the miseries he suffered at school and at home. They were laughing at the disastrous relationships he had with girls, women and other men. They were laughing at him as a human being. This laughter went straight to the centre of him and he – momentarily - lost control.

It was impossible for him to stop what he did next, this extremely stupid thing. His brain had taken over and, as he was outside of the scene at the moment, there seemed to be little in the way of consequences that he should consider. This was a big mistake because these guys were just waiting for a chance like this. This was the moment that their taunts and tricks in the past, had been designed to bring about.
The strong rarely look after the weak – they usually prey on them. These guys had consequences written all over them.

Drew turned and swung his arm holding the gloves at Keith and hit him squarely in the face! Time, for a moment, stopped. The fitters were like a pride of lions that have finally singled out their victim and, as if by telepathy, they all knew exactly what each must do. There was no outward sign of sheer delight from them but it was there. They knew exactly what they were capable of. They had brawled side by side in most of the nightclubs in the town and on the football terraces. The fitters had finally managed to get a violent action out of Drew and they could now react, and after that moment, react they did!

When it was over Drew had been given a good slapping. They dare not use their fists because that might have meant hospital, police or dismissal. Slapping is what it was and it was done with wet rags and lengths of old inner tube. It would not have been so bad if he had been wearing clothes but they stripped him first, laughing all the time. They tied him to a pile of old tyres out the back. They stripped him, slapped him, left him. He could hear them laughing in the distance now, just like they laughed and squealed during his punishment.

It was the manager who cut him free. It was the manager who blamed *him* because he had swung the glove – the gauntlet. It was the manager who told him that if he continued like this he might have to leave. It was the manager who had words with the other fitters and asked them to cool it but he was laughing all of the time with them. It was going to be impossible to stop this treatment because the manager was the worst of the lot.

All the next day Drew worked with tears in his eyes. He tried to avoid the others but they went out of their way to make contact and ridicule and poke fun. They were laughing at his life again. His life was a joke, he had no power over anything. He didn't even have power over himself anymore. As the day lengthened the depth of his misery increased and his brain took over. His brain started to torment him about how inadequate he was. He made promises and started to fantasise. He would work out, build himself up, sign up for some martial arts combat lessons and come back here and wipe the floor with these guys. For a second, he believed it but it didn't last. He was on the downward slope of misery and he could not put the brakes on.

* * *

James could not get on his bus. He was perfectly capable of getting on the bus but there was no room. The bus was full and the door was shut in his face. No room. This was a common problem but it had not happened to him before, he was usually quick enough out of the school gates to get on and get a seat.

It was easy for the driver to close the door because *he* didn't have to walk home in the rain. The bus was full alright but it was full of the kids who had no right to be on it! The driver never checked the passes and never listened to the pleas of the kids who *should* be on the bus. The bus was full, the door was closed, James had to walk. With his head bent down and the drizzle hitting his face he set out to walk home from school. There was no other way. He wasn't happy, in fact he was downright angry. It was dark and wet and late.

The bus ride as usual went all round the houses but as the crow flies James lived only about two miles from his school. He knew all of the alley ways and short cuts but he just didn't want to walk for half and hour. His bag was heavy there was a dinner waiting for him, good stuff on telly and warmth.

All of this didn't matter.
His homework would never get done, he had already had his last meal, he would never see telly again and ... warmth? That was to leave him very soon.

He was passing through the shadows of Eastleigh Towers, round the back, when he met another hapless soul bent against the rain and cold, also taking a shortcut in the opposite direction, hurrying to get home. You could call it home but it was a miserable place. It was a one roomed bed-sit. There were dishes in the sink, papers and magazines on the floor strewn amongst the socks and briefs. It was clearly a bachelor pad of the worst type. A bachelor who had no regard for himself. A bachelor who never had any visitors. The dark and dingy bed-sit belonged to Drew Treevill and he was angry. He hated himself because he was a coward. He was weak. He was hurt and he wanted to get out of the rain and get home.

There should be something which warns us of events which rip through our lives. Volcanoes at least rumble. You can feel the prickle of electricity before lightning strikes. We see it all the time in the movies – the army guys stop and tilt their heads and say "It sure is quiet .... too quiet!" just before all hell breaks loose.
There should be some sort of St. Elmo's fire glowing around evil people who are about to do extremely evil deeds. If that was the case then we could all give them a really wide berth and avoid such earth-shattering trauma.

But that's not the case.
Evil people look normal. You never suspect the guy next door. He looked like an OK guy. The lady in the chip shop? No..... not her!

Poisoned thirty people with her saveloys? Never! Oh yes, she did, but she looked like a normal person. They all do.

The two hapless individuals came together without warning. No rumble or prickle of electricity. Two ordinary *looking* people but there was a demon inside of Drew. It was very close to the surface and it took very little to let it out.

The bump set it off. It was a touching of the shoulders really. Nothing too spectacular. If it had happened on a busy high street, it would not have been out of place. The demon, though, weighed up all the odds instantly. This is a smaller person. I can dominate him. It is dark and there is no-one around. There is no one looking and we are in the dark. Dark and alone. I can control this person. Let me out!

For that instant when the shoulders touched there was a moment, a moment when the universe and the lives of everyone in it hung in the balance. It could continue to plod along in space and we could all live happily ever after or it could swing the other way. The other way was destruction. In that moment words were exchanged. Drew very gruffly muttered under his breath.
"Get out of the way"

Even now there was a chance. Even now, if the right actions were taken and the correct words were spoken there was a chance. There is an etiquette which must be followed but James was too young and did not know the ways of the world yet. He did not know how to treat half crazed, miserable, self-loathing creatures like this.
How could he? Most of us don't know, because we never see them coming in time to get out of the way. He *thought* he could make a smart remark to this adult and get away with it. It was cold and wet and dark, a throw away comment here would probably not provoke any reaction. It came easily to his lips.
"Watch out yourself, you pratt!"
Drew spun and reached and grabbed and held.

The demon was out and it was not about to be contained until it had spent itself completely. Drew was powerless to stop. He was not really there. This was somebody else! This was who Drew wanted to be. Going forward. On the front foot. No retreating. The other person was cowering and holding up his arms. Drew stood tall over his victim. He could feel some pain in his hands as he dropped some heavy blows on the boy's head. It was a new sensation, a pleasant pain that he could endure. This pain was a pain that he liked. The demon really got out now.

James' first sensation was a crunching, piercing pain in his throat. Try as he would he could not make a sound. He wanted to scream with the pain but he only burbled. He was thinking about the pain when he felt the thuds to his head and shoulders. He felt the wet grass come up to his face and fill his nostrils. His arms would not work his legs were bent at a strange angle and there was tremendous pressure on his back. For a few moments he saw the towering side of Eastleigh Towers, the lamp post going straight in to the air. He was moving, being dragged in to a disused lock up garage. No more rain on the face. No smell. He could hear though. He could hear the heavy breathing of the man. He could hear the words that he was muttering.

"Strip ME will you? Slap ME will you? I'll show YOU what I can do. I've got a life too you know. I have feelings you know. You lot are disgusting, all of you. I'm not going to take this anymore. You'll see!"

It was almost unreal. It seemed like a dream to James. Who was he talking to? Was this really happening? It all became very clear what was *going* to happen when he saw Drew pick up a piece of iron from the corner of the garage, something used to change tyres with. It was then that all of his strength came back to him. He raised his arms and tried to struggle to his feet. He caught the first blow on his shoulder and he managed a low howl. As Drew recovered from the first swing and wound up for the next, James lunged and caught a handful of cheek. It pulled Drew's lower eyelid down and gave him a hideous 'phantom of the opera' appearance. His fingernail went deep in to the soft flesh of the cheek under the eye. Blood appeared. No, it did not just appear, it stampeded across Drew's face and it was like a scorpion sting. It completely paralysed him.

He stood there gasping, gaping, bleeding. He was shocked. The demon had left him. The demon that was the misery in his life was gone, was spent. He was no longer driven by that monster. This was the new Drew.

He was now in control. He was the powerful one and a smile grew on his face.

There before him was *his* victim. His first victim. So, this was how it felt. This new feeling must be power. This was good.

Drew lifted the piece of iron over his head and brought it down again on the boy's arms. They lowered. He did it again and the boy died. All the blows after that were not necessary.

To Drew they had a cleansing effect. He had washed away all of his hatred of others right back to his junior school days. Each blow had an empowering effect. He gained strength with every thud and kick. He exhausted himself. He gorged and purged himself. The universe would not continue to plod along. Something was wrong with it, it was a blacker place. There was an evil growing here inside this lockup garage behind a block of flats.

He never passed out but when Drew 'came to' he was cold and in pain. It was the sound of the rain beating on the corrugated iron roof that brought him to his senses. His cheek was swollen and his clothes were covered in the blood of two people. It was still dark and raining even harder. Anyone outside would not see him in the dark, the rain would give him a good excuse to pull something over his head. He stole into the night with his jacket over his head and he kept to the shadows. He managed to get to his bed-sit unseen. He had a deep cut on his cheek and it was very swollen. After a hot bath be double bagged all of the clothes he was wearing that night, even his shoes. For the first time in many months, he gave his room a clean. Finally, he lay down in the dark and stared at the ceiling.

Tomorrow he would call in sick and spin that out until the weekend. Those disgusting bastards would think they knew why and probably understand. They would be laughing all day, probably well after the weekend. He showed them though. Drew was a new man. He had a new power. He was capable of *much* more than any one would ever know. He looked up at the ceiling and smiled.

* * *

Victoria Casey was an exceptional girl. She showed promise in all that she did throughout her entire life. She was smart and always stylish within the reasonable bounds of her parents' means. They were supportive parents and had brought her up well. Now that she was fifteen, she was causing a bit of concern at home but in the dark quiet moments when her parents were alone, they smiled and said that it was natural and they would have to ride out the storm.

She was their only child and they had invested much joy in her for the future. Her mother could actually see her unborn grandchildren. They were not even a twinkle in anyone's eye yet but she could see them. She had pencilled herself in for *all* the baby-sitting jobs that would be needed. Her dad often practised how he would react when the boyfriends would come calling and his favourite scene was when someone would ask for her hand in marriage.

"You are talking about my baby! You want to take my baby away from me? I am going to have to think about this carefully son. This is a big decision for me because you are taking a part of me when she goes. What do I know about *you*? How can I be certain that you are the right one for her? This is a big decision."

He always smiled when he went through this scene in his head but there was a little voice right there at the back that kept telling him that it was deadly serious and he should prepare for it. The decision was really going to be out of his hands in the end and he knew it. In those dark and quiet moments both he and his wife knew that Victoria would make a good choice and be happily married and have kids and mum could baby-sit and dad could build cupboards and help keep their old banger of a car on the road.

At school Victoria was not a person to be too close to only one group of friends. For her there was no clique. She got on well with everybody. She moved through those types of barriers and this made her happy. She was not stunningly popular but a steady soul who was reliable and trustworthy. In fact, she didn't have much time for gossip so people didn't divulge too much to her. She often heard but was rarely interested.

Victoria was on the fringe, not the centre of things. Someone who was at the centre of things was Jackie. Jackie was a year older and full of responsibilities. It was so important to have the latest style and be at all the popular places. She organised parties and was invited to the best of the rest. She tried out all the boys and talked about them afterwards. Jackie was full of joy and hate at the same time. She couldn't live when her boyfriend of late had dumped her. This was, in no small part, due to her broadcasting some of his shortcomings, to the assembled year eleven in the common room at school. When the news reached his ears, she was history!

After she got over that tragedy she went on the offensive and really spread the gossip about him. Truth did not come in to it but gossip from Jackie was gospel.

Vicky and Jackie were like chalk and cheese. They did not mix and they steered different courses. Victoria loathed a confrontation and Jackie knew that many people liked Victoria and she would be a hard target to smear. People would not believe it if she were to sling the dirt about Victoria. Dirt and Victoria did not mix either.

Victoria had all of her life in front of her. It would have been a life to brighten the lives of everyone she encountered. Her children would have been bright and loved. It is sad that they didn't have a chance to see the sun. No doubt their spirits went on to be somebody else but if they only knew what they were missing they would have led a life of sadness. Unfulfilled. Victoria would have made the world a better place there is no doubt. Instead, she briefly made friends with Jackie. Their paths crossed and a light went out in the world.

Jackie organised a disco in the premier night club in the town. She didn't actually organise it, the nightclub, Darby's, sometimes opened their doors to teenagers before the more serious punters started to prowl through the town. That Friday night was such a night and Jackie was organising a group to go. It was always so much better to go as a group. You didn't feel so alone and if you were a girl you didn't look like a tramp. The boys went around in twos, which must be a boy thing but the girls could link arms in lots of eight and ten! Victoria heard that there was a disco on at Darby's and she let it be known that she wanted to go. It was arranged. As simple as that.

There was the usual anticipation, the preparation, the delivery by her dad and the fatherly instructions for behaviour and collection, the queuing and then the lights, the music and the dancing!

There were masses of kids from all the schools in town and Jackie was at the centre of attention as usual. Victoria was with a few friends near the shuttered bar and they were looking over the room. Everyone there was under age and so the bar stayed shuttered. There was security but they were not on their toes because this event wasn't even a warm up for the action to take place later in the evening. They also turned a blind eye to some of the concoctions brought in to the building which were then secretly drunk in the darker corners of the lounge and in the toilets. Sometimes there would be a flurry of activity when a drunk was hustled out in to the street. The drinks would be put away, hidden more cleverly, and everyone would take it as a warning. On this night, for some unexplainable reason, there was more alcohol than usual and the security staff was more lenient.
Jackie was getting very drunk.

The disco ended at eleven o'clock. The club was cleared and the doors were opened to the night shift. The bar was opened and the security staff was on their toes.

It was too late though. The damage was done and fate was now going to take over. The world was going to become a fouler place. A light was about to be extinguished and nothing was going to prevent it.

It is difficult to know when this chain of events was set in to motion. If she hadn't gone to that school maybe. It was not the school's fault. If she had not been so bright and cheery. Perhaps if she had a plain face, sterner parents, if she were more shy? Where do you put the blame? Is there any blame? Should we not just shrug our shoulders and say – Oh well, what will be, will be! Where is the justice in that? You can be the best driver in the world but it is the drunk who kills you. You cannot escape. We don't know what is going to happen. We can't see the evil ones. But they are out there.

Jackie had too much to drink. The night air all in a rush, made matters worse as she left the club. She could do nothing but slump up against a wall and try to recover. Most of her friends were too worried about getting their lifts so they left her there to her own devices. She would be ok, her lift would come and she would be ok. Headache in the morning, a good telling off maybe, but she would be ok.

As Victoria walked by, she was concerned about Jackie so she went over to see if she could help.

"Jackie, where is your lift? Is your dad coming to pick you up?" Victoria had seen Jackie picked up at school by her dad many times.

"He said he would wait for me in the car park in the back..."

Victoria decided to wait with Jackie for a while. She was concerned that she would miss her dad when he pulled up. As the minutes went by it became more difficult to make her mind up what to do. If she had gone at the start she could have been back by now. The crowds seemed to be much thinner now and Jackie seemed more in control of her legs.

"Come on Jack, I'll give you a hand to your lift."

Jackie's dad was furious and much slamming and banging of car doors showed his anger. He thanked Victoria and she started back down the street towards the main road where she could meet her dad.

She was now alone.

*   *   *

David Brenner stood in the dark entrance to the alley way, that led to the refuse area which served the row of neglected shops on an adjoining road. He had been standing there for about an hour, drinking from the whisky bottle at regular intervals. He had a good vantage point there in the shadows. He could see and not be seen. He watched two girls stagger by about ten minutes ago and almost made a move then but his courage was not established yet. Two girls? That would be too much to manage even though one seemed worse the wear for drink.

David was always full of excuses as to why he should not do something. He missed the moment and spent the next ten minutes arguing with himself. He should have taken the chance. Damn! Another missed opportunity. Maybe next time. Definitely next time. Knowing that there would probably not be a next time he could boast to himself like that. He was full of what he would do, knowing that he wouldn't.

When Victoria walked past on her way *back* to the street he was overwhelmed with fear and guilt. He had made a promise to himself that he would take action. How could he miss this opportunity. It was dark. It was deserted. She was a teenager for gods sake. He could manage this. He stepped in to her path.

Victoria was startled and had no time to prepare herself or to resist. He stepped out at the last possible moment and grabbed her by the back of the head with one hand and pressed his other hand over her mouth. He spun her around into the shadows and still holding her head he dragged her down the alley.
There was no sound.

He was panting and she was fighting for air. She could smell the whisky on his breath. She could only hold on to his arm to prevent herself from falling because she was off balance. When they were deep in to the shadows, he threw her to the ground and fell on top of her. With one hand on her throat, he fumbled and tore at her clothes with the other. All the time he looked into her terrified eyes.

She looked in to his and pleaded incoherently through his fingers.

The cold began to grip her body as she lost some of her clothes. The cold also clasped around her heart as she realised what was happening. His first task complete he prepared himself for the second by loosening his belt and trousers. Now he held her like a vice. With his knees he drove her legs apart. Then he spoke.
"If you make a sound, I will kill you."

Her nightmare began. Floods of pain and guilt and horror washed over her for the next few minutes. There in the dirt and refuse of a disgusting world, a flower was crushed. There should have been wailing from witnessing angels to bring this unholy act to a stop. In reality there was nothing but weeping, shuffling and animal grunting. The background noises of the night masked these very well.

When he was finished, he stood over her and he looked down. The girl lay motionless.

He arranged himself and drained the last fiery liquid from the bottle and threw it to the side. Feelings welled up within him. Feelings of power and pride.

He would no longer mock himself for his inability to fulfil his inner boasts. He stood over this broken creature as the victor. He was temporarily free from that primal urge to spend himself. These good feelings were short lived and a feeling of self-preservation took over and he ran.

He ran in to that dark universe-shattering night to join the shadows and attempt to blend in. He must hold back his smile. He must choke down his need to tell and laugh about it. He thought about the consequences now but it was too late. The deed was done. Fate would not be harnessed or diverted. He ran and she heard his footsteps for a short while and then, there was only darkness.

She lay in the hospital bed and thought about the activities of the night. The attack, the rape, the cold and the rescue. Ambulance and police. Loads and loads of police. Questions and statements, notepads and pencils. Sympathy and sympathetic looks from everyone.

Someone said that everything was going to be alright – they said it over and over again while patting her hand as she sobbed. People, all the people, gave her that 'Poor wee thing' look. The hospital suite was a hive of activity. Her flesh was scrubbed and smelled of soap. She had been examined and swabbed. It was all coming back to her now slowly but rushing faster.

Up to that point all of this had been a dream. It had happened to someone else. She could not possibly deserve this. She was helping someone else for god's sake. She had only gone to the disco. How far away from evil can you get?

Scratch the paint girl, it is closer than you think!

The people now came in to recognisable focus and, with a rush, the reality of her situation washed over her. She completely collapsed in upon herself when she focused on her mother and father sitting there on the end of the bed. Her mother was crying of course, but you can never tell what weight of sorrow made her do that. She could cry watching an old movie.

It was her father's tears which meant so much. He was holding them back. He was contorting his face, trying not to let her see that he was destroyed. His face was fighting with an expression that it never had before. It was very uncomfortable for him, but it spoke volumes to Victoria.
She had lost her parents.

She would never be the same, in their eyes, again. It was not her fault but that is the way it is. Where is the justice in that? She broke down and that was the signal for them all to do the same. They let it all out. The police had all of their statements and they were ushered out by the nurses. The nurses left and they closed the ward door behind them.

The family cried their despairing cries but that does not take away their pain. These cries come from deep within the soul and cannot be held back. The cries are not generated by pain, just despair. The sound was a desperate one and those who could walk away did so, shielded their ears, counting themselves lucky.

* * *

It is late at night.
Hospital late. That peculiar lateness that you encounter only in a hospital. Rubber wheels, rubber shoes and echoes, fluorescent lights and warmth. Long corridors mean you can hear the foot traffic long before it arrives and long after it departs. It is always too hot in hospital. Time always goes by to slowly in hospital. It is always difficult to get any sleep.

Too hot, too noisy, too bright for too long.
Victoria lay awake. She had no feelings outside of her emotions and they were in a dreadful mess. She couldn't get to the end of one thought at all. Her brain kept on switching tracks. She kept changing her train of thought because she could see where they were all leading to.

All of her thoughts led to the fact that she had lost her parents.
School would never be the same and it was probable that she would not return.

The people in the town would always know. Her friends would never accept her again as they once did.

Oh, how she missed what she had. It gave her a small gem of amusement to know that she never even tried to get all of these things – they were just there.

Oh, how she missed them.

Then there was that black thought in the hidden blackness of the back of her mind. It was like a dark black disgusting odour in the shadow in the corner. It was in the corner because that is where it was told to stay. It was not wanted. It was bad but it had to be dealt with. It had to be confronted. It peeked out into the light as if it was saying 'Shall we talk about it now? Do you think you have kept me here long enough? Are you strong enough to face me? Here I come.'

This was the one train of thought that would not be derailed. It was like a locomotive on straight shiny tracks. It had noise and emotions and pain. This thought always maggoted its way to the front. It would not be suppressed. It was evil and it brought evil to stay.

She knew that there was a good possibility that she was pregnant.

It kept coming to her brain over and over again. There, inside of her, was the seed from the evil one. She felt like she was harbouring the devil. It was a filth that she couldn't wash away. She could see his face, smell the stench of his breath and hear his guttural voice. This was the father. This was the *Dad*!

Oh, how could such an innocent word which held such trust and love, be attributed to that drunken monster.

Her brain would not give up.

She would nestle the baby but always look upon it as the product of a violent act. For her the child could not be loved for love never was part of the equation which created it. There could only be hate and misery and despair. For the rest of her life. She could not face her parents or her friends. She could not live in the town, or any other, any more. She could hardly bring herself to look in the mirror and a child by that fiend she would always hate.

It was too easy and in a way it was delightful.

The window was easily opened and the cool breeze took away some of the overheating from the ward. It is surprising what you think about at times like these.

For a moment she was worried about closing the window after she was finished but she decided that the ward could use a bit of fresh air anyway. The night was cool and traffic noises distracted her momentarily. She savoured the moment because it was a moment that she had decided upon all by herself. True it was only a minute ago that she made up her mind but now she had a course of action. Now she was determined that this action would solve all of her problems.

She swung her legs over the ledge and sat there. It just took a second. One last look. One last smile. In a funny way she was happy.

Then she was gone.

No scream. No hesitation. After all she didn't want to draw attention to herself.

She was alone in the world. She could only help herself. She didn't want to be talked down from her perch eight floors above the cool green grass below.

* * *

Two

It took John Deverall exactly an hour and a half to get to work. He travelled the same way every day, by foot and by bus. He got the same buses at the same time, there and back. His working day would be a boring one to you and me but that was the way he liked it. Not too much thinking to be done. He liked working on automatic. He didn't like surprises. He liked an ordered life. After the torment of his waking time he would wash and shave, make a frugal breakfast, wash up the dishes and leave them to dry. He would go to the door and open it and then turn to look back around the room.

Looking around the room was always like a punishment. He looked at his life and saw how empty it was. There was no life in this existence. His wife was the last life to go. She had to go because he wouldn't share his pain and she could not stand there and watch the pain devour him. He did not blame her. If *he* could have gone, he would.

There were times when he thought about subtracting himself from the human race but that was the one thing he could not do. There was something inside him, a little voice that he did not often listen to, partly because of the shouting raging sorrow that took up all of his time and partly because it was a little ray of hope for his life and he felt betrayed by any hope. It was a voice that said that someday he might make a difference and there may be a purpose to this life. It was a voice that said, that to kill himself would be a betrayal to Helen.
He still had something to prove to Helen.

Helen would have made the difference. Helen would have curled his lips into a permanent smile. Helen was the brief joy in his life. Helen was gone now and his life was empty. He looked around the ordinary lifeless empty room then closed the door and left.

It was a twenty-minute walk to the bus stop. It was made at the same pace every day no matter what the weather. Habit meant no thinking. Thinking just brought sorrow. On a good day the bus was on time, late meant waiting and thinking, hurting. The bus stop was a place where he had the chance to mix with the outside population of the world. He didn't get much of that. In fact, the people he met on the bus and in the street, the regular people, didn't like to have too much to do with him! John was rarely told about how lovely the day was or if he had ever seen such rain. He seemed to always be in deep thought. He was a dark creature and a powerful one at that. He was best left alone, you could see that at first glance. People who had those thoughts about him, had them confirmed one day when a hapless youth made a late run for the bus. There was plenty of time to make it but he decided to jump the queue. It was thoughtless, it was unfair. This brought about the usual light weight protestation from the rear of the queue but it was not serious and it was duly ignored. People shook their heads and tutted, but none of this from John. He left the line and moved slowly to the front.

This is where it started. On any other day he would not have noticed the thoughtlessness of the lad but something inside him today made him act. Later in his life he could pinpoint this moment as the time of the change. His act was not wild and reckless, but it was planned knowing the outcome. He was always sure of the outcome of his actions – especially these actions. This could get physical.

He stood beside the youth. As the young man began to step up John moved his hand across his chest and eased him back.
"Hey! Leave off!"
"You're out of line." Said slowly, coldly and deliberately. Said with head forward and eyes unblinking and slightly raised. Said with feet spread ready for an assault. Said without menace but with promise of deadly peril.
John followed this comment with "This is not your bus." He then lowered his hand and stood there and stared deep into the young man's eyes.

All the time this was happening the other passengers were boarding the bus. They were doing it faster than usual. They didn't want to get caught up in a brawl in the street. They wanted to get to their seats. They wanted to see what was going to happen from the safety of their ring side seat behind the glass. There were a few seats left when John boarded last, but the young man was so shaken by what might have just happened, that he stood there as the bus doors closed and moved to the next stop. John sat there and let life cover him again. There was still a reluctance for the other passengers to engage him in conversation. They let life cover him as well and the status quo was re-established. Everything was back to square one and everyone was happy with it.

John Deverall was powerful. He came from a powerful background. Not his family but what he had done in life. Very early he decided to become a Royal Marine. The decision was made at school. Everyone said that he was a natural, he would go far in the marines, it was just the job he would do well. In fact, a career in any of the services would have been best for John because there was no possibility of him ever passing any exams. He never studied. He never worked. He caused a tremendous amount of trouble, most of it physical and mostly to other people. When he attacked a member of staff in his final year at secondary school he was asked to leave.

He left and walked into the marines where they accepted him with open arms. His life there was ordered and some of it was painful but he loved it and he responded. He was dependable and hard. The officers knew they had a weapon here. There is not a great deal of need for human weapons in peace time so they did the next best thing and transferred him to the Military Police. This is when John Deverall began to mature.

With the Military Police he was thrust into every sort of situation involving other hard men doing very nasty things to each other. His job was often to separate the fighting factions and then to systematically sort them both out. There were many occasions when the original brawling groups would be so brutally beaten by the peacemakers that they would join forces, forget their differences, and start on the MP's! The military police were a brotherhood. They looked after themselves and each other. To be a military policeman was to be part of a world-wide group. To be in the Royal Marines as well, was very thick icing on the cake.

John liked the order and the timetabling of life in the military. He had no time for brutality but he appreciated that sometimes punishment could be dealt quickly and sharply without the need for paperwork and toffs with university education arguing over points of law in a court-martial. If you gave a private a good smacking for being drunk and disorderly he would remember it and maybe not do it again. Send him to the stockade and he would just become resentful and probably be worse when he got out.

John's second bus was not well populated. It was the bus that led out of town. The people on this bus were rarely regulars. They were seen once and forgotten. They are the type to never hold small conversations. They are real travellers. They are going on longer journeys. They do this rarely and so they want to be left alone and not bothered for great lengths of time by the person sitting across from them. Everyone on this bus seems to have a seat to themselves. No doubt, as the journey nears its end, they will have to double up as the bus fills, but for John the bus is never full. His part of the route only takes thirty minutes. After this half hour he is left at the end of a country lane. It is five hundred yards long. He walks. He has taken these buses and walked this lane for eight years now. Every time he walks the lane, he stops and looks at the impressive building which is at its end. It is big enough to be a country seat. It is functional enough to be county hall. There is a sign. The sign which brings so much understanding of what the building is. What it does. Why it is way out here. Who is at home.

H.M.P. Renkill
Maximum Security

The big gates were meant for deliveries and departures. Everything that went into the prison was checked here. The cons, the visitors, the remands. The food, the furniture, the rubbish. All of the day-to-day stuff of the prison, goes through the big gate. Here there was a special squad of guards who checked everything in and out. There had to be a balance. What went in that gate had to sometime come out of that gate in some form or another. That way you knew what you had inside and what you should keep out. This gate always dealt with the unexpected. The guards controlled the gate and the unexpected they didn't like. They were always a little bit itchy about the unexpected.

John made his way around the side of the building, the tradesmen's entrance if you like. This was where the trusted people were expected. There was a timetable here and only one timekeeper who greeted you with a smile and a kind word. Big difference from the main gate. John went to the door and keyed in the code and swiped his security card. There was a short buzz and the door clicked. He was in, out of the world again. He was inside the order of the prison.

"Morning Sarge" This was from Ted, the early watch orderly. He checked John in on his clipboard and hung it back up on the nail on the wall. John was called 'Sarge' because of his respected rank in the marines. All the officers in the prison knew about John's marine background. They were mostly service men themselves. Some were ex-police, some were ex-army. It was rare to get a civilian in a prison officer uniform.

"Morning Ted, how are the numbers today?"

"We are light again, three down on west wing and two on the east. It is the flu bug, but it is still early, they could go up or down before the shift starts."

John was interested in the number of officers that would call in absent because being short staffed made his job more difficult. If the numbers were too low it meant calling officers from leave or worse, making a temporary transfer from another prison. He had to adjust the numbers so that there was a decent ratio of guards to inmates in case there was any trouble. The moment the 'residents' knew that the guards were under-manned, there could be real trouble and he did not want that. A new face in the ranks would be a liability. This was a maximum-security house and you didn't take chances here.

He moved to the changing rooms where he met the others from his shift. The others were a hard core of hard men also like himself. Over the years these men had evolved as his team. There were some who came and went but these men found something amongst themselves that they needed. They needed to give and to draw from this group. They only met here at work and each one had a need to be part of this whole. They all had a physical presence, a no-nonsense attitude that they wore. They all acknowledged John as he walked in to get changed. They were like holy men ceremoniously robing themselves with vestments while praying. Each was deep in his own prayer-like thoughts. They put on their uniforms. Checked their keys and their badges, leaving behind personal items. No pens, no combs, nothing that could be used as a weapon. No notes, no letters, no photographs or wallets. Nothing to give the residents a clue about where you lived, or who your family was.

It was silent. They were preparing themselves and each knew that this 'job' could get you killed or injured – if you didn't take it seriously. They were focusing on the task in hand. They were about to take charge of some of the most dangerous inmates in the country and they could be putting their lives on the line. Their preparations were over now and the clock was calling them. Now there was eye contact – a little cough and perhaps a joke. 'Made your wills guys?' There would be a nervous laugh but there was a serious mental note made by some, to get on top of paperwork just like that.

"Let's get to the briefing and get stuck into the day" this from John. This from the authority. This from the man who everyone looked to, for strength.

The briefing room was not a welcoming place. It was a room, posters and fliers on the walls, uncomfortable chairs and tables, a few bins and a double barred window with reinforced glass. It was not supposed to be a nice place. You were not meant to dwell there and casually read the literature.

The posters were about safety, caution, regulations. The fliers were about recent Home Office changes to rules. There were rota's, menu's, lists of names of new officers with new duties. There was a timetable and shift hours. You could be very bored by reading the material on these walls. This was a place where information was posted by the officers for the officers. There were three shifts in the prison and it did not pay to forget what you were supposed to do. Ignorance was never a good excuse. You had to keep up with what was posted on the board. It didn't matter that some pinstriped pencil neck in Whitehall decided to change the rules, to make your life with the residents more difficult. You had to read the board and do what you were told. These men were used to that. They knew how to take orders and they didn't like their orders ignored.

Doctor Malcolm Endersley was the chief of the prison. He was a doctor of Psychology, college man, politician and not from the world of his men. His world was meetings, planning, finance, seeing the bigger picture and not immediate action. He trusted his men to take the decisions needed out there on the landings. They were his tools and he wielded them skilfully. He was already in the room as the men filed in led by John. The Chief gave John a fleeting smile and a nod but only the nod was returned. Only the Chief knew that his greeting was returned because their eye contact was different. Anyone else who didn't know these men would have seen nothing. The Chief was glad to see John. He was glad because he knew of the torment that was John's life and for him to show up every day meant that he had not ended it all. He was also relieved to see him because he led these men from the front. John's requests were never ignored or questioned. When John was on the landing the men felt safe and in control. When he was on the landing the residents thought twice about everything. They were more respectful. The men filed in behind John and spread out through the room claiming the uncomfortable chairs. It took a minute to settle. This was work.

"Good morning gentlemen. I would like to draw your attention to the advice from the Home Office concerning transport of prisoners from place of sentencing to prison. As you know these modifications to the rules were drawn up because of the incident last month concerning PO Roxburg at Lewes Crown Court. We, as receiving officers, must inspect the 'restricting implements and their effects' when prisoners are handed over." There was a sneer from many of the seated officers because they all knew the full story.

PO Roxburg was transporting a prisoner, Bill Davies, from court to Renkill Prison. Davies was a vicious animal and had just been sent down for eighteen years for his part in an armed robbery in South London. He and two others robbed a jeweller late on a Saturday afternoon just before Christmas. The shop was full and so was the cash register. Davies carried a sawn-off shotgun to the robbery and would have done less damage had he used it! During the robbery he systematically and brutally beat five of the people in the shop. They were scum and they didn't look at him properly. They got in his way. They were weak and he was strong, powerful and unfeeling. This was how he proved it. He gave the staff and customers a selective going over.

During the trial, the security video was so appalling to watch, that some of the members of the jury looked physically sick when they were made to view it. Davies snarled and grimaced throughout the trial. The robbery had gone dramatically wrong. Davies scared even his accomplices. There was a tactile sense of relief which ran through the crowd and the nation when he was sentenced. The trial was a very big story and made all of the papers. Now the nation was secure once again. The monster has been put away. Even the others sentenced with him felt a sense of freedom because when they were at large Davies was a difficult ally. The judge gave Davies thirteen years for his part in the robbery and a further five to protect the public.

PO Roxburg had the unenviable task of picking up Davies from the holding cell prior to his delivery to Renkill. All of the officers are used to verbal abuse from prisoners but Davies offered very little. He was a man of little words and this should have been a warning to Roxburg.

Davies was angry. He, like all punished people, tried to shift the blame for his predicament. It was society, he was poor and needed money. He had a habit that he could not feed. He had no job. That was the fault of the school that did not teach him or prepare him for life. It was those foolish people in the shop. If they hadn't looked at his face so keenly, he wouldn't have beaten them up. His fellow criminals, they were a pussy bunch, they rolled over on him too easily. He must give a thought for them in the future. It was that judge. He really focused on that judge. He probably had a most comfortable life and was not living in the real world. An extra five years to protect the public? The system. The police, the judge, the jury, the schools, the employers they were all to blame, how could he reach out and make *them* pay?

There, in front of him, was a member of the system. PO Roxburg. Here was a focus, for his hatred and malice. Here was a uniform. This was an avenue for release, and release he did. Davies was secured at the wrists by means of rigid cuffs. When Roxburg came near he swung both hands as one and caught the prison officer high on the temple, stunning him for one moment. Roxburg was not a slight man and he gathered himself, threw his arms around Davies and they both fell to the floor of the holding cell. The outer corridor was occupied by the defence team and the officer of the court. There were two other prison officers attending but the cell seemed to be filled by the two struggling men. It took several seconds to respond but they did.
Davies was overpowered and made to stand up. Roxburg faced him with a shaken smile on his face.
"Was that an escape attempt Billy?"

The cell was now full. Everyone was facing inward and Davies was the only person facing out. He was up against the wall. The story of his life. He faced Roxburg with cold eyes.

"If I wanted to escape, some little shit like you would not stand in my way. I just wanted you to have something before I go. Something you can remember me by."

His head moved. Actually, it was his whole upper body. From his waist to the top of his head moved, like a human lever and it moved quickly. There was no seeing it coming. It just arrived. Davies brought his head forward and shattered the nose of PO Roxburg. It could be heard all the way down the corridor. The cell filled with action again. It was made a great deal more difficult because blood was now everywhere and everything was slippery. Davies was bound even more securely. There was not going to be a recurrence of *this* event if it could be helped. His hands were forced behind him and the locks were tightened. Guards held an arm each and manhandled him from the cell to the waiting vehicle. Roxburg spent the night in casualty. His cheek had been gashed, his nose was shattered and he lost both of his front teeth.

The following day Davies made a formal complaint against Roxburg. His wrists were covered in red marks where his restraints contacted the skin. His upper arms showed bruising from the grip of the guards who took him to the van. Roxburg was the prison officer in charge. Roxburg was responsible. Roxburg was hauled up in front of a disciplinary committee to hear his punishment. He had to stand there with the hospital bandages still crossing his face. He could not speak because his mouth was wired up. He had to listen to the punishment that was meted out by this committee. He had to stand there and take it. Davies sat in his cell and laughed.

Where was the justice in that?
The news spread through the prison service like African drums.
This was the reason for the modifications in the rules concerning the handling of prisoners. This was the reason for the sneers from the prison officers. This was the tail wagging the dog and the guards didn't like it but they sat there and listened all the same. They listened to other items about changes in timetable, sick prisoners, sick guards, releases and arrivals.
Briefing over it was time to go.

There was always a little feeling of dread in the pit of the stomach when it was time to go. You were entering a different world. You were leaving sanity and safety behind. You were moving in to a world of violence that was always just below the surface. Don't scratch that surface too hard. Along with that feeling of dread there was also a thrill. The men knew that they could take care of themselves and they were confident but there was something else. They also knew that as a team, when they faced violence as one, they were invincible. This feeling was the thrill. Being a part of the team was the thrill.

The transformation from outside world to their world of work always starts slowly and imperceptibly. Leave the briefing room and walk down the corridor. Sounds of stout shoes on lino. There is a military squeak to that sound. There is a team feeling to the noise. There is a rhythm. That rhythm was comforting to those men because they knew that each could depend on the other. There were no loners in this business. You led or you followed. You led bravely and you followed without question. The corridors are full of gates. Metal gates with locks. For every gate there is a guard. The advancing group of guards did not need identification. They did not need to know the password. They were coming to take charge and when they loomed in to sight the gates were unlocked and swung open.

The locks made the first prison noise. They clicked and tumbled. The keys on chains. Metal clashing on metal. The second prison noise was full of emotion. If you were there for the first time it brought hopelessness. During your stay it would generate hate. If you worked in the prison, it gave you security. That sound is the sound of the slam and the spring lock as the gate is closed behind you. It was a final sound. It was the punctuation of your sentence. The residents hated the sound. The guards could not live without it. Each of these walking men listened for that sound. They did not turn and wait but they would walk through the gate and listen for it to be closed and locked. It always came and it always pleased. Each small journey from gate to gate was not complete without that sound. The sounds of keys and locks and gates could be heard throughout the prison all the time. There was only a reprieve from these sounds at night. There was a myriad of sounds in the prison and each was at home within the walls. The people there, got used to the sounds and when they occurred out of sequence, mental alarm bells rang!

There was another sense that was continually assaulted.

The sense of smell.

The smell of the prison. It could be touched. It was right out there in your face all the time. As this group of guards walked towards the containment area of the prison the smell started to catch their nostrils. It was a mixture of healthy smells like polish, cleaning fluid and paint, but there was a menacing smell there too. This smell was the core smell that everything else could not shut out. It was always there in some form or another. It was a mixture and each of the components constantly vied to be dominant. It was the smell of sweat and noxious body odour mingled with faeces and urine and cheap tobacco. This was almost the complete prison smell. But there was one other. You had to live this life to know what it was. You needed to *experience* this smell.

It was the smell of fear.

The residents lived in constant fear from each other. They were not like this band of brothers who could depend upon each other. They were prey for each other and those who hunted went hunting every day.

John passed through the final gate, filled his ears with the sounds and took a deep breath of the prison smell. He was home. Now he was happy. He knew this world. He belonged here. John clicked in to automatic and let his work life cover him. Eight hours would pass before he would retrace his steps, retake his buses and find himself in his bed once again. He had eight hours of this bliss before his nightmare life began again. For the first time in his day, John actually smiled.

*   *   *

Drew Treevill planned to stay indoors for at least a week. He phoned work and spoke to the manager saying he was not well, the walk home in the rain had given him a cold. The manager was sympathetic but he also thought that it was a good idea for things to cool down around the workplace. The stripping and slapping incident earlier in the week was not handled very well and if Drew had brought an official complaint, he could see himself being reprimanded and maybe one of the fitters losing his job. He was sympathetic. He told Drew to get well before he came back. Take as much time as he needed. He hoped it would blow over.

Drew only went out after dark because of the gash on his cheek. He did not want too many people to see his injury. Even so the few people he had to see did comment on it.

"That's a nasty cut you have there Drew, you should see the doctor."

That was the last thing he wanted to do.

"How did you get that gash on your cheek?"

He stuck to a story about walking home in the rain and due to poor visibility, he walked into a rose bush. Drew stocked up with the groceries he would need for the week and stayed at home. He thought that when the cut did not look so raw and angry, he would go back to work and pick up the pieces of his miserable life. He made some distant unformed plans to move out of the area for good. Start a new life. A complete change was needed. He didn't need to make these plans. They would soon be made for him.

Every serious event is built upon a series of smaller events and that is what happened now. Event one was the report by James' parents to the police that he was missing. They now sat at home and waited. There was nothing else they could do. All of the usual questions were asked. Did he get along well with his parents? Was there a reason why he should run away? Was there a problem at school? Drugs? These questions all angered Mr. and Mrs. Thomas, the police were suggesting that James was a problem child and he had done this of his own free will. He did have problems just like every teenager, he did argue with his parents, he was somewhat rebellious at school. He did not do drugs and he was considerate enough to let his parents know where he was if he was going to be out late. He had now been gone for two days.

Event two was a problem with the local dogs. There were a greater number of them in the area than usual. The council was called and some were caught and returned to their owners. The others seemed to congregate around the old disused garages behind Eastleigh Towers. They were becoming a nuisance at night. Howling and fighting amongst each other. The situation got so bad that the dog warden had to be called out at night.

That is when James Thomas was found. Now the media took over.

"The body of a boy was found last night in a disused garage on the Eastleigh Estate. Police say that it may have lain there for several days.

A spokesman said that death was caused by a severe blow to the head and they are treating this as murder."

This was a shock. People were horrified that it could happen in their area. There are no monsters here that could do something like that. Surely the animal who did this must have come from somewhere else, why did they have to come here to prey on our children. To the public it was easy to put two and two together. It must be the boy the police were appealing about. How coincidental can you get? Why is it that news people are so clever but never put two and two together?
The parents lived in hope.
Every time the thought crept into their mind that it could be Jamie, their little Jamie, the thought was chased away but deep inside they knew it was possible, no, it was probable. The request came to them very shortly. The world waited with bated breath. They all wanted to know. The police came to the house and they had with them some personal effects from the body found in the garage.

The tear scarred faces of the parents were terrible to see. The smell of fear was on them and the officers recognised it because they had experienced it before. The couple tried to be strong and hold it back. They looked calm and orderly. They looked at the books, the bag, the watch and the key ring. They held out bravely until they saw the bus pass. James had a bad hair day the day that photograph was taken. Nobody has a good photograph in one of those booths. As it turns out, this photograph was the last one to be taken of James. It would be the one used by the media to break the news. The life filled eyes would look out from newspapers and television sets all over the land. The life is now gone from the boy and was about to be drained from his parents. The floodgates opened and misery flowed in. The misery that would fill their entire lives even if they lived forever.

Mrs. Thomas fell forward towards the table and Mr. Thomas caught her and held her. They both wept openly. The lumbering, suited policemen could do nothing. All they could do was to make some inner promise to these people, drink in this pain, wallow in this grief. They were determined to experience all of this agony so when, at the end of a long day, when they wanted to go home, take a break or have an early night, they would remember these poor people and redouble their efforts. It was not over for the parents. They were asked to view the body to make a positive identification.

"It is now confirmed that the body of the murdered boy found on the Eastleigh Estate is that of missing schoolboy James Thomas. James was last seen leaving school on Wednesday evening..........."

Now the story was in the face of the neighbourhood and the nation. Every paper had the details. Every news bulletin on the TV and radio had more information. It seemed to be everywhere. The face of the boy the crumpled parents and the suited policemen. The garages were closed off and the police scientists were hard at work sifting through the scene of the crime.

Every word that was spoken, printed or televised, was absorbed by Drew Treevill in his spotless flat. At the end of every day, he would drift into a fitful sleep and when he woke in the morning his confidence grew. He often smiled. It was not a crime that he planned and it looked like he was going to be lucky. Soon he would be able to get back to his life and this episode would pass. He would never bring suspicion to himself. He would go back to work, act normally and when the interest had died down, he would move north.

His face did start to heal and after a week he went back to work. The others left him alone. They were under strict orders from the manager but they often smirked and sniggered within his hearing. Life was tolerable. He kept to himself and so did they. It lasted a week.

Police work is always done by the book. The book says if you do not have a smoking gun or bloody knife then you start to investigate. Follow the rules, look at the leads and in the end – with luck and persistence – you will clear up the mess. In this case there were no witnesses and no motive. It was time for the police to ask the public for help on this case so they went on television.

"And now to the murder of schoolboy James Thomas. What information do you have about this case, Inspector?"

There followed all the information that the hungry and grief-stricken audience needed. Refused entry to the bus. Bus driver severely reprimanded. Very rainy night, that should jog some of the memories. Vicious attack but James put up a struggle. There were skin tissues under his finger nails. The murderer left blood at the scene. The murderer may have a large gash on his head, arms or face. Call this number if you have any information.

The phones began to ring.

Drew Treevill's grocer, landlord and employer were all on the phone while he sat there watching the television like a rabbit in the headlights of an oncoming car.

* * *

There were policemen searching the dirty alley where Victoria was violated. They were not the same policemen who had to speak to Victoria's mum and dad but inside they were the same. Strip off their skin and they were all the same. They always seemed to be clumsy in their suits. They should have worn overalls because of the dirty things they had to do and the filth that they dealt with every day. Don't look into the statistics for alcoholism, lung cancer, stress related death amongst this profession. Every time they have terminal news to give to next of kin it takes its toll. Every time they see the ravages of some thoughtless youth, or maniacal pervert, it kills them a little bit inside. They see it all. This girl was now dead. Some guy would never be able to pay this price. Not even with his own life would he make anywhere near enough payment to bring these parents back from the torment they feel. Their agony would never be removed.

Like all police they too stood there looking clumsy as they broke the news of the death of Victoria to her parents. It started all over again. They were only just getting to grips with the situation and it was now everything was out of their hands. They reached a depth of pain and hopelessness that they thought could never exist. Care now should be taken because the only relief for their torment was to follow Victoria. Take the direct path to oblivion and relief that she did. Their lives were over because they lived for her. She was gone, where can they go now? The officers were aware of this possibility so constables were posted, nurses were notified. The family doctor was called. Everything was done for these people. The hunt for the rapist went on.

The police scoured the area of the crime.

Victoria had given them very little to go on. Approximate age was about all she could offer. The picture was of a male, white, about thirty to thirty-five years old and he had been drinking. Whisky she thought. The detecting machine went into full swing. The scene was well trampled by people looking for clues and as it was an alley way, used by many during the day eliminating footprints was a waste of time. Swabs from the hospital provided DNA samples but they could only be used if a suspect was detained or had a criminal record. There was one piece of evidence that it was vital to find. The bottle. The whisky bottle that was discarded by the rapist. One of Victoria's last conscious memories of that black evening was that he threw it away and she did not hear it break.

Every solution to every crime comes with the first break. There is a sense that it just takes time so you keep at it. It might be tedious and messy but you keep at it. You could be doing something more interesting than crawling through dog shit and sifting through rotting garbage. But you keep at it because if you are looking for a particular grain of sand in the desert, and you search *every* grain of sand, eventually you *will* find what you are looking for.

The officer who found the bottle was treated with some celebrity status. He had been scrabbling through filth for hours and painstakingly searching every inch of his designated area. It was some distance away from the scene. His call to the attending detectives was the turning point. The mood of all of the officers changed. Some were glad that they could go back to pounding the beat but everyone knew that this was a break. This was where finger prints could be lifted and if the man was on the police files he would be caught. The bottle was ceremoniously carried like a flag at the head of a procession. There was a pencil inserted in the neck and the bottle was carefully deposited into an evidence bag. The police computer would do the rest. As things always go there was to be a deflating of the bubble that was hastily inflated by these searching officers. Unfortunately, the enquiry was back to square one for the prints that were lifted from the bottle were not on the police file.

The search for clues widened. All of the local shops which sold the brand and quantity of the whisky were visited. Some had video surveillance equipment installed and these tapes were viewed. Each tape had a time and date logged on screen. There were only three people who made purchases on that night which interested the police. One was a middle-aged woman, one an elderly gentleman and one was a slim man, aged about thirty. Investigate by the book, ask the obvious questions.

His name was David Brenner.

He was twenty-eight and at the precise moment the police focused on him he was sitting in the park with a can of strong lager in his hand. He was totally unaware of what was happening to him. How could he know? According to him his life was trundling along much as it usually did. He sat in the park and eyed all of the people. He had regained some power now. It had been a long time since he felt this power. He could make older people uncomfortable with his presence. A stare usually did it. Ladies who walked their dogs gave him plenty of room. It was the drinking in public that gave the game away. You never know what you get from a drunk in public. Stay clear. Kids were a problem sometimes but a few choice swear words were usually enough. He did behave himself when men came near. He was not that brave yet. He did not have that sort of power. His actions a week ago, when he got this new power, did not give him *that* much bravery. He picked and chose who he could intimidate. When he finished his drink, he threw the empty can in the bushes and stood to leave. The effect of the lager was not as good as the whisky but it would keep him going until the night. He knew that he had done wrong. He knew that if he were caught, he would be punished. He also thought that he had committed the perfect crime.

He lived with his mother and she worked at night. He did not have a job so he stayed out all day and went home at night. *That* night he went out after she left. If she were asked, she would say that he was at home. That is what she thought, that is what everyone would think. He didn't leave any clothes at the scene, it was dark, it was over in a few minutes. No one saw him arrive or depart. He got home, washed and made himself a meal and went to bed. He slept very well that night as he recalled. He had to be woken by his mother as she left for work. His clothes were washed the next day and that was that. The perfect crime. It would all blow over and he would never do it again so there would not be a pattern.

But people were making plans for him. His life was going to change drastically and he was not going to be a party to the changes. He was the missing link in the chain of events. The police knew everything about him but did not have him in custody. The manager of the off license recognised him from the video still, that the police produced. He did not know the name. In this business with this type of customer you wanted to know as little as possible. Take the order, produce the goods, wrap it up, take the money, give the change and say goodnight. There was no time for niceties with this type of customer. Sell them what they want and then hope that they get as far away from the shop as possible. He remembered David as being already slightly drunk on that night. He bought the whisky and left the shop. He remembered being relieved. He also remembered selling a six pack of strong lager to him only this morning!

It took two weeks.
Two weeks which the off-licence manager had to put up with a clumsy plain clothes police constable breaking bottles and putting the wrong prices on stock. He did not know the difference between Cadburys and Cockburn but then where do you learn that in the police training school? The constable was there for one purpose only. This was the off licence where the suspect bought his alcohol and if he came in, he would be detained.
It took two weeks.
That evening David still felt the nagging necessity to put more alcohol into his bloodstream. The slow drip, drip, of the lager was not enough. He had a few quid in his pocket. Whisky was the thing. Buy a small bottle and go home. Watch some telly, drink the lot and cast off! He was finding it more and more comfortable to reach oblivion like this. His mother was starting to worry as well. She could smell it on his clothes, on his breath and in his attitude. Poor dear, he was between jobs at the moment but when he got himself sorted out things would be ok again. His footsteps took him to the off licence again and into the waiting arms of the police.

"Stall him!" The two words from every detective movie. The constable sent a message to the station and then began to stack bottles near the door. The proprietor tried to comply from behind the counter. David was engaged in polite conversation but this conversation troubled him. Why was this old duffer so interested in which football team he supported? Why did it take so long to wrap the bottle and look for a plastic carrier bag? The lager he had already consumed had not dulled his sense of self preservation. If it had, he would have heard some mental alarm bells ringing and he would have bolted from the shop. He would have become uncomfortable by the young man aimlessly working near the door and the way that he constantly glanced at the manager. There was something not right about this situation. He was having that moment that we have all experienced. If he could turn the clock back only one minute. Please let this little moment not have happened. It is a pivotal moment and we have all had them. Everything would change from this moment and in the case of David it is a moment that changed his entire life.

Instead, he stood outside of himself looking in. He was not in control now, other people were. He was now at the centre and not on the periphery. He had to get out to the blurred edges of this situation again because once out there in the light, it follows you. It hounds you. David left the shop. David was followed, challenged, detained and examined. The world became a noisy place, police cars, uniformed officers and plain clothes suits. They seemed to descend upon him from every direction. He was taken back to the station and legal counsel was called. Later blood was taken, finger prints were recorded and saliva was collected. He could not believe how polite everyone was. It was please and thank you all the way. The police knew they had their man and there was no need for the rough stuff. Good cop and bad cop could stay at home tonight. In his cell David was miserable. The lager was not enough. Its effects were gone. The adrenalin was sobering him up fast. He was in a pit of misery and the police upstairs could not contain their joy.
Everything was done by the book. The forms were filled out and the statements taken. All of the pieces of the jigsaw were slotted together as the police built the case against David Brenner.

*   *   *

Even though the officers were still taking phone calls from the public, Drew Treevill could mentally hear them coming. A pressure noise developed in his ears and his face became very hot. His colour changed and became redder and beads of sweat started to appear on his forehead. The sound of the television disappeared and the movement on the screen was ignored. He just sat there his mind raced his jaw dropped. From a moment where he believed he was in the clear he now found himself in the frame. The evidence was overpowering and it would only be a matter of time before they found him. Drew decided to act and from his stupor he now moved very swiftly.

He grabbed a bag and went to the bedroom. He gathered the minimum of clothes he might need. Wallet and money. Check book, cards and keys. Take the keys because there was that optimistic voice that said that he may still be in the clear and would need to come back. To come back in the dead of night and clear out the flat. Move north later. Shit – he should have done this a week ago when he was in the clear. In the clear? He would never be in the clear, just one step ahead. He had to keep his wits about him and keep one step ahead. If he had moved out a week ago, he could have been miles away by now. Never mind, the events dictate his moves now. Last look around the flat pull on the coat and open the door.

They were big and well dressed. They were well groomed. They were grim.

"Drew Treevill? I am Detective Inspector Carr and these are Detective Sergeants Terrence and Moore" this said in a calm voice as a warrant card was displayed "Are you going somewhere?"

It did not take long for the police to find Drew Treevill. He felt that if he just denied everything, they could not prove anything - but he was wrong. There was the material found under James' fingernails and Drew's blood at the scene. The flat had been very well cleaned and there was little evidence inside but there were traces of blood from the boy and Drew on the doormat outside the flat.

Drew had lost all of the power that he had gained. Now he was pathetic again and he was in the hands of people who loathed him. Every glance told him how lowly he had sunk. He felt miserable and at times he thought he could not go on. The police were aware of this and a close watch was kept. This man was not going to cheat society of the pleasure of punishment. Special level headed officers were assigned to look after Drew. There were some in the force that would have dealt out justice themselves. They were kept well away. Drew had to be held at a secure station in case the public got impatient and decided to side step the legal system. In all of this he felt very small and unprotected, rather like James Thomas felt during the last moments of his life.

The trial was a very high-profile affair. It was of national interest and the public hungrily consumed every word written about it. Every fact was now known about Drew from his birth to his imprisonment. They interviewed his colleagues at work. They painted Drew to be a loner and an easy-going sort of chap, they liked working with him but thought him a bit weird so they left him alone. The defence tried to paint a better picture for Drew but there was little it could do. The facts were there. It was an unprovoked attack on a boy on a wet dark night, the boy was beaten to death and Drew had confessed. The only mitigating circumstances were his constant torment at the hands of his work mates. It was hatred pent up and unwillingly released. The boy was in the wrong place at the wrong time. It was a defence that was little to cling to and the grip was soon loosened by the prosecution.

The interest shown by the public brought even more pressure to bear. He was a pathetic figure standing in the dock and the country wanted blood. The judge wanted to send a message to the country that justice can reflect the mood of the people so Drew Treevill was sentenced to twenty years in prison. The hammer fell and the court was cleared. No one wept for Drew, there were gasps and sighs at the sentence but it was from relief. The monster is being taken to the cage. He was taken back to his holding cell where he sat with his head in his hands and there, alone in that barren room, with his power all gone, he finally came to terms with himself. He was worthless. He was weak. He was inhuman. He felt sorry for himself and he began to cry and he was still crying later when prison officers came to take him to Renkill Maximum Security Prison.

*   *   *

For David Brenner there was also a trial. It lasted one week. The defence did not have a case to argue but they pleaded mitigating circumstances. The boy had no father, no job, a drink problem and it was really the influence of the alcohol that made him act this way. His mother spent little time with him and she was the sole earner and was presently between jobs. He stood in the dock, brushed and combed and suited. He spoke very little but when he did it was extremely polite. The defence could not deny that the actions took place, the facts spoke for themselves. Victoria was last seen with Jackie, a notoriously promiscuous young lady. This, by association, tarnished Victoria in the eyes of the jury. It was also assumed that because Jackie was very drunk it was possible that Victoria had been drinking also. Counsel for Brenner suggested that the girls could have seen him in the alley and that Victoria actually returned to try and pick him up! The trial was the rack for Victoria's parents. They had to sit there and listen to the impossible permutations of the defence counsel. Victoria was never like this.

How could this be justice? As a result of the actions of this monster their little cherished child was dead. There could be no other way of looking at it. He is responsible, for her death. The anguish and the grief in their faces were pitiful to look at, but everyone knew. Everyone knew that a portion of that grief was there because they could not expect the court to see it their way. The boy was not responsible for the death. That had to be put to one side and forgotten. The jury was instructed to do just that. Just forget it please. Victoria was here once and now is not. She was driven to madness by being raped but just see if you can put that to one side please.

The mob was there for the sentencing. They knew that there would be a controversial decision. There was the press in full, banks of them, because the story had caught the imagination of the nation and paper circulations were up! The neighbourhood well-wishers were there ready to offer comfort. There were strangers, activists, all with a particular axe to grind and this free national publicity could be good. There were also ordinary people who just wanted to see that this great justice machine of ours, does the right thing.

After the verdict there was a rushing of people from the court. There were scuffles in the corridors and a man and woman emerged from the building. The man was Mr. Casey and he was physically supporting his wife. She was crying. She was more than crying, she was mourning. She was mourning the way that only a woman mourns, a woman who has seen the child of her womb, the hope and joy of her future, savagely ripped apart in front of her. She was near to feinting. Mr. Casey was holding her. In him we see the man who has a supreme task to perform and perform it he will but first he must just do this. First, he must see that his wife is comforted and safe, then there is other business to attend to. The jury had swallowed all the whitewash drip fed to them by the defence. They felt that perhaps Brenner was also a victim and they gave him the benefit of the doubt. The judge sentenced Brenner to six months in prison, but as he had already spent two months on remand as a model prisoner, he released him to the community to be held over to keep the peace for two years.

David Brenner, that day, walked free from the court.

* * *

Three

John Deverall walked the landing. He never took anything in this place for granted because every day, in this place, was different. Every day was different because the hierarchy of the residents changed every day. Sometimes it was subtle and other times it was notable and usually violent. The violence could be physical with broken bones, teeth and spilt blood or it could be mental. Threatening. The promise of violence in side these walls was never an idle threat. Here, a promise *was* a promise. If you did not carry out your threats then you dropped, plummeted, down the pecking order with new levels of predators looking hungrily at you. Any promise with the surety of it happening, was something that was palpable, it could be touched and felt in the air on the landing.

This pecking order was very important. For the guards it helped keep the inmates in their own place. Knowledge of this order was compulsory. If you knew the order you could keep the peace and prevent anarchy. That was their business, to be the human line between order and chaos, to keep these men hidden away from an even larger innocent prey, society. It was not unusual for the residents to solve their own problems. The guards always preferred it and would only interfere if security could be breached or harm could come to a prisoner. The officers would allow this to happen as long as it did not get out of hand. Damaged prisoners always reflected badly against the staff. When you have a barrel load of violent men all crammed cheek by jowl in one building there has to be a pecking order and it establishes itself very quickly.

It can be simple. Allowing another to pass through a doorway before you, establishes order. The type of eye contact establishes order. Unfortunately, the order usually evolves through violence so fights are very common. There is a tremendous amount at stake in a fight. It's result will dictate how you live tomorrow. It could even mean IF you live tomorrow. But a fight can take many forms. It can be simple affair like just walking up to a man and flooring him without reason. This is a mad dog way of establishing yourself. The mad dog in prison holds a very high perch in the pecking order. They are impossible to reason with. They can blow up for no reason, they have no fear for themselves and no care for the damage they may do to another. On the landing every move you make has to be calculated because the effects may be felt for a long time and they may even be felt forever. Men on their way to prison will make conscious efforts to establish themselves quickly. These men, the new men, are the most dangerous and feared among the prison community. They also make the hairs on the back of the neck bristle amongst the prison officers.

The arrival of new 'meat' meant that the air would be full of tension. The established pecking order would attempt to strengthen itself. The residents braced themselves for the threat by reaffirming their places. They would meet the new arrivals and fit them into the chain. Some would be demoted some promoted but there was always stress. There was always some sort of violence. Sometimes there could be serious trouble.

Every sort of man could be found in Renkill. The meek the mild, the vicious and the mad, the sadistic and the calculating, they had all found a place in the pecking order but the word was out that Bill Davies was not happy with the way things were going for him at the moment. Davies was a new, mad dog, prisoner – the worst kind. John Deverall was expecting some friction from him but he hoped it would be on a different shift.

The first sign of Davies's displeasure was when his food tray, toilet contents and cell mate were thrown out on the landing, when they returned from breakfast. Then there followed books, shoes, chair and portable radio. It happened fast and the reaction was swift. The officers approached the cell from both directions along the landing. It was something they all expected.
Their first task was to get the cell mate away and attend to his injuries. His injuries were many because Davies had beaten him thoroughly before throwing him out of the cell. One of the officers, the first on the scene looked at John Deverall "How do you want to deal with this Sarge?"
John looked around and saw the other officers waiting to hear what he had to say. He knew from the look in their eyes that no matter what he said they would support him. He also knew that he could count on them.

"Talk first." He took a step forward and turned ninety degrees to the left filling the cell doorway. The light of the cell fell on his face revealing a forced smile.

"Redecorating Davies?"

Davies was slightly out of breath but he was facing the door from the far end of the cell. He was waiting. He knew what these actions would cause. He was creating a stage where he could play out the next scene in his life. It was something he had to do if he was going to rule this place and create an easy life for himself. Do some easy time. He looked up and saw the guard smiling at him. The guard filled the doorway and must be the biggest guy on the shift. Poor sod! All of his mates must be cowering outside or he would never have made this move.

Davies knew that he was going to get a beating but he would take this guy out first, then be over powered by the other guards, there was no shame in that. He stood up and took a pace forward.

"I've had enough of this creeping around, keeping the peace! Everywhere I look I see cons who are allowed to walk about and have visits and shit like that. I have to wear prison issue and it stinks. How long do I have to wait until I get mine?" Davies said this very loudly, he was not only talking to this guard he was talking to the landing, talking to the other inmates who were undoubtedly listening. John Deverall spoke.

"Look Davies, you have not been here long and you are being assessed. It all takes a little time and this sort of behaviour is not good. It upsets me."

"I don't give a shit about you!" This said as he moved further forward towards the doorway of the cell. The officers on the landing could not see this being done but they knew what was happening. The sound was closer, they did not need to see - to know. They inwardly braced themselves. Davies was still grandstanding. Deep inside they all held a quiet unseen smile because they knew exactly what was going on. They knew the script and the role that Davies was playing. They also knew that John Deverall never read that script. This play would have a twist in the tail, there was only going to be one conclusion and Davies never even considered it could end that way.

"I don't give a shit about anyone in this dump! I don't give a shit about your rules. I want something done now!"

Davies advanced to within striking distance of John and then stopped. All the time he was moving he was making calculations and looking at the body language of the guard in front of him. The guard unexpectedly stood his ground. He was either very stupid or there was a shitload of backup out there on the landing. Another calculation - there may be another reason for the brave stance and he saw it in the officer's eyes at the last moment. This guard felt that he was capable. He thought he could handle this situation. This was a prize for Davies and it would send the perfect message to the population.

John looked at the advancing inmate. Davies was screaming and waving his arms but John was calculating with his eyes. Davies was making a lot of noise but it was his movement that John concentrated on. He must hold himself in check until the proper moment. It was going to get physical, he could feel it. When the moment came, he had to be ready. The whole scene was like watching the television with the sound turned off. The solution to this crisis would come with that one false move.

Then something else crept into his thoughts. Something distracted him. His thoughts dangerously went there. He considered himself to be a decent man. Why did he have to put up with scum like this? How did he find himself trawling down among the garbage of this earth? Was this thug worth it? This is the bastard that assaulted Roxburg. Nothing in the legal system is ever going to change the attitude of this filth. It just took an instant but Deverall completed all of these thoughts as Davies closed the remaining distance between them. Now his full concentration was on the man in front of him.

Two handed, Davies grabbed Deverall by the lapels as if to haul him out of his way but John made his own move. He caught the prisoner's upper arms and complimented his movement. Their combined weight moving in the same direction spun Davies fully around and forced him back into the cell. Davies broke the grip and swung a punch from the hip. It formed an arc through the air and hit Deverall on the shoulder who instantly lifted his arm and reversing his hand, he gripped Davies by the wrist and twisted. Davies grunted and twisted himself to negate the move. They stood there for a moment and looked into each other's eyes. In that look was everything that Davies needed to know. He had to win this one or his prison life would be over. Nothing but droppings to look forward to in the pecking order. It had to be all or nothing. John saw this too.

Now they went at it with a will.

The next assault by Davies took John by surprise because of its desperation. He was caught high on the temple by a wild punch. This made Davies smile and some spittle and drool escaped from his heavily breathing mouth. John was hit again, this time behind the ear but it transformed him. He now felt nothing and could hear nothing. He seemed to stand calmly in the face of the frenzied assault. He didn't blink or flinch. He moved in close, risking the savage blows. He moved in closer and cobra-like his arm shot out from his body. His hand opened and met the other man's neck. Davies and Deverall both moved towards the back wall of the cell. Davies was pinned high on the wall with only his toes on the floor. The expression on Davies's face instantly changed. Both of his hands gripped John's arm. John stood there, arm outstretched and Davies struggled to break free. Davies looked into John's eyes and saw something new. Davies saw, that to John, he was nothing. He saw that his life was insignificant. He saw in those eyes that this officer had the ability to kill without regret. He knew that he was in deep trouble. He thought that he was going to die. All of these sights were projected by John's eyes.

John looked at the man on the end of his arm. Those rogue thoughts came back. They distracted him again. He decided that the world would be a better place if Davies were to perish. He would be doing the people a favour. He could dish out the justice right here right now. His grip tightened.
Davies stared oblivion in the face. He increased his efforts to break free but the grip was like a vice. He was starting to choke and his vision was beginning to blur around the edges. He did not have a good life but he did not want to lose it. His lips curled and he formed a word. It made no sound because his last breath was trapped in his body. His lips formed the word "Please" and now there was begging in his eyes. His body began to lose its rigidity and the muscles relaxed. The grip tightened.

Davies knew it was all over, his bladder emptied and the cell filled with the smell of that unique moisture.

It was at that moment that the other prison guards moved in to the cell. A light touch on his shoulder by a firm friendly hand brought John Deverall back to reality. He heard a calm soothing voice encourage him to release the prisoner.
For the first time in minutes, he blinked and his dry eyes stung and filled with tears. He loosened his grip and Davies fell into the pool of piss that he had created on the floor. John looked down on the body. He stood there unmoving while the other guards tended to Davies and when he was certain that the man would live, he left the cell.

When he was certain that Davies would live, he experienced a new feeling, a feeling of disappointment. Something inside told him that this might have been the cure for his torment. There was that nagging thought again. The same thought that had distracted him earlier. He felt that he had missed an opportunity to do some good. He had come away from the episode without having brought it to a conclusion. He felt that the job was not done. There was another feeling. The feeling handed down from all men who have ever lived. He had fought and won during single handed combat. He was the victor in a conflict where he could have stared death in the face. He was pumped up and adrenalin was coursing round his body. It was the first time in a long time that he had felt good.

*   *   *

Martin Casey had an overpowering urge to make sure that his wife was comforted and protected from the evil world. She was in a very bad state. Her grief was the loss of Victoria and she felt that her own life was now over. He was a man who can find strength in tragedy and puts all of his needs and feelings on hold until the lives of his family and loved ones are on an even keel.

There was another feeling within him. It was related to anger but much worse. Hatred was the wrong emotion. Revenge was closer but as nothing would bring Victoria back, revenge would only please him. He did not want to be pleased. He wanted justice. He wanted the system to see that Victoria was unjustly treated and her attacker was unjustly freed.

Her attacker was walking the street and Victoria would only ever be a memory. He could not get the image of David Brenner, smirking and walking and living in the community, out of his mind. He had to do something. Now all he could do was watch his wife career down a hill of depression, which was making her physically ill. He threw all of his efforts to making life easier for her. This gave him a distraction, something else to worry about but it made her worse and worse. She knew what he was doing and why and it made her focus even more on the gaping hole in her life.

When his wife was safe, he would do something. Exactly what he would do, he did not know. He had gone over many scenes in his head but they all resulted in his being convicted for a brutal act or worse. Every scene ended with his wife visiting him in prison, doubly miserable having lost both of the people she loved. What he could not live with was to do nothing. To let things heal and go on much the way they did in the past was out of the question. Martin just knew that he would do *something*!

The doctor had provided a prescription for sleeping tablets and advised him to administer them. Even the doctor saw that she was in a terrible condition and her suicide was a possibility. The doctor gave strict instructions about dosage and times but tonight Mrs. Brenner was very bad, at least that is what he told himself. He used this excuse to give her an early pill and when she went to sleep, tucked up in bed, he knew he had at least six hours to himself while she slept. He was going out in the cold and would not feel the warmth of a room again until he returned. He was going to do something.

Martin Casey took a bus to the other side of town. Within twenty minutes he had walked to the address that he had memorised. He had never been to this address before, he had never been to this part of the town before. When he arrived, he did not approach the door but instead he found a place along the road where he could see the building, see all the exits and see all of the windows. He placed himself near the bus shelter and drew his jacket collar up against the cold. He lit a cigarette and stood watch. This was his plan, it had plenty of room for development, but it was something. All he could think to do, was to stand and watch the doors and windows of this flat. This flat that he had never visited before was the address of one David Brenner, rapist and indirect killer of his beloved daughter. He would stand there and maybe a plan would come. Maybe David himself would come and the plan might take care of itself.

* * *

Mrs. Brenner was also living in a hell of her own. The son that she thought was hers had turned out to be somebody else. She knew that he had problems. She had always made excuses for him but now she looked at herself as part of his problem. After the trial it took a long time for her to be in the same room as David. It took even longer for her to bring herself to speak to him. They occupied the same space but the air was tense and filled with questions and reproach. Best not say anything at all. Thankfully David felt this tension and avoided contact with his mother. He stayed out of the house most of the day and during the night he lived in his room while his mother wept in her bed. Mrs. Brenner had lost her job and the time during the day weighed heavily on her shoulders. She had taken to wandering from window to window and looking forlornly at the street below. People down there had a different life and she would have changed with any of them in a second. No questions, their problems could not have been as bad as hers. She needed an escape but there was none. Life was long and heavy. It had to be endured and not lived anymore. She was waiting, waiting and hoping that someone else would make things better for her because she could not do this herself. It was one morning while wandering the flat alone that she made a discovery that would cause even greater grief and lead her to make a decision that would haunt her for the rest of her life.

David had left the flat that morning after grunting over his breakfast while she ate hers in the kitchen. She listened to his noises as she picked at the meagre meal she had prepared. Food was an item on the timetable now, not a time for sitting and sharing lives with family. She had no family. She only had this person who she shared a space with. He ate noisily in the silence and muttered something when he finished. That muttering could have meant anything but to her it meant that she could now have the flat to herself and not avoid him.

He left and she emerged from the kitchen to the quiet flat. She cleared up the breakfast things and dropped into automatic, going around the rooms, tidy this, straighten that, things she did every day. She did these things the same way an animal would, that carries her dead infant. Not knowing why, not accepting how, just moving and doing things on automatic.

There was no pride in the actions. The flat did not bear the scars of everyday living. It was just a place. He spent all of his time in his room. God only knew what it was like in there. As she automatically freshened the room, her eyes, driven by her thoughts, automatically glanced to his door. This caused her to stop and stand up. The small yellow cushion she was fluffing, she now clutched to her chest.

His door was open.

The door to David's room was ajar and it was like an invitation. The door to the room of the person who she shared a flat with, was open and it was inviting her to enter. The walk to the door was physically short but there was a lifetime to cross. The feelings and emotions that it generated were immense. She was walking towards her son's life and at the same time towards the life of a man who had committed such evil that she could not think of him as her son. She had been alone, apart from him for so long that she felt the need to see his room, to see the place where he lived, to look upon the trappings of this person. She needed to understand. She needed to be brave. She accepted the invitation and walked towards the door.

She pushed the door open and stood in the doorway. All of the objects in the room were familiar to her. She had been in the room thousands of times in the past to clean and dust. To put clean clothes in the drawers and cupboards. To wake him with a kiss. To soothe his brow when he had the flu or a cold. A smile started to creep across her lips but it was quickly killed by the sight of lager cans on the window and the pile of magazines on the floor.

Pointlessly she made a mental note to visit the room more often and tidy up. She would never do that again. She felt that she was looking at the room of a stranger. A lodger. These things were unfamiliar to her. The history of the occupant was unknown to her. Where he would go in the future she did not know. Where he was now, what he was doing, what he was thinking, feeling, she did not know and she did not care. The stranger was out. Her heart was breaking because until recently, in her way, he was her life. She had given him to the world and look what he had done. It was her fault. How could she make amends?

Like the light from a lighthouse her gaze steadily and without pausing scanned the room. Unmade bed, cans on the window, magazines on the floor, drawers open, dirty clothes and trainers on the floor, wardrobe open and clothes hanging haphazardly on the rail. There were many familiar things like his clothes and the furniture but he had brought new trappings, foreign items. A jacket and some personal items of clothes were hung or slung around the room. There were books and magazines stacked or strewn in many places near the walls. Reading was a good time filler and he did have empty time to fill. The magazines were glossy. The magazines were disgusting and left in open view. Why hide them, she never came in here and he never brought a friend home. His bed was not made and the pillow held a head shaped depression. As she scanned the room her eyes fell on the wardrobe. It was half open and contained a small empty hold all, some shirts and trousers hanging up, more magazines and a small book the size and appearance of a photo album.

It seemed out of place so her gaze would not move any further. Her curiosity was getting the better of her so she put down and knelt on, the cushion she was clutching. Sticking out from one of the covers was a piece of newspaper. Before she lifted the book, she took a quick look at the door and crooked her head to hear if there was a sound. She made a mental note to return the book just as she found it.

The book was a scrap book. It was filled with newspaper cuttings and pictures. As she turned the pages the blood drained from her face. Her breathing had stopped and her eyes rapidly scanned the words and images. Her open mouth was covered by her free hand and tears started to well up in her eyes. The book was filled with clippings and photographs from papers about the trial. Everything was there from the first report of the rape of Victoria, her suicide, his arrest, trial and sentence. There were pictures of Victoria and her parents. Her grieving parents on the steps of the court house. It was morbid, macabre. What did he do with these things? She sat back on her heels and tried to recover her thoughts. The book was still open and she was about to close it when she noticed that she had only been reading the material from the ending. There was more at the front.

These pages were older, sporting the yellow tinge associated with old newsprint. The dated pages were from fourteen years ago. There was a lesser amount of material but it was more serious. She read everything and pieced it all together. Now she felt cold inside and scared. It was as if she had just discovered that her life was in danger and an enormous urge almost overcame her to get up and run and keep on running. She could not outrun her emotions though. Wait, these were only clippings from newspapers. They didn't mean anything. They probably came with the album when he found it or borrowed it from a friend. Then, just when there was a chink of hope that she could be wrong, fate twisted the knife.

One of the clippings was torn from the pressure of the book closing on something solid behind it. She felt it and forced it with her fingernail to the edge of the page.
Now she lost all hope.
She had to sit.
Her legs were weakened by what she held.
The tears in her eyes dried almost instantly and she began to feel sick. She drew out a silver chain with a dangling silver letter. Closing her eyes, she gave out a silent scream to God, the angels – anybody who could rescue her from this deep, deep agony that she felt. When she was finished, she found that she had made a tight fist around the chain and letter. She released her grip and the letter dropped and dangled in front of her. She spun it around. It was a child's silver necklace with a small silver "H".

* * *

When Drew heard the words from the judge and the cheer from the gallery, time seemed to stop for him. He wished that he had not gotten the job at the garage, wished he was bigger, wished that it had not rained that night and wished that he had never met James Thomas. All of these things would have changed his life. Now his life was to change again but he did not have the imagination to see what it was going to be like. Now he abandoned himself to others. They were in charge now, all of his power was gone. He stood there with no emotion on his face. Many of the people there mistook this for indifference. The press would dwell on this perceived attitude and painted him as a remorseless child killer and a prison sentence was not good enough.

His attitude even opened the hanging debate. He felt a hand on his shoulder, the hand of the constable, and he was led from the court. He sat in his cell, the same cell he had occupied only an hour ago. Only an hour ago there was a chance. There was still a thread of his life that he had control of. Now things were totally different. He was directed by everyone. It was time for him to be transported.
"Stand up."

Drew stood and realised that the attitude from these uniformed guards was different. They were cold and official. It was like they were working from a script. There was no sorrow or hate in their eyes, they were doing a job, they did it every day and they always did it the same way.
"Step back from the door and turn around."

Drew asked, "What is going to happen now?" There was a pleading in his voice attempting to draw some emotion from the officer but none came back.
"You are going to get changed into these overalls, you will be handcuffed and taken to your transport. You will then be taken directly to your place of detention and there you will start your sentence."

Now the dawn of the future began to break over Drew. It was not the warm, fulfilling, life giving dawn which we get from the sun, but a cold depressing, despairing dawn that we get from the certain knowledge that this is the way it is going to be forever!
Drew stripped awkwardly under the gaze of three prison officers and he pulled on the ill-fitting overalls. When he finished, he turned and offered his arms to be cuffed. The officer snapped on the manacles and stepped back.
"You will need this."

He offered a blanket and Drew returned a puzzled look.
The officer broke from his script and for the first time he spoke with some feeling.

"Put the fucking thing over your head when we take you through the yard to the van. We don't want that crowd outside to get out of hand. With this on you won't have to see them and they won't be able to see you!"

"There's a crowd outside? What do they want? Why are they going to do?"

Drew blurted out the questions further infuriating the guards. They had to offer their own words again. This was outside their brief. In fact, they would have enjoyed giving Drew a piece of their mind. They had some choice words for him. They would have loved to have spent a few minutes alone with him in his cell. Drew could not possibly have known how much he had been spared.

The officer who seemed to be the senior guard walked from the back as the others gave him room. He walked up to Drew, towering over him. From the waist he bent over and placed his face just a breath away from his prisoner and spoke.

"That crowd outside want to tear you to pieces. They know what you look like. We have several other prisoners to transport. If they see you the whole thing might kick off and *we* might not be able to protect you. Everybody goes out of here today in overalls under a blanket. If you have any other questions just keep them to yourself. Do what you are fuckin' told or I might just let the mob have you. Get in the corridor."

Drew moved, his eyes darting from one officer to the other. There was a smell of fear in the air. These men were part of a very strong team but they knew that if things did get out of hand, they might be victims as well. The fear was born from the feeling that they were putting their health and maybe their life on the line for what? This little child murderer? This waste of skin? Deep down there was a cold smouldering feeling in them all that throwing this guy to the mob might be the just thing to do!

They moved to the end of the corridor where there was a door flanked by two policemen. The first reached out to the door handle and the other took the blanket and draped it over Drew's head. From somewhere someone spoke.

"The van is on the other side of this door. You will need to take about five steps. There are three steps up into the van. Let's make this quick!"

Drew heard the bar of the door being punched, the light around his feet increased but there was a new sensation. The wall of sound. He squeezed the blanket around his head. Rough hands on both arms pushed him forward quickly. Something hit the blanket and there was a momentary pause followed by a thrust that took him almost off of his feet. They covered the distance to the van in a second and he was catapulted up the steps. New hands grabbed his arms and pulled him down a short corridor. He was turned to the left and shoved through a door. The blanket was hauled off of his head and he looked up blinking in the light. The face that he saw was sweating and angry.

"Sit there you little shit! Stay away from the window!"

The face left the small cell and slammed the door. The sound of the lock could not be heard over the sound of the crowd. Drew could not help but look out of the window. It was a small piece of darkened armoured glass. The whole world was there. They were all over the street and in all of the overlooking windows. There were some people on the roof. Almost in equal numbers were the police, their yellow jackets the thin dividing line between the baying crowd and the prison van. They were pushing with all of their might attempting to create an exit for the van which was being pelted with eggs and stones.

It started to move. It had to move out of the courtyard into the street where there were two police cars and four motorcycles waiting to be the escort. The last hurdle was the photographers, they sprang into action holding their cameras to any window in an attempt to catch the face of the killer. The van passed through this last line of people, turned right and started to gather speed. The police vehicles fell in, front and back and sped down the road which had been closed to traffic for the last hour. The crowd took some time to disperse, there were eighteen arrests for public order offenses all of which were dealt with by a warning which showed the sympathy held by the police.

Drew Treevill was on his way to prison, and there was no hell that he had ever lived through, no torment or pain that he had ever endured that was going to compare with what lay in front of him. Drew Treevill was on his way to Renkill.

*   *   *

Phil Brooks was the first guard into the cell when the fight started. He assessed the situation almost immediately. There was no need to panic,

John had the situation under control and no 'claret' had been spilled. John was standing there with his back to the door and he held the semi-limp figure of Davies at arm's length. The furniture was broken all over the place and there was a pool of liquid on the floor being supplied through his trousers. This was something that could be sorted out. This was good. A message would trickle through to the inmates and the stature of the guards would be raised. Close on the heels of this relief there came a feeling of unrest.

John had not released Davies. Brooks realised that he had to do something. He had never seen John like this. He seemed to be in a trance and if he did not snap out of it, Davies would be history. That was too much. That was too far but how do you tell a man like Deverall to stop? You did not give him orders and he only did what he wanted to do. How do you tell him to stop doing what he obviously wanted to do?
"OK John, we can take it from here." He said this softly near his ear. There were other officers entering the cell and he could see that John was not in control. No need to let everyone know. "Come on John, let some life back in to the guy." There was no reaction. It needed something else. He put his arm firmly on Deverell's shoulder and raised his voice one perceptible level.
"John? You're going to kill him."

John Deverall slowly turned his head to stare straight in to the eyes of his junior officer. The eyes told the whole story. He was not out of control. He was in full control of his actions. He held the existence of this prisoner in his hand and was making a decision. He was weighing up the situation. Something in his eyes told Brooks to wait, the decision had not been made yet and Brooks felt a fear well up in him. Brooks had to go along with this. At the moment it was just a clean-up job but, in a few seconds, he would have to make a life changing decision. He would either have to go along with Deverall or fight with him to free the prisoner. Each of the actions was not going to be good!

Inside John's eyes, a fire went out and he released his grip on Davies who slumped to the wet floor. Two other guards immediately lifted him and dragged him from the cell. Other officers were busy on the landing shutting down cell doors and packing the cons back to their holes. This was a situation that did not need a big audience.

Bill Davies had to be taken to the infirmary. His neck was badly bruised and it took a while for his breathing to go from gasping to normal. He stayed unconscious for a long time but the nurse was not unduly worried about that. All of his vital signs were returning to normal and it was better to have him out cold than tearing the place apart. The nurse was a man who did not need to come face to face with the prisoners too often and Davies' reputation was well known.

The guards were not worried about reports and paperwork. Davies fell over and caught his neck on the handrail. He was not going to make a complaint. He could be charged with assault on an officer. He assaulted a prisoner. He destroyed personal property and government property. More importantly his reputation in the prison just took a nose dive. He would not want the story of how he was beaten or how he soiled himself, to get around. One thing was certain though and every guard knew it, they had seen it hundreds of times before, Davies would now need an avenue for his anger. The prime suspect for his attention would normally be the person who humbled him. That was John Deverall and everyone felt that Davies would steer clear of him. No, someone else would have to catch the fury, someone else would take a beating. The guards would not know until it was over. It would be done when it was safe but it had to be done. There was a balance with these things.

Phil Brooks approached John in a dull moment later in the morning. He made sure that no one was near or could overhear their conversation. They were on the top landing standing side by side looking down into the well of the prison. When Brooks started to talk, he did so in a joking way hiding a serious thread.

"For a moment there John, I thought you were going to squeeze his head right off."

John did not reply at first and gave the impression that he was thinking of an answer. Measuring up what he was going to say, looking into the distance not really looking at anything. He turned his head then his whole body towards Brooks.

"Phil, it crossed my mind. I looked at him and I knew that I would be doing society a favour. He is scum and we have to walk around him as if we are walking on eggshells. Did you see what he did to Roxburg? Did you see what he did to his cell mate? I have to tell you Phil I was seriously thinking about it. I held his life in my hand and I could have done it. I gave it a really good thought. I heard you talking to me and in a way, you brought me back."

Brooks took a little praise from this, looked down and shuffled his feet but raised his head slightly and spoke.
"We all have those thoughts Sarge, if we didn't, we wouldn't be doing our jobs right? I know that it sounds like I am a company man but we *are* here for a purpose. We are responsible for these men while they are here and choking them to death is not in the job description. We have to hold it together John or we become just like them. The thought of losing control frightens me because of the consequences and of how it would change my life. I could not go inside for it. If it happens you can't go back. Life would be different and it would have to be like that forever."

John looked at Phil and spoke, "We are responsible for these men. Who is responsible for the people they violated? There are innocent people out there Phil whose lives have been destroyed by these men. Some people do not even exist anymore because of these men. Think about how we have to treat this scum. We have to be civil and polite or they can report it to the prison complaints board. We have to provide a level of care that is higher than that experienced by the majority of the people in this country. We let them set up their own society in here and sometimes turn a blind eye to their wheeling and dealing. Then there are the friends of our wonderful guests. The other scum whose collars never get felt, the ones who get away. We are the victims here Phil. We are the ones who are being punished by being held back from doing what we know to be right! Where is their pain, the retribution, the hand of real justice not just the weak political shit dealt out in the courts these days? The real justice could be dealt out by us, the people down here with the filth. We stink of these people. They taint our lives. We are martyrs for the society we protect." John felt himself losing some of his self-control so he decided to paint a different picture
.

"Think of a pond Phil, and the ripples that are caused by dropping a pebble in to the middle. That is what has happened to all the innocent people whose lives have been touched by the actions of these men. Now don't think of a pebble, think of a brick and you are starting to get some idea of the real effect. You talk to me about how our lives might change if we take the law into our own hands?"

John shrugged his shoulders and readjusted his stance. The conversation was over and John Deverall turned to look into the body of the prison again. He made ready to move away but turned his head to Brooks and spoke.
"You talk about life Phil? What life?"

Davies was comfortable in sickbay. In actual fact there were remarkably few marks on his body because he was never struck, just his windpipe was a bit bruised. He would croak when he spoke for a few days. It was likely that he would not speak at all. Form said that he would be very stroppy and moody but not rise to physical anger. There would be glances and the other inmates would give him a wide berth. He lay there in the dark thinking about what he would do. He knew that the whole block must know about the incident by now. By tomorrow the whole prison would know and by the end of the week the story would be common knowledge throughout the system. He would have to put up with the whispers and the glances. He would have to put up with the sniggering and the jokes. It would last only as long as it took for him to demonstrate his potential. It would have to be a very big, very messy, very clever demonstration to everyone, of what *they* could get if they did not show him the respect he deserved. It would not be a guard. It would be a worthless, weak and miserable, scrape of life. He would have to spend some time searching for the perfect victim but it should not be too hard. There was always a bottom link in the prison food chain. He would find him. A smile crept over the features of his half-lit face. He even chuckled which made the ward officer turn his head towards the noise. Bill Davies now drifted off into his violent dreams.

*   *   *

Martin Casey was not tired. After standing in silent vigil for about four hours he was cold but not miserable. He kept himself pumped up by going over in his head what he might have the pleasure of doing if his prey ever showed his face. It would have to be sudden and quick. He was an old man and Brenner was younger and stronger. He would have to follow him until the moment was right. He would have to follow from a distance because Brenner knew what he looked like. If he spotted him, the game would be up and the tables could be turned. That would not do. Brenner must pay for the grief and loss that the Casey's were feeling. He would have to use something, a weapon. If he had to wait for the right moment it could come at any time. He would have to carry the weapon at all times just in case. He made a mental note – think about a weapon. Something ordinary so it would not arouse suspicion. Something he could carry. Maybe a knife.

Martin pushed these thoughts back because he was a decent man and to contemplate sticking a blade into someone was completely alien to him. He pushed the thoughts back because they weakened his resolve. He deliberately thought of something else.

He looked towards the flat. There were lights on but there was no movement. Shadows never crossed the curtains. No one came and no one went to the flat. He wrestled out the crumpled piece of paper he had in his pocket to reassure himself that he did have the correct address. He was in the right place but nothing was happening. It was getting late and a glance at his watch confirmed that he had stayed the allotted time. Coincidentally the lights in the flat went out. Nobody came out of the door so he decided to call it a night. Martin Casey's first surveillance was over. He pulled his jacket closer to his chin and headed off to the bus stop.

* * *

No shadows crossed the windows of the flat because there was no movement in the flat. David had come home late in the afternoon and he had obviously been drinking. When he was like this he came in and went to his room. There were some noises, some movement and then he went to sleep for the rest of the night. As he was home late in the afternoon, he never turned his light on.

Mrs. Brenner sat in the small, tidy front room of the flat. She sat there with her feet drawn up beneath her. Her fingers were intertwined and her knuckles showed white with the pressure of the squeezing they were being given. Her upper body leant forward in an uncomfortable tilt and she stared at the photos on the mantel piece above the electric fire. Those little children. The innocent faces of those boys stared out from the photographs. Who were they? It was obvious that they were pictures of the same child taken at different stages in his life. She was asking impossible questions. She asked questions that a mother should never ask. Who was that child?

He could not be hers.

He could not be the sweet child she pushed in the pram, the child who she played with in the park.

Where was her little boy? Where was the human being that she poured so much love into? Thoughts now crystallised in her mind. They had been coming for a long time. She knew that he had changed even before the court case but she was his mother and she would cling. She would hold on to any hope that it could all be turned around. There was no hope now, nothing to cling to. The faces that stared out of those photographs were of her son who had gone away and she would grieve him. He would never return. His place had been taken by something evil and she had to do something about it. That thought – there in solid form – shocked her. She had made a decision. There was a certain amount of relief that came with it. What to do? That would have to wait for tomorrow. The thoughts from the last few moments had exhausted and weakened her. Suddenly she felt the pain in her fingers, back and legs. Think tomorrow about what to do. It was now time to go to bed. She looked at the photographs once more and took them off of the mantle and placed them in a pile on the table. She moved towards the bedroom turning the light out as she passed through the door. Mrs. Brenner undressed in silence letting her clothes fall on the floor. The light from the street was enough for her to see the bed and she turned down the blankets. The sheets felt cold as she gently rolled herself in and covered up. She turned her face to the street light and closed her eyes. That is when the tears came and they kept on coming until she slept.

* * *

It had been a long day. It had been the longest day of his life. This morning, he was innocent but since then he had been found guilty of murder, transported to prison, processed, reclothed and rehoused. Drew Treevill now lay in his cell and reflected on this day and the rest of his life. His first thoughts were, that it was over. He knew he was going to end up here ever since he had opened the door and the detectives introduced themselves. Here in his cell, he did not have others pouring over his life, asking him questions and giving him disgusting looks. He felt a strange relief that it was over. He lay there in his prison clothes and looked around his cell. Having just arrived, he only had a few personal items, things he needed to wash and shave. There was prison issue of toilet paper and towels and a pot under the bed to relieve himself in. These were the trappings of his new life. This life that would not change for years and years. He could not look forward so he tried to look back.

He looked back to his childhood when he was happy but it was hard to find a time that he enjoyed. All of his memories started well but just seemed to be a short introduction to sad times. He was not wanted, always being neglected by his parents. He was a burden to them because he was so clingy. They resented the time that he spent with them, they never had time of their own. He came between them and split them apart. He remembered an argument they had when they were making claims to possess the remnants of their marriage. He remembered the heated conversation about who he should live with, neither wanted him. His mother, the weaker parent, took possession and never let him hear the end of it. Life at home was poor. He really loved his mother but he could not stop showing it, which drove her further away. When he was able to leave home, he did. His mother found a new partner very quickly and left the country. He never heard from his father again and his recent high profile only drove his parents deeper under cover.

His life as a single male was a disaster as well. He showed too much emotion and was hurt too easily. He made a few attempts to find a girl friend but they all ended with him walking home alone. There was no hope there. Men? He just could not get along with them because he did not fit in with them. He did not share their views, he could not reflect their ideals or agree with the male character. Drew stuck out like a sore thumb, which had been grafted on the wrong hand!

But Drew had dreams. All the time he thought of the things that he had dreamt he would do, he realised that they would never come true. Not even one. He was going to be in this place for the rest of his life. Even if he got out after twenty years his life would be over. He looked around the cell again and the full weight of his sentence fell on him. Twenty years of staring at walls. Twenty years of humiliation from the worst

people on the earth. There would be beatings, it was inevitable. Who would he be kidding if he thought people would treat him differently in here. Inside these walls was a collection of the worst bullies in the world. They would soon sniff out his fear. They would soon make his life miserable again. Tears welled up in his eyes as the cell lights went out. He lay there in the darkness and sobbed. Any strength he had left deserted him and his sobbing became cries. He spoke through his tears and sobs to his tormentors of the future.
"Leave me alone … leave me alone…….!"

He would never be alone again. This was made clear by the response he received from the cells nearest to his own. The words froze him. He lay there wide eyed and silent with the tracks of his tears still wet on his cheeks. Drew Treevill did not have the luxury of crying himself to sleep.

* * *

John Deverall did his shift and retraced his steps to his tidy flat. He was more tired tonight than he usually was, but that was to be expected. He granted himself a very little smile as he reflected on the events of the morning. Being tired though, brought some depression. He would have to go to bed and that meant his torment would start all over again. It could not be helped. He looked through the door to his bedroom and saw his bed. His smile was just a memory now. He gave a deep sigh and shuffled through the door. Sleep came easily, that was not what he feared. It was the waking early in the morning to the ambush by his brain and those oh so terrible thoughts.

Sleep seemed to last but a second then he woke with his hands again squeezing the sheets and sweat rolling down the back of his neck. He closed his eyes tightly shut and braced himself for the onslaught.
And again, it came.
All of those so familiar terrible scenes were played again. Helen being tortured and helplessly allowing her attacker to do whatever he wanted to do. These were pictures that were hard to endure. He was so strong and able and she was his daughter, a little precious thing that it was his destiny to protect. It was impossible. He lay in bed, in the dark, sweating and straining, trying to do something for her but he could not. He was

also standing there in the woods watching the whole scene as hands curled around her neck and began to squeeze.

"Fight Helen! Fight for your life! Scream Helen! Scream my little angel!"

Helen looked at her father, she opened her mouth and words clearly came to him.

"Daddy, you have to do it for me, I can't do it myself. Daddy? ....Daddy?"

John Deverall opened his eyes and the scene was lost. All tension stopped in his body. It was as if he had heard a noise and he was listening hard for another to confirm what it was. He sat up in the darkness and switched on the bedside light. There was a hissing in his ears and he could feel and hear the sound of his own heart. He was shocked by what he had just seen. He could not believe it. This was different. He walked over to the bathroom and pulled the light on. He stood there looking at his reflection sweating in the mirror. His head dropped and he closed his eyes and began again to cry.

This was a feeling that he had not felt in a long time. He let it happen for a moment and then struggled to regain control. Again, looking at himself in the mirror, more composed, John spoke.

"I'm sorry Helen."

From behind him in the bedroom his alarm sounded and he listened until it shut itself off. Now he thought about the day, knowing that it would be different. He felt different. He did not feel so exhausted. He had made a connection!

* * *

Four

Morning.

For most of us it is a new beginning and we are refreshed. It is not only a time for us but it seems that all creation is refreshed. As we look out in the morning, we see a time to renew the assault on what we have started because we have been rejuvenated. Our aches and pains have gone, our strength has come back and the worries of yesterday might still be there but we can face them today. It is a new day. Another day, another dollar. Good day sunshine. Morning fresh. There is a new freshness in our lives. The very rays of the sun seem to be new. There is a tremendous difference between the rays of the sun in the morning and those just before dusk.

Dusk rays seem to be tired. They seem to just have enough energy to make the effort to give us light.

These were morning rays and they were plentiful and shining on everyone. These morning rays were shining freely through any window, you just had to close your eyes and let them hit you in the face. Their warmth gave hope and energy to most people, but it depended on who you were, where you were and what you knew the day had in store for you. They could give you that extra energy you needed to make a change in your life. They could put you in a good mood, a mood that could infect everyone you meet and ultimately make the world a better place.

But what if your curtains were closed? What if you had a hangover and knew that the day just gone was not going to be better than the one breaking outside? How much could a morning do for you, if you knew that your life was just a bore full of bad memories and bad people and there was no way of changing it? Would you look out on the fresh, energy-giving morning rays, and bless them or would you utter a curse? David Brenner hauled himself up in bed and squinted his eyes. The sun's rays found their way through the solar system and impacted upon his retina. A bless or a curse?
"Shit!"

It was a predictable response. He stumbled to the end of his bed and pulled the curtain closed. He turned back to the bed and lay down again. It was no use, he was awake now and it would be impossible to go back to sleep. His head throbbed from the excess of alcohol he had consumed yesterday. It was a hollow feeling that he could only cure by replenishing the blood with alcohol again today. That would come later. There was a bad taste in his mouth partly because of his poor oral hygiene, partly because of junk food consumed yesterday and partly because of the ever-growing cavities situated in his molars. His saliva was thick and he needed a drink. David threw back the covers and stood among the debris of his room.

He shuffled to the door and opened it. It was like entering a different world. This new world was clean and orderly. There was the refreshing sunshine cascading all over it. It brought out the colours of everything. He squinted to try and shut the brightness out. He shuffled to the toilet and bent his head in the sink. He let the water from the tap run directly into his mouth and he drank heavily and noisily. The cold water seemed to course through his entire body. It was refreshing him, making him feel better. It was also waking his body up to the fact that it had a good quantity of water on board!

When he finished drinking, he looked at the toilet seat and, deciding that standing was too much of an effort, he dropped his underwear and sat on the bowl. The liquid drained out of him and the decreasing pressure was a good feeling. Holding his head in both hands with elbows on knees David let a smile loose on his face. He was feeling better. Bodily functions made him feel better. Alcohol made him feel better. When he could get them, a variety of soft drugs made him feel even better. His thoughts turned to other things that turned him on.

Some of the pictures in the books he had in his room made him feel better. Actually, it was the women in the pictures, it was the thought of them making him feel better, that pleased him. He was finishing his toilet task but he was beginning to … stir. More thoughts were going through his head. More thoughts of pleasant feelings and the time when he had the extreme. He had that night in the alleyway. He had the soft yielding flesh. He had spent himself with that young beauty and had not been punished. He was really stirring now.

It is strange how we can change the facts in our minds about reality and real events. Reality was that the rape of Victoria was a dirty affair. It was down in the dirt disgusting. In fact, it was painful. Victoria had resisted and his penetration, there in the dirt, was painful. At the time he had to push the pain out of his mind and get on with the act. Dwelling on the pain at that time would have made him hesitate and the opportunity had to be taken. There wasn't much time. Much later, he discovered that he had ripped his skin quite badly robbing him of replaying the events in the dark solitude of his room. To David now, it was a beautiful event. He could hear her voice sweetly saying things that she did not utter. She welcomed him, she needed him, she enveloped him sweetly in her embrace and she gave herself to him freely. She was warm and smooth. It gave him the feeling that he was born to have. He was fulfilling her and giving her the opportunity to be a woman. Allowing her to do what a woman was destined to do, to give herself to a man.

Sitting there in the bathroom David had become fully aroused. He was feeling much better, his bladder was empty and he had the drink he needed. Now he had another urge that he rarely denied. There was only one place where he could guarantee not to be disturbed. After making sure that he would not be seen, he covered the distance to his room and closed the door. Now he could indulge himself and make his life better. The images that came to him now were from his perfect world. He could live here. The images came faster and faster until both body and mind were spent.

Now his head really hurt. It hurt because of the increase in blood pressure. His perfect world was gone and he was left there amongst the debris of his room and the sordidness that was his life. The sun, having inexorably moved, was in his eyes again. He dropped his head heavily on the pillow again as all of his body went limp. For the second time in the morning, he spoke. For the second time he uttered the same word. "Shit!"

* * *

The same sun shone on Renkill Prison but Drew did not see it with hope of any kind. These sorts of things did not concern him anymore. He was now caught up in a system where there was no hope and each day did not offer any prospects. The lights in his cell went on as they did in every cell. This light was now his sunshine and it shone the same for everybody. It filled all the inmates with the same feeling, the feeling that today would be the same as the last and a prelude for the next.

He was new to the system and he would have to learn how to survive as he went along. First, the lights went on and new noises filled his world. He did not know what to do so he waited. The sound of the latch on the door was the next spike on his new and predictable learning curve. A guard filled the door.

"Grab your pot and stand on the landing."

His pot was empty. He had been too exhausted to function during the night but he grabbed it anyway. The empty pot caused the guard to comment.

"You are going to be given time to sluice out your pot every morning, after lunch and before lights out. We don't have the time to watch you have a shit any time you want to. Slop out at the right time or you will have to keep it in your cell. Is that clear?"

Drew stood there looking into the pot and suddenly did feel the need to purge his system.

"Yes sir, can I go now? I have to go now."

"Leave your pot here and go to the sluice room. There is a toilet next door. This won't happen again will it Treevill? We are not going to get off on the wrong foot, are we?

"No sir."

The guard took a step back and pointed to the right. Drew stepped out on to the landing. He could see other prisoners opposite moving quickly along the landing on both sides of the well and on landings above and below him. Each was carefully carrying his pot, filled to different levels with the night's effluent. There was a smell. The smell of urine and cigarette smoke. There was noise. The noise, of distant shouting of orders and of other prisoners talking loudly, filled the prison. There was the noise of doors opening and closing. The scrape of metal on resisting metal. The prison was stirring in its organised way. There were other guards at the end of the landing supervising the ablutions of the prisoners. The guard at the door called down the landing.

"One for the toilet Mr. Brooks!"

One of the guards paid attention to the call and beckoned Drew to follow. When they met at the end of the landing the guard spoke.

"Treevill, this only happens once. You slop out in the morning, after lunch and before lights out. This is not a primary school where you raise your hand to leave the room. I am not a nursemaid and I neither have the time nor desire to watch you have a shit! Do we understand each other Treevill?"

"Yes Mr. Brooks."

"Get in there, do your business and be quick."

Drew entered a room tiled from floor to ceiling. There were several cubicles with half height dividing walls and no doors. In each cubicle, there was a toilet bowl. On the wall at each end of the room were hand basins. Drew turned to look at the guard. The guard knew that expression and the question, which was behind it.

"You are all the same in here Treevill. You do not have the privilege of privacy. I want to know about everything you get up to. Do your business and get back to your cell. This will not happen again."

Drew moved to a cubicle and prepared himself. He sat down and averted his eyes. The guard was watching him and he felt humiliated. He felt powerless again. He felt cold, small and insignificant. It hampered his previous need to go. A new fear gripped him. If he didn't relieve himself what would this guard think? This was only day one and he was making a mess of it. He had wanted to make a good impression. This thought gave birth to a new feeling of reality. Who was he kidding? He was a child murderer, the lowest scum of the earth and every single guard in the prison knew him. Soon every inmate would know him. The guard at the door frowned and took a step towards the cubicle. The internal grip on his waste products gave up and Drew relieved himself. He cleaned himself and flushed the toilet. Sensing the need for some urgency, he quickly and shyly arranged his clothes and trotted to the hand basin. A quick splash on his hands was enough and he turned to shuffle out to the landing. Three officers barred his way. They were like mountains and Mr. Brooks stood in the middle as their peak.

"Treevill this is the first and last time we are going to give you some good advice so listen very carefully. Every single con in this house knows about you and the thing you have done. They are all capable of sending you out of here in a box and they would do it gladly if you give them a chance. People like you are not held in high regard among the population. Every con in here is your enemy. Things like this give you a high profile. Follow the rules and do everything you are supposed to do, when you are supposed to do them. Keep your head down and maybe later, much later if you can survive, things might settle down into a routine. You will not get special treatment from us. Do we make ourselves very clear?"

Drew looked at the three huge men. They were waiting for an answer but his mind was racing. There were no words that he could say. He had been given no option to express himself and instantly, that new reality, surfaced again. He was in very big trouble in here. His eyes began to show his tears. The officers moved, creating a path between them which suggested that the conversation was over. Drew wiped his eyes quickly, passed between them, and shuffled towards the landing.
The officers stood back and let their breath out. They each knew what the other was thinking. They looked at each other and unprompted they spoke.

"I give him a month."
"Two weeks!"
Phil Brooks led the way out between his colleagues muttering.
"This guy is going to cause us a shit load of trouble"

* * *

Martin Casey did not wake when the sun began to shine. The sun was well into the sky when he woke. He woke because he was alone. His body felt the absence of his lifelong partner beside him. It was a feeling that was so alien to him that his body responded with instant consciousness, ready to act. It was not the gentle waking that we experience but one that sees the body ready to fight or flee.
His eyes opened and he assessed the situation. There was something wrong, he was alone. In the real world that in itself was not a problem but he and his wife were not living in the real world anymore. They were living in a nightmare. She was teetering on the edge of insanity and it was his place to look after her and see her through this mess. He sat up in bed and listened for any sound. He was rewarded with a noise from the

bathroom, flowing water. Wide awake now, despite the fact that he was out for the most part of the night, he moved quickly towards the noise.

He found his wife bent over the sink with the bottle of sleeping pills in her hand.
The blood drained from his stomach and he suddenly went a deathly cold. There was a ringing in his ears as his heart rate increased. How could he have been this careless? In his haste to get out of the house last night, he had left the pills in the cabinet. When he returned, he was tired so he went to bed. He never thought to make sure that the pills were in a safe secret place. Now she stood there staring at him without blinking. She looked angry as if she had discovered a secret, a secret that he had been keeping from her. He summoned the courage to speak and his words whispered out of his mouth. The question had to be asked even when he knew that he was terrified of the answer.
"Cheryl, what have you done?"

She did not take her eyes from his. She moved a step back from the sink and drew herself up to her full, if limited, height.
"I have disposed of the sleeping pills Martin. I have poured them down the sink and washed them away."

Cheryl Casey showed him the empty, lidless bottle. He looked into the sink and there was nothing to be seen. The pills, if they had gone that way, left no trace.
"I don't understand." He muttered
.
She passed him in the doorway and went back to bed where he found her sitting up with her knees drawn to her chest, under the covers.
"Martin, I woke up with the rising of the sun. It is such a good day. I was looking at the clean bright rays and I thought about how much Victoria would have loved them. She was created for days like these. She really was the sun in our lives."
Martin could only slowly walk to the other side of the bed and listen, amazed, to the words from his wife.

"I have watched you, Martin. I see how this has destroyed you and I have not helped. You have been there for me and you always would be." She put her hand on his as they sat face to face on the bed. "But if I am ever going to be able to look at the sun and see the goodness it gives, I must make a change. There is so much that is good in this world, and I have to see it, not the evil side. I have been sitting here thinking for hours. It would taint the memory of Victoria if her death were all that I remembered. I must remember her life. The joy that she gave to us."

Martin was getting it back. His world, at least the world that was left to him, was coming back together. He could feel the despair fleeing from his character and being replaced with hope. He was not foolish enough to think that everything would be cured, he would have to work at this, keep up the momentum that Cheryl was offering. He searched for words but everything that came to his lips seemed to be the wrong thing to say. She sensed this and stopped him with words of her own.

"Don't say anything Martin. I just want you to promise me something. I will do all that I can to put this horror behind me and look for the good. I want us to celebrate all the wonderful things that Victoria was to us, from the time she was born. I want to sit with you with our photos and smile and laugh about all of the times we shared. That will get me through each day but I have to have something else. It is something that you can do because it will be beyond me. Only you have the determination and the strength that is needed. Will you promise me something Martin?"
Martin looked at his wife as her expression changed. He was looking at a different woman from the one he put to bed last night. There was something else though. There was something changing in her attitude as she came to press him for his promise. He had not seen her like this before. It was in her eyes. It sent a chill through him because they were filled with pure hate. He could feel the stiffness in her body across the bed and her grip painfully tightened around his fingers.

"Somehow that Brenner bastard has to pay. You have to find a way to make that son of a bitch feel the pain that we feel. He has to feel the pain that Victoria felt. I don't need to know what you are doing. It would probably be best if I didn't but I must know that you are doing *something!"*

She waited for an answer and now he had the words. He knew what he had to do. Everything was going to be all right again because they were pulling in the same direction. His answer chased the hate from her eyes and they filled with joy.

"He will pay Cheryl, he will pay dearly. I promise you!"

* * *

Bill Davies spent about two days in sick bay. It was a cushy number and he knew that he could swing the lead a bit while his minor injuries healed. He knew exactly what was happing out there in the prison. The old lags were having a wry grin about what happened to him. They knew that he had been put firmly in his place, they had seen it all before. They were a bunch that knew how to stay away from trouble, mind their own business and do what they were doing now, having a wry grin amongst themselves, but they would never let Davies see them do it. The younger more able men were bracing themselves because they knew that it could be one of them that would have to pay the price for Davies's humiliation. In their minds they were creating scenarios with Davies to predict what they might do or say if the time comes. It was important not to get caught cold, you always needed to know what was going to happen next. Knowing what Davies was going to do next was difficult, because he was one of those mad dog prisoners whose actions you could not predict. There was a distinct nervousness amongst these prisoners.

There was another category of prisoner, the prey. These prisoners were divided in two, those who were wise to prison culture and knew what was going to happen and those who had no idea. If you were one of those who knew, you would be trying to do favours, find a buddy, get somebody who could protect you and stick to him. Never get caught out in open ground by yourself. Their days were filled with heart stopping moments until the event was over and then they hoped that the next crisis could mercifully be a long way away and didn't affect them. The prisoners who were unwise were usually the weak new arrivals. The stronger ones might be able to fend for themselves so they were rarely selected as prey. The unwise weak, went about their daily routine oblivious that one of their fellow inmates was waiting for his moment to pounce.

Curiously, none of the other prisoners let on what is happening. They could have sent out a warning that Davies would be looking for a victim but this would only have prolonged the event. The event *had* to take

---

place before Renkill could settle down again. The sooner the better so, everyone kept their mouths shut. Eyes wide open and lips tight shut. Drew Treevill, unwise, weak and a prime candidate for the role of prey, found himself in this climate. He was so out of place in amongst these men. It was like being back at work with the other tyre fitters. Every direction he looked he could find a bully, a parasite or pervert. His body language was wrong. He gave way allowing others to pass. He thanked, pardoned and excuse me'ed all over the place. He would not have been easier to choose had he painted the word 'victim' on his back.

Davies was discharged from sick bay just before lunch. He was escorted by two guards back to the landing and his cell. Few words were spoken. "Lunch in ten minutes Davies." The guards left the cell and door was locked. His cell mate had disappeared and he gave a little grin to the wall as the door closed behind him. At least he had achieved something with his little demonstration. He reached up and rubbed his neck and his grin disappeared. He lay down on the bed and stared at the ceiling. He was not making plans because whatever happened would be spontaneous, spur of the moment, fast and unexpected. He was hungry and his mind wandered to thoughts of food and guessing what was for lunch today. His thoughts were interrupted by the sound of the key turning in the lock. "Grab your pot and stand on the landing"

Davies could see two other guards on the landing and he let his grin loose again. They were taking no chances. This was status but it was not enough.
"No pot sir, just got back from sick bay."
"OK then stand on the landing and prepare to go to lunch."
The guards moved down the landing and allowed Davies to exit. He stood there and saw the other prisoners along the landing above and below opposite. Some gave him a look, some avoided his glare and others were just unaware. He moved towards the iron stairs. Another grin escaped across his face when he saw that the meal was curry. He liked curry. Davies made his way to an empty table and he was sure that it would stay that way. He sat there and ate slowly and when he was finished, he concentrated on the others in the hall. He was aware that his presence was causing some concern among some of the cons in the room. No one wanted his gaze to dwell on them for very long. He knew that if he looked long enough their movements would give them away.

The scurriers would be hard to catch. The motionless showed no fear and could be tricky, but the unaware, the ones acting normally, they were the prey.

Drew Treevill slopped out and was happy at having been part of the routine. He joined the others and entered the dining hall. When he got to the hot plate, he was happy with his meal and he made his way to a table where some others sat. He gave them all a quick glance and decided not to say hello! He sat down and began to eat.

The hall was filled with the smell of food, murmured conversations and loud noises of crashing pans from the kitchen. Some men near him spoke in barely audible levels but he kept quiet. He did not know how to start to talk to these men. 'Do you come here often' was not the way.

After a short while he sensed a change of attitude among the men he ate with. Their conversation stopped and they seemed to be uneasy. Some picked up their empty plates and left, others finished quickly and his last remaining table mate picked up his tray and just moved to another table. This left him alone and bewildered. He hadn't said anything, he didn't smell and he could sense that the noise had died down in the hall. He looked around but no one was looking at him. It was as if he was being avoided deliberately.

Then he felt the gaze.
He could feel someone looking at him. He turned to see a prisoner two tables away just sitting there looking at him. The man had finished his meal and was grinning. The smile did not show happiness but rather it was the smile of surprise at finding something lost, like the last piece of the jigsaw. The other man stood up and carrying his tray came towards Drew.
"Hi there, you new here, aren't you?"
Drew looked around at the other inmates but could draw no information from their expressions. The noise levels went back to normal and eating continued. It seemed an innocent question so he decided to answer.
"Yes, I just got here this week."

"I bet you are scared shitless about what to do, who to avoid, when to sit, when to stand. I know I was when I first came here. My name's Bill by the way."

"Hello Bill. I'm Drew. Yeah, it's not been easy."

"Look, come and see me sometime during the exercise period and I'll show you the ropes."

"Sure, maybe, uh … Bill."

"Good, I'll keep an eye out for you." This was said but not intended. Davies looked like a man to be avoided.

Bill Davies felt good. He now had the guards on their toes when he was around. He had a cell to himself. He had just filled himself with his favourite meal and he had found the perfect victim for his event. His grin was now promoted, to a smile!

*   *   *

John Deverall washed and shaved just the same way he always did but this time there seemed to be more feeling in what he did. He could feel the razor slice through the bristles. He could smell the soapy freshness of the shaving foam and the heat of the water in the bowl. He stopped to take all of this in. He looked at himself, half shaven, in the mirror. John was pleased with what he saw. The half shaved, half dressed man staring back at him seemed to have a question. Why are you doing this John? Who are you living for, who are you trying to impress?
He looked at the reflection.

It was puzzling, it was a good question. He looked into the eyes in the mirror and without sound he replied. The purpose was to make himself presentable, to have a good clean shave and smarten himself up, wash the night out of the system and get ready for the new day. But why? This was not the way things usually were.
Something made him think about the way he looked. He went back to shaving with renewed care, he wanted to give himself a good close shave because it made him look good, it made him feel better. When he was finished, he towelled himself down and gave his reflection a sideways glance. He left the bathroom and turned off the light.
The sun was beginning to rise now and the beams of light penetrated his flat in horizontal bars. He went to the window and opened the blinds

fully. The sun shone on his face and upper body. Looking in you would have seen the naked form of a man, eyes closed, seeming to drink in the energy from the sun. He stood there motionless but his mind was racing. His life had changed somehow. The terrifying script that his daughter always stuck to in his vision, had been different. He took pleasure in the chore of preparing himself for work and now he was basking in the pleasure that the sun was giving him. Opening his eyes, he looked down into the street and saw it stirring with people preparing to continue their lives. Suddenly he wondered about their lives, what were their problems and their joys? Who were they? What kept them going from day to day? Until that moment he realised he had only existed. He had struggled from day to day, getting by and no more. Now he had discovered a capacity to see something good. To feel something good. Where had all of this come from?

It came from the feeling he got when he held the life of Bill Davies in his hand. He could still feel it now, the way that he became oblivious to everything around him. No sound or light triggered his senses. He had stood there, a supreme being, and it was his sense of right and wrong that mattered. He was the ultimate court and his decision was final. He held the life of Davies in his hands and had he not been brought back to reality by Brooks, the sentence would have been carried out.

John made his way over to his still unmade bed, the scene of so many horrible dreams. He sat down and looked around the room. Looking at his bedroom was something that he rarely did, it was just a place to sleep and endure the tortured thoughts that his brain would send. The room was functional, it did what it was supposed to do. The room had no personality. He stood and moved to the hall and then to the lounge. Another sterile, lifeless room surrounded him. He looked closely at what the room lacked, pictures, pieces of the past, something to stir his memory. A voice in his ear, an inner voice spoke to him, warned him.

'You don't want that sort of stuff John, they will only dredge up feelings from the past that you can't cope with, feelings like love and joy. They will give you a whiff of happiness that you once had and you will never be happy like that again.'

He shut the voice out. There were so many thoughts running through his head that he could not get to the end of a single one. He let his thoughts do whatever they wished, like silly children they could be dealt with later. He moved through the entire flat and opened the curtains of every window. The flat filled with morning light and warmth. There were two things he had to do, get dressed and phone in to say he would not be coming to work today.

John Deverall now realised that his life could change, he knew that he was not stuck with anything. He had the rest of his life to make a difference. He would start today.

*   *   *

The news that 'Sarge' would not be at work sent a small imperceptible shiver through the guards on his shift. They were all capable men but he gave them a sense of unity. They worked as a unit when he was there and none of them could remember the last time he took time off. It was a rarity. In his absence Phil Brooks took the lead and took charge of the men during the morning briefing with the governor.

Phil was much younger but still had the respect of the men. He was a talker, he weaved his way through problems by discussion and planning. In a pinch he could easily hold his own if things became physical but he was best at gathering information and 'heading off' trouble before it started. Phil was worried about his friend. He saw the way he dealt with Davies and now he was drawing a picture in his mind of Deverall, at home, tormented and wracked with guilt. He needed to discuss this with someone, he would have a chat with the governor.

"Good morning gentlemen. We are a bit short handed again today. The court list is posted." He gestured to the paper on the wall "So the lockdown hours will have to increase while staff do escort duty. Four officers from HMP Southurst will be arriving in about an hour, to take up the slack."

The men shuffled. It was not unusual for prison officers to move between prisons in times of need. Officers from other prisons were always welcome. They made the job easier and as the system was the same everywhere they already knew the ropes. The men who did this job belonged to a brotherhood and got on well together.

The briefing was over, the men began to get ready to file out. Phil Brooks walked up to the warden and spoke.

"Mr. Endersley, can I have a word with you?"

The men stopped, they were used to moving together at this time so they stopped to wait for Brooks and not out of curiosity for what he had to say.

Brooks looked at them and said, "Go ahead and I will see you on the landing."

The two men waited until all of the other guards were gone.

"Sir, I am worried about John."

"Worried? Why?"

"There was an, incident, on the landing with Davies."

The governor looked up from the papers he was arranging and took greater interest in the conversation.

"John had to restrain Davies and that is why he ended up in the sick bay."

The governor knew that the inmates had to be controlled and that sometimes the control had to be physical. He also knew that the injuries to Davies did not come from a fall as had been reported. He had spoken to the doctor and was going to let the situation drift in to the past. These men had a hard job and they dealt with hard men. Davies was one of the toughest to deal with but he had not made a complaint so it was best left.

"Are you making a complaint Brooks?"

"No sir, on the contrary, John dealt with the situation competently but there was something that I saw in him at the time. You see, I know about his history and the things that have happened in his life."

"We all know that Officer Deverall has a tragic history Brooks, what does that have to do with Davies?"

"I felt that he could have killed Davies because he had nothing to live for, as if he thought he was dealing out punishment. I spoke to him about it afterwards and it was something he said that also worried me." Brooks waited for a reply.

"What did he say?"

"He told me how he felt about the damage some prisoners have caused to the lives of others, the innocent, and how these men deserve to die. He led me to believe that his life would not be ruined if he were to … take the law into his own hands."

The governor, who had been leaning on the back of a chair, now stood up. It was a way of saying that the conversation was over, but he had one more thing to say.

"Brooks, I want to thank you for bringing this to my attention. Let's leave it as it is, unofficial, and we'll keep an eye on Deverall. I will have a word with him when he gets back. Right now, your men are waiting for you." He dismissed Brooks with a thin smile.

Phil Brooks made his way to the landing where the men were waiting for him but he could not shake off the feeling that the governor was not as concerned as he should be.

Malcolm Endersly left the briefing room a full minute after Brooks had gone. He went straight to his office pausing at his secretary's desk on the way. She looked up from her work as her name was spoken.

"Mrs. Whittle, I want you to cancel my tasks for this morning and schedule them for later in the week. The Deputy Governor can take my calls."

"Yes Governor. Where can you be contacted?"

"I will be with the Minister."

* * *

David Brenner was woken by sounds in the flat. He had slept for most of the morning and now his mother was pottering around outside his room. He would have to face her soon. He had long ago stopped worrying about the disappointment he saw in her eyes. He just didn't care anymore. He didn't look. She provided him with food and a place to stay. He lived in his room for most of the times so they rarely met. He dressed and shuffled out into her world. She stood in the kitchen drinking a cup of coffee. She looked at him as he came in and confirmed the thoughts she had about him. He was not her son. He was here, he had a right to be here but he did not belong.

"Any hot water left?"

To ignore him would give him a clue about the decision she had made. To ignore him would probably start a row and peel back the skin she was growing over her pain. She would cry and he could not comfort her. She would not want him to, she would be abhorred by it so it was safe to be civil.

"There is some in the kettle."

She left the room as he made his drink. She went to her room and sat on her bed. Now she could hear the noises of him moving around her flat. Her coffee grew cold and she put the cup on the bedside table. She sat there on her bed staring straight ahead. She showed no concern about what happened on the other side of her bedroom door. As the time went by, she was aware of the smells of food being fried, the sounds of the television and finally the door closing. It was some time after that when she snapped back into full consciousness again. The flat was now silent. She was cold and cramped, and it was dark. She had sat on her bed for the entire day. In her trance like state, sitting there not thinking, it seemed like only an hour had gone by.

She stood and walked in to the darkened flat. He must have turned the lights out when he left so she turned them on again. She went to the kitchen and put her cup on the worktop which was now strewn with the cooking debris of the day, his day. While she washed up the plates her mind was constantly being drawn to the items in his room. Having only half seen the album she needed to see it again to confirm that she had not been dreaming. The washing of the dishes was a ploy to keep her busy, something to delay the act of going in there and confronting her worst fears. When the kitchen was back to a standard that she liked she hung the dishtowel over the taps and turned toward the door.

She needed to do this quickly, like taking distasteful medicine, move quickly, do the deed, don't think, just act! Deep breath taken she moved quickly towards the door, through the hall and to his room. Without slowing she pushed the door and entered his world. Nothing gained her attention. The room was much the way it was the last time she was there. The album was in the same semi hidden place and she made straight for it. Removing the book was her main concern so when she had accomplished that she turned and left the room as swiftly as she had entered.

She took the album to her room and placed it deep in the bottom drawer of the linen cupboard. She shoved the drawer home with excess force and closed the door heavily too. This part of the medicine taking was over, the distasteful part was done, unfortunately she knew that browsing this book would not make her feel better but she had to know. Her breath was coming quickly now and she made the effort to control it, bring it back to a normal pace. Stealing his book, being in his room, made her feel dirty and her body was still feeling the cramp of inactivity so she ran a hot bath for herself.

* * *

Martin Casey felt odd standing there in the night looking up at the lights in the Brenner flat. It was odd how things turned out, his wife making a complete turn around. It was odd the conversation he had with her as he left their home.

"Where are you off to dear?" She said this as she caught him getting his warm clothes on in the hall way. He looked at her but he did not know what to say. What he couldn't say was that he was going to stand in a bus shelter for most of the night, just staring at a window.
"I'm doing … something," was all that he could say.
She looked at him and started to fuss over his collar.
"Make sure that you look after yourself. Make sure that you come home to me."
Tears came to his eyes. They were tears of pride, not of sadness. This woman had such a well of strength and for a moment, he drew from her all that he needed. He could face anything if she were on his side. He turned to the door.
"I'll probably be late, don't wait up for me." He kissed her lightly and opened the door. From behind him he heard her speak.
"I will be here, waiting for you to return."
The door closed and he made his way into the oncoming dusk.

* * *

David spent his day lounging around the flat. He ate when he was hungry and watched television most of the time. Every minute that went by his need for a stimulant gnawed at his system. There was nothing in the flat, his mother did not drink and his room was barren also. He was getting desperately low on money and his next handout from the government was four days away. This desperation called for desperate measures. He would go out tonight and score. How? He did not know.

The day dragged on and his need became acute. He had made it through the day but would not last out the night. He went to his room and dressed in warm clothes preparing to go out. As he left the apartment, he turned out the lights, an act that was keenly awaited by a darkened figure standing in the shadows of the bus stop.

David emerged on to the street and looked both ways. He chose the route which took him past Martin on the other side of the street. He began to walk.

His hands were thrust deeply into his empty pockets and his mind was scrolling through all of the ways he could get the cash needed for a drink or if he scored really well, something chemical, to take him to a temporary oblivion. Being so engrossed by these thoughts made him unaware of the man now following some thirty yards behind. Martin too had thoughts of his own. What would he do if David stopped, what if he came back the same way? What if he hopped on a bus or taxi? What would he do if he was seen and David confronted him? Let these things take care of themselves.

David was still walking at a steady pace and not looking back. He was walking further out of the city. He knew that anything he did, had to be far from home. He had no money so he must walk. Any place where there were few people around was best and his mind was made up that he must try burglary. Get in to a house fast, find something small and expensive, take it to a pub and get the best price he could for it. Others do it all the time. He walked, and was followed, for forty minutes.

The area became darker as the street lights thinned. There were more houses and fewer groups of shops. Martin watched and worried from his safe distance. Pedestrians were also thin on the ground and he was aware that it must be obvious that he was following the man in front but the man in front had other things on his mind. He was looking for a darkened house, a rarity in the area, and his needs and frustrations were taking their toll on the caution he took.

David was approaching a small row of shops. They were all dark except one and his mind went from burglary to robbery. It would be easier to sell a new item than one which was obviously second hand. He decided to walk past the shops and see what they had to offer, pick one out and then make his way around the back to see if he could gain entrance. In the middle of the terrace stood a Laundromat, the only lit building in the street. It was occupied by a lady who sat and stared at the only moving washing machine. David looked in and then walked on to the end of the terrace, where he stopped.

Martin had not reached the shops yet and when he saw David stop, he just took a step to his right and stood in a leafy entrance to a private house. From here he was concealed but also had a good vantage point to see what David did next.

David was making new plans. Never mind breaking and entering, here was a woman, a small woman, she must have a purse or a bag. He could just go in, make the grab and disappear into the night. It was perfect. It was cash. He didn't have the reinforcement that alcohol gave him. He stood for a long time making up his mind, listening to the voices in his head, trying to weigh up the pro's and con's but it was useless. He needed money and this was the only way to get it. Go in, be bold, be quick. Make the grab and run out. He walked into the full fluorescent glare of the shop.

The lady was dressed in sweater, trousers and canvass crepe shoes. She was attractive and although she was over forty her face still held the traces of her youth. Her close-cropped hair was stylishly done and her make-up was conservative. She was not the usual type of client commonly seen in the Laundromat. Much to her distress her washing machine had broken that day so she had to get these loads done tonight. She had two children at home and they needed clean clothes for tomorrow. When she decided earlier to get the washing done this way, she was worried about being alone. Dismissing it as nonsense she now wished she hadn't because she didn't like the look of the man who walked through the door and the fact that he did not carry any washing!

David walked in and the woman immediately looked at him then looked straight ahead. Worse, she moved her oversize bag across her body to the bench, putting herself between it and him. She crossed her legs and folded her arms and bit her lip. There was no way he could grab the bag and run, he would have to push her out of the way to get what he wanted. There was still a hope that he could intimidate her into handing it over.

Big front, get her scared and she might just hand it over without a struggle.

"Give me your bag."

The lady turned to David. Her face had gone white. The fear was there to see in her face and this gave him the bravery he needed.

"Your bag!"

She stood up and clutched her bag as she backed away. Fear was still there but dignity and resistance also surfaced. This woman was not used to being pushed around. She could look after herself and what she had – she held!

"Get away from me. You're not getting my bag. Just get out of here!"

David didn't expect this. In his mind everything would play out as he had planned so he never had a plan 'B' to fall back on. He had committed himself to this action so he had to make it work. They were both going in the same direction towards the back of the shop and their pace was quickening. There was no escape for the woman. The dryers at the rear halted her retreat and David made a lunge for the bag by reaching over her shoulder. The moment he grabbed the bag she brought her knee up into the soft flesh below his ribcage and the wind completely escaped his body. One of her hands was tightly gripping the handle of her bag and the other had found his hair. His head was being forced back and the pain in his scalp was unbelievable! He let go of the bag and gripped her by the neck.

She screamed and lunged forward but he was too tall for her and he did not topple. Instead, he turned, threw her to the floor and fell on top of her. Now he had some strength, now he had some power, distant memories ran through his body. The woman was screaming and squirming beneath him and he had to shut her up! The bag that he so desired was pressed to the floor beneath both of them but the damned woman was making so much noise. He reached over and placed his hand over her mouth. The woman now knew she was fighting for her life and every weapon she had was brought to bear.

She opened her mouth and the pressure of his hand pushed it between her teeth which she brought together. Now it was his turn to scream and the pain gave him the strength to wrench his hand from her mouth. He arched his back and for a moment they looked each other in the eyes. Hers said she would fight. His said I am going to kill you. David was the first to react. She was a millisecond too late. His hands shot out and clasped her neck. She could not make a noise, or breathe. She had to make a noise to live. She had to scream or she would die. She had to *breathe* or she would die. Her eyes were wide open, disbelieving that she could possibly be in this situation. All she could see was the salivating grimace on the face above her. She was blacking out. It was over.

Martin stayed on the path for about five minutes. When he saw David enter the shop, he did not know what to do. If he moved too soon, he might get caught as David came out. He waited what seemed an age and then moved from the deep shadow towards the shop light. He was reluctant to give himself away so he crossed to the other side of the street. He chose another garden gateway where he could have a clear view of the shop which he now saw was a Laundromat. He also saw that it was empty!

David must have gone out through the back! This sent him into a mild panic because he didn't want to lose his prey. Something he saw in the shop broke his chain of thought. David's head suddenly popped up from behind a bench inside the shop. Hemust be laying on the floor! Intrigued he crossed the street but avoided the light from the shop. Something was wrong. The movement was wrong, David seemed to be struggling with something.
Then he saw a hand reach up and grab at David by the hair!.

Martin left the shadows and bolted straight into the light. He hit the door with his shoulder and it crashed back on its hinges. There before him lay David, his hands gripping the neck of a woman beneath him. Her eyes were rolling backwards in her head and only the whites were showing. She was gradually giving up the resistance to his chokehold. David was leering, grimacing through his exertions and he slowly lifted his head in response to the crashing of the door. Martin could not match this man for strength but something had to be done now! He instantly scanned the room.

Nothing but plastic laundry baskets were available but there was a fire extinguisher clipped to the wall. Two steps were all it took. The red bottle came off the wall easily and in one movement, he swung it across David's head.

David dropped like a stone. He dropped on top of the inert body of the woman below him. Martin dropped the cylinder and pushed David over to the side. He gently picked her up and started to revive her. No longer being choked she dragged huge gulps of air into her lungs. He held her in his arms gently saying that everything would be all right. He looked over at David. Here he was at last, at his feet, at his mercy. All the time he worried what he would do and in the end David did it to himself! The worry flowed out of his being, to be replaced by relief. His body relaxed.

The scene, when the police arrived, was a puzzling one. There, in the Laundromat, was a man lying unconscious with a large bleeding cut and bump on his head. A dishevelled woman sat rasping for breath, clutching her bag. Most peculiarly of all, there was an older man who sat, shaking his head, while he chuckled and laughed.

* * *

Five

John Deverall spent the day changing things in his life. They were little changes but his life had been the same for so long, they were major to him. He moved the furniture around and changed some of the décor in the flat. He opened the windows that had been shut for so long. He was letting life back into his existence. The exertions made him hungry and he found that there was precious little in the way of food in his fridge. He had to go out to do some shopping and he felt a peculiar fear to do it. The fear amused him but he dismissed it quickly.

He put on his coat and went out into his local world that he knew so little about.
It was a voyage of discovery but it did not last very long. Late in the afternoon he was overcome with a sense of futility. He told himself that this would all come crashing down and he would drop back into that existence again. This world was for these people, the ordinary people, who were untouched by the horrors that visited him and the dross he dealt with at work. He felt guilty because he was not meant to be like this. He was more comfortable the way he used to be. This was not punishment enough for failing Helen, for not being there when, at the end of her life, she really needed him.

When he returned, he sat in his newly rearranged flat, looking at the changes he had made. He would need a new strength to keep this up and put some of the past behind him. He wondered if he had the strength to do it. A different man closed the windows. The man who opened them was filled with a pipe dream of new beginnings and a will to change his life. The man who closed them was more practical, a realist who knew that he was just kidding himself. It was getting late and there was a ritual to endure. He left the kitchen very untidy and went to his bedroom. That too was untidy, he had not gotten around to straightening the bedclothes that day. It would have to do. Tomorrow, or when he could find the time, he would recreate his old world and carry on. He was tired again. The brief promise of change had taken its toll so he went to bed. He knew he would sleep his dreamless sleep and after that? His ritual torture would begin.

He woke, as usual, without opening his eyes. The darkness stayed dark but the images came again. The images were the same tormenting images he had endured for years but they were moving faster. They sped through to the point where, last night, the change had taken place there in the woods with Helen. He was not sweating. He was not straining. He was waiting to see what was going to happen. The same hands curled around his daughters' neck and she said the same words.
"Daddy, you have to do it for me, I can't do it myself. Daddy? …….
Please?"

Eyes opened and scene lost. He was not in pain. He was not covered in sweat. He was filled with the need to do something. Helen wanted him to do something but for the life of him he did not know what. He did know that his life had changed and he would not go back to the way it was. His alarm sounded and he prepared himself to go to work.

The twenty-minute walk to the bus was different. There were more colours in his surroundings, the air was fresher and there were sounds he had not heard before. Of course there was no change in them, it was him, he had changed. He was being opened up, revived, brought back. The optimism was blunted by that fear again, did he want to start living again, did he deserve it? Soon he found himself standing at the bus stop with the usual collection of fellow travellers. As he was experiencing these new feelings, he was also looking more closely at everything around him.

The others in the line were looking at him fondly and quickly looking away when their eyes met. He sensed a peculiar feeling from them, they seemed to be pleased he was there. They seemed more relaxed, comfortable, safe. One elderly lady even spoke!
"We missed you yesterday, I hope you are well."

He looked at her as if she was speaking a foreign language. He looked around at the expressions on the faces of the other passengers in an attempt to confirm that she had spoken. But all of their faces were expecting an answer. She had spoken but she had also spoken for them!

"Er, No. I'm fine thank you," was all that he could afford to say at the moment. He needed time to think. The other passengers nodded to each other as if, upon hearing that he was not ill, they were pleased with his good health.

From the other end of the line, a bespectacled man made his presence known.

"We were very grateful for what you did the other day." More nods and confirmation. The responsibility of 'spokesperson' had been passed on. Not knowing what he was talking about, John had to ask.

"What did I do the other day?" But the answer came from beside him, a completely different quarter, a young lady holding her infant offered the answer.

"You stopped that hooligan pushing through the line and barging on the bus."

The conversation went back to the elderly lady.

"More people like you should stand up to these thugs." It was the turn of the bespectacled man next.

"There is no respect these days, they get away with murder!"

John looked at these people. They had shared the bus stop with him in this routine for years and he had never seen them. He had never looked at them closely but now, because he had righted a wrong, they had opened themselves to him. Things were becoming clearer. These were the people being protected by the prisons. These were the decent ordinary people whose lives were constantly being ruined by the mindless thugs that he held at bay every day. He looked at them more closely and saw that they were worthy of more, much more.

John Deverall looked at the bespectacled man and repeated his words.

"Yeah, they get away with murder."

* * *

It takes about three months to settle down into a routine in prison. The world is new and you are constantly trying not to step outside of the usual routine because it could mean that you miss something. It could be something as innocent as not getting a library book, but even the most innocent tasks can be blown out of all proportion. Riots have occurred because there was no second helping of custard. Drew Treevill was struggling with the transformation. He had no support because no one would give him the word to the wise. His association with Davies had branded him and he didn't know it. The word had travelled all over the prison that he belonged to Davies.

The word had passed to everyone to keep clear, everyone but Treevill. There are times when prisoners will give a message of impending trouble to the guards. When an inmate is going to do something that will cause suffering for them all, then the guards might be tipped off. There was no point in suffering needlessly. In this case though, the suffering was going to be limited to a single individual, it would clear the air of the tension and anyway, the guy was a child killer and probably deserved it. So, when the word went out that Davies wanted Treevill, the information never reached the guards and certainly not Drew.

Drew was oblivious. He was spending his time getting used to things but he was not so foolish as to make friends. He knew who was in here. These men were all dangerous and he was so vulnerable. He felt the vulnerability at the start but the feeling was wearing off. He was becoming bolder with his knowledge of the system. He was becoming familiar with this place and it was time to make a few acquaintances. It would make the time seem a little less heavy if he could occasionally talk to someone, but most prisoners had little time for him and tended to shamble away from him on contact. They restricted their comments to single syllables, affirmative grunts and negative shakes of the head. Drew was in this state of mind when he came across Bill Davies in the yard.

Davies was standing by himself leaning up against a wall with his hands firmly shoved in his pockets. He had been watching as Drew wandered aimlessly through the clusters of other prisoners. They gave him distance and were not drawn to a conversation. Davies waited and counted himself lucky that his quarry was being delivered straight into his hands. A wry smiled attached itself to his face as the distance between him and Drew lessened. To get his attention he had to speak.

"Hi there, how is it goin?

Drew was taken aback by the words. This was the first time that anyone other than a guard had chosen to speak to him first. His second reaction was of uneasiness. He wanted to speak but something inside told him that he shouldn't. He had to be on his guard but the need to develop a relationship was too great. The last time he had met this man was in the canteen and he seemed alright then. Remembering that distant conversation, he pushed his fear back and decided to reply.

"Oh, Hi. Yeah, I'm still getting used to things. It's not easy." Drew stopped and faced the taller man.

"It's not supposed to be easy, this isn't a holiday camp but there are ways of making life bearable. Have you got a connection on the outside?" Drew needed to know more. "On the outside, no, what would a *connection* do?"

"They can get you things to make your life more bearable. Tobacco, soft toilet paper, magazines and books. Delivery would be during visiting hours. I knew a con who could get anything past the guards and as long as you kept him sweet, he would share his connection. It gave you something to look forward to. There is nothing like having something that makes your life bearable. There is nothing like having something to look forward to. Next time you have a visitor let them know that you want something and they can bring it in for you."

Drew frowned and confided in Davies. "I haven't had a visitor yet."

Davies looked with sympathy at the young man, at least that is what he appeared to do. Inside he was roaring with laughter. This was going to be too easy. This man was easy pickings. It is a pity that he had other plans because he could form a relationship here. He would be able to get Drew to do anything he wanted.

"Look er …. It's Drew, isn't it?"

Drew nodded.

"I'm Bill … remember ...? Look Drew, I have someone on the outside and I know a lot of the lags in here. You let me know if there is anything you need and I will see if I can get it for you."

Bill held out his hand and Drew shook it. Drew felt more comfortable. He had made contact with someone. The handshake had not gone unnoticed. Every prisoner in the yard knew what was going on. The first step had been taken, it wouldn't be long now.

* * *

She was surprised to hear the ring of the doorbell. She had very few friends and none of them ever called round. It could only be David who had forgotten his key. She braced herself to see him. She knew what state he must be in and she made up her mind to just let him in and then go back to her own bed. Their lives would briefly touch again and then run along parallel lines, together but apart. Expecting him she opened the door fully but immediately stopped and became fully awake.

There were two men standing there, two big men with an official air about them. Behind them stood a policeman, uniformed and helmeted. She put the door between herself and her visitors, quickly clutching her night clothes and dressing gown to her neck. Looking around the door she spoke.

"Yes? What do you want?"

"Mrs. Brenner?

"Yes."

"I'm DS Roper and this is DC Langham." The first man said this as they both flipped out their warrant cards. Her eyes briefly flicked to the small documents and then back to their eyes. The whole story was there in their eyes. There was sympathy and pity in their eyes. They knew that she was not to blame and the sorry figure that she presented in the doorway, prompted these emotions in them, which showed in their eyes. They were men who dealt with raw emotions all of the time and it was impossible to hide their own sometimes.

"May we come in?"

Mrs. Brenner turned and went into the lounge. The officers looked at each other and entered the flat. The uniform stayed outside. She stood there as they spoke. Words passed her ears and filtered out the unnecessary information. She stood there and stared at the window as they spoke.

'Arrested' made its way in,

'attacked … woman … laundromat … hospital … concussion …. custody.'

An emotion brought her attention back. The officer had spoken of an injury and she was concerned and had to know. Oh God she hoped that it was not serious. Out of sheer compassion for another human being she had to know, she had to ask.

"The woman …. Is she OK?

The officer stopped speaking and relaxed.

"Yes, she will recover, she has some nasty compression injuries to her neck but she will be fine. As I said David is in …."

Mrs. Brenner turned sharply and looked at both men. In this moment her life had pivoted and changed direction. The connection that she so tenuously held with her son had broken. He was out there now by himself. She could not help him, he could not even help himself. He had his chance but was not strong enough to use it. She held his secret, that would be safe but now these men were in charge and she must let them get on with their work. Let's get it done and over with.
"What can I do?"

The sympathy from the officers was gone, replaced by determination. This was now a crime investigation and evidence needed to be gathered.
"Mrs. Brenner we need to ask you some questions."
The questions lasted long into the night.

* * *

Mrs. Casey was waiting for her husband to return as she did every night that he went out 'gathering information' as he put it. When the phone rang, she was startled, because it broke the silence so sharply. It was very rare to get a call and never at that time of night. By the second ring fear had set in. There was a buzzing in her ears and a heat in her face. She looked at the phone as it rang. Its ring was compelling and she moved to answer it.
"Hello?"
"Mrs. Casey?"
It was the voice of a man, he was a stranger. She was caught between acknowledging the question and hanging up to avoid receiving dreadful information. She spent too long wrestling with this dilemma. The strange voice on the other end of the line repeated the question.
"Hello, is that Mrs. Casey?"
She cleared her throat and spoke. "Yes."
"I am Sgt. Coombs from Northbank police station."
She had to sit down because her knees weakened. She became dizzy because this was the moment that she had dreaded but knew was going to come. This call could only mean one thing. Martin had not been able to resist attacking Brenner. She was filled with a feeling of total loss. She had lost her daughter and now her husband. The feelings alarmed her. Until that moment, she always felt that her sorrow would be for herself, thinking about being alone for the rest of her life with nothing but

miserable memories pushing out all others. But her thoughts went out to Martin. She switched from feeling self-pity, to bracing herself to give all the support Martin needed. She had to summon up strength for him. The voice on the phone brought her back.

"Mrs. Casey? Are you there?"

"Sorry, yes. What has happened?"

"There is nothing to worry about Mrs. Casey. Your husband was a witness to an assault this evening; in fact, he may have saved a woman's life. He is here at the police station being interviewed."

"My God, how is he?"

"He is not hurt Mrs. Casey, but we do have a problem. It seems that the man we have in custody is known to both you and your husband, a Mr. Brenner?"

Her focus immediately changed. The muscles in her face completely relaxed. This was not worth being concerned about. She would find out all the details later. Now she must be with Martin.

"How do I get to your police station?"

The reply from the sergeant was so quick and organised that it could only have meant he was expecting the question.

"A car will be with you in five minutes."

*   *   *

The life that John Deverall now led was not vastly different on the outside. It was on the inside where the changes had been made. His life was now more bearable. The nightmare still came but that too was different. There was a small part of him that looked forward to the dream. It looked forward to the soft words spoken by Helen just before she departed. It looked forward to the look in her eyes, a look that gave him hope but also made him yearn for more. John knew that there was more, he had to go further but he had no guide. He did not know what to do so he played it by ear, trial and error. Something would tell him when he was doing right and he hoped that he would not destroy everything by doing something wrong. In the meantime, he lived his meagre existence, changing something little every day.

The changes were not conscious changes but he was more aware of his environment and he started to interact with it. People said hello, they always did, but in the past, he never took any notice so he never replied. Getting no reply people would hold back the greeting.

He experimented with his diet, breaking from his weekly routine. He turned on his long-neglected radio and allowed music into his world. The style was not to his liking so he played a record. He chose one at random from the pile in the cupboard beneath the phonograph, the pile that had not seen the light of day since the movers placed it there years ago. He placed the record on the turntable and the music soon filled the flat. He sat back on the chair and looked at the sleeve of the disc. He looked past the sleeve into the distance and across the years of his life.

These sounds brought back memories of when he was courting Naomi. There were parties and days out, there were smiles, hugs and kisses. He was very clumsy around her because she was so delicate and he was like a bull in a china shop. His awkwardness around her always made her laugh and she would throw her arms around his neck and kiss his ear. He never bent under this pressure, he always stood firm and held her off the ground. He would gather her up and look into her eyes to see her love for him.

Another track played and he changed his focus towards another part of his life. This was a torture, because the sounds brought back such sweet memories from wonderful times that would never come again. They can never be recreated because they are lost to the past. With every good memory came the realisation that they were gone, never to be revived. The good times had rolled and were gone. Once he would have stood and ripped the playing arm from the record and something inside him urged him to do just that, but his life had changed so he resisted that urge and just sat there listening. He sat there staring into the past and tears welled up in his eyes. He did not cry but he could not stop the tears, they were not many but they were tears of sorrow and regret, so different from the tears of pain that he had shed for so many years.

The record played itself out and the arm lifted to return to its rest. The speed of the record decreased swiftly until it stopped. John sat there as he had done while the music played, the tears had passed and his eyes were dry. The silence tugged at his subconscious and he came back from the past to the present. He rubbed his face and with an embarrassed clearing of the throat, he stood up and looked around the flat. It was getting dark now so he closed the curtains and turned on the light. Normally he would make a meal, eat it and clean up after himself. He would take his time because there was a lot of time to fill. The change in him was making itself evident again. He had been filled by the music and the pictures from his past. He remembered having fun and enjoying the company of others and the feelings gave him a new courage.

John Deverall decided to go out. He put on his jacket, picked up his wallet and keys and walked to the door. He turned and looked back into the flat, which gave one last pull at his emotions. 'Where are you going John? You're not leaving me here all alone by myself, are you?' John looked around and with determination stuck out his lower lip, he flipped the light switch and closed the door. Life would never be the same again, he hoped.

* * *

Sometimes the planets are in alignment and everything goes according to plan. The heavenly beings who look down upon us, don't put any obstacles in our way and everything runs smoothly. It doesn't happen often and so we see it as a blessing but when our plans are evil and they run smoothly? Who is looking after us then? Is there some evil entity looking after evil people so they can do their ghastly deeds without hindrance? Why is evil stronger than good? Why is it easier to do wrong than it is to do right? Why does pain linger while joy is a just a fleeting emotion?

The guardians of evil were all on duty the day the prison landing needed to be cleaned. They were looking down and rubbing their hands at the prospect of the guards choosing two prisoners to mop the landing. They exercised their powers and influenced the choice that was made. The guards chose Drew Treevill and Bill Davies to mop the full length of the landing. Davies could not have planned it better.

The two prisoners were given mops and buckets and instructed to start at the head of the landing and clean to the other end where the toilets were located. It was a distance of about forty yards. They collected their tools under the supervision of a guard and were led to the head of the landing. They looked down the landing to where their task would end and they

were told that it would take them about an hour to complete. The guard would supervise the work
.

Davies knew that the guard would stay at the head of the landing and watch as the prisoners slowly increased the distance between him and their mopping. He would not venture onto the wet floor. It should take less than a minute for Davies to pound Treevill into a pulp. Once he started, the guard would react, but it was only one guard. He would take time to react and then cover the distance separating them. This guard was a podgy wheezy man and again Davies thanked his luck. He would have time to sort out Treevill and he might even be able to overpower the guard. A whole lot of trouble would come from this but he needed to let people know that he was not going to stand for any shit anymore! He was driven by this violent desire. His feelings had been held in check for far too long. He started the rhythmic mopping of the floor as he spoke to Drew.
"Well, this is a bonus."
"A bonus? How is this a bonus?"

The mops first slopped warm soapy water to and fro, were squeezed and then used to soak up the excess. Drew was unfamiliar with the motion but studied Davies for the first few feet and he soon fell in with the rhythm.
Wet mop – side to side – step back.
"Yes, this is a bonus. Most of the exercise we get is just walking around the yard. That's just walkin'. This gives your shoulders and arms good exercise, your back too." Davies spoke between heavy breaths. "The air aint as fresh as it is outside but you work up a sweat and maybe there might be the chance of an extra shower."

The mopping went on and with every stroke the distance increased between them and the guard.
Davies stood up and squeezed the mop into the bucket. He leaned on the mop and faced the guard, he spoke up so the guard could hear.
"Is that right Mr. Janson? Will we be able to have an extra shower today or some extra grub for doing this labour?"

The guard stood alertly at the head of the landing. He had been listening to the chat and watching every movement of the prisoners. This was an easy task, the prisoners couldn't get away or cause any trouble so only one officer was appointed to the job. It was usual practice for there to be two but the numbers were down again.

"I'll see if I can get you an extra spud for dinner tonight, Davies, let's get the work done first."

Davies grinned and turned to look at Treevill who had stopped to listen to the conversation.

"You see Drew, it's a bonus and we have to accept every little bonus."

They went back to the mopping. The distance increased between the prisoners and the guard. The floor shone slickly between them, daring anyone to spoil the shine with a tread. Beyond the halfway mark Davies began to slightly increase his motion and he stole a lead on Drew. The malevolent visions in his head were starting to take over and a skeletal grin attached itself to his face. The grin was created partly from his exertions and partly from the glee felt by that evil person within him. It would be soon, they came closer to the sluice room and toilet, that is where it would be.

The sound of keys interrupted the regular sounds around them. Janson, at the end of the landing, looked to his right and spoke to someone out of sight. It was another guard sent with new orders. The prisoners stood up to see what was going on. The guards were talking and Janson was indicating that he had this to do first, pointing to the prisoners as he argued about his instructions. He paused his conversation with his fellow guard and looked down the landing. Raising his voice, he gave his instructions.

"There is no need for you to stop, get on with it. We have got West landing to do next!"

Davies smiled again. When he heard the keys, he thought that another guard would be posted behind them. That would have scuppered his plans. He made increased efforts to get closer to the door and not arouse the suspicion of the guard. He must be seen to be doing what he was told. Then the final twist in Davies' favour took place. The guards at the end of the landing took their conversation out through the door.

Davies *felt* that he was not being watched. It was a sixth sense you pick up in prison.

He grabbed Drew by the front collar of his shirt and hauled him to the sluice room. Drew had no time to react or call out. Inside the door, he spun around and slammed Drew's head against the solid tiled wall. Davies was breathing heavily now, through clenched teeth. The muscles and blood vessels in his neck stood out and his face had gone red with the exertion. He held Drew on the wall and pulled his fist back like an archer drawing a bowstring. The impact of the blow split Drew's upper lip and drove the bone of his nose into his brain. There was an instant spasm of his body before it went limp. Davies held him to the wall but his target, the face, was not available because Drew's head fell limply towards his chest. Davies loaded another punch, this time high above his head. He brought his right fist down on the back of Drew's head, releasing the grip with his left. There was a sharp crack as vertebrae separated, followed by dull thud of Treevill slumping to the floor.

Davies stood there and looked at his handiwork. His whole body was bursting with energy. He had his power back, he was on top of things. He would gain such respect and fear now, from the cons and the screws. He would laugh as they all gave him a wide berth. He could have anything he wanted! He was breathing heavily, sweat was dripping from his nose, and spittle ran from his lower lip. He looked down at this miserable piece of garbage. Was this such a trophy? This was a poor defenceless kid. The beating was a sham, too easy! He looked at the bleeding pulp on the floor and listened to the gurgling noise coming from the face. Drew was paralysed and probably brain dead but he was alive and breathing. Davies looked at Drew's chest, it was pulling in air, somehow! Davies took a step back and then leant forward with a kick. He put his hands on the shining white tiles of the wall, towered over Treevill and kicked him again and again.

The entire assault lasted only thirty seconds. The guard reappeared after ten, stood puzzled for about five. He took another five to recall the other officer and they both got to the sluice room in time to see Davies retreat from the lifeless body of Drew Treevill.

*   *   *

When Martin dropped the fire extinguisher, he knew that he had gone too far. He stood over the body of David Brenner, which showed no signs of life. The earlier feeling of exhilaration, at being able to deliver a body blow to this animal that he had stalked, now left him and guilt took its place. He stood there wondering what he should do when David started to move. The movement was not natural, it was as if David was not in control of the movement and indeed, he wasn't. It was the desperate struggle of the woman beneath David, trying to get up. Martin instantly went to help her. He rolled David on to his back and carefully lifted the gasping lady to a sitting position. She was still clutched her bag but was having great trouble breathing! There were nasty weals already forming on her neck.
"Are you alright?"

She looked, with her tear-filled eyes, into his. She reached up and put her hand around his neck and he stood taking her to her feet. Standing, she could drag more air into her lungs and she did. He put his arm around her to give her more support because he could feel, through body tension and the weight on his shoulders, that she was near to collapse. When she had recovered a little bit more she turned and looked at him. Her voice was hoarse and laboured but she mouthed the words.
"Thank you."

She then broke down and started to cry.
Martin felt that he could not leave her but he desperately wanted to call the police. It was the first instinct of a law-abiding person. He needed to call the police even though he knew he had killed the man.
"I have to leave you for a moment, I have to find a phone and get the police and an ambulance for you. Will you be all right?"

She didn't look up but reached into her bag and pulled out her mobile phone. She raised it in his direction and continued to sob and fight for air.
He took the phone and within a minute had alerted the police and ambulance. He gave the phone back to her and she held it in her hand, not wanting to waste the energy needed, to put it away. She looked up at him again. She had stopped crying but her mascara had run with her tears, leaving black lines down her face. She had recovered enough to speak.

"Is he .... dead?"

Martin almost said yes, but instead he went to the body lying on the other side of the room. David was on his back and there was a three-inch gash on his forehead. His breathing was imperceptible but the wound was bleeding. Prompted by this Martin made a closer inspection and found life in the limp body. A wave of physical relief washed over his body and he became giddy. He stood up and the sudden movement caused his head to swim. He stumbled over to where the lady was sitting and he sat next to her.

"The bastard is alive, which is more than he deserves. I never knew that things would work out like this. I knew that if I kept it up night after night something would happen. I thought I could get something on him and maybe send him back to jail but this is even better. His type just can't stop. There will be no saving him now. Are you sure you are alright? This is really sweet. Such a turn up for the books."

Martin was quite giddy and he began to chuckle and shake his head. The lady was looking at Martin now with a mixture of feelings. Here was a man who had obviously saved her life but now he was ranting and raving! A little thought crossed her mind that she could still be in danger so, without looking, she took a firmer hold on her handbag!

The sirens could be heard in the distance and both of the conscious occupants of the Laundromat looked towards the door. The blue flashing lights appeared then the vehicles and then the police. The paramedics stabilised David and when he was on a stretcher with a neck collar, they took him, under guard, to hospital. Martin, having no need for medical attention, stood in the middle of the scene being interviewed by a police officer. The lady was to be taken to hospital too, but in the doorway, she stopped and turned to look back at the man who had saved her life. She was safe now so she walked up to Martin and on her tip toes she reached up and kissed him on the cheek. The hardened officers, in the middle of a serious crime scene, exchanged glances and smiles, but then almost immediately returned to their work.

* * *

Mrs. Brenner answered all of the questions that the officers asked. Their questions created a profile of David. He was a loner with a drink and occasional drug habit. He had not found a job since the last trial, so he depended on money from the dole, his mother and probably various unlawful activities. The officers searched his room to get an idea of the type of person he was. As they went casually through his things, she sat there feeling guilty. A voice told her to go get the album, show it to them, and get all of this out in the open. David was on a downward spiral and the album would finish him. It would release her too. She could start another life somewhere, a limited existence where she could make a few friends, maybe get a job and gather some happiness again. She should not have to bear this weight of guilt for having brought David into the world. She should not be punished any more.

The officers were finished and stood together filling the lounge of the flat. Their body language told her that they were ready to go.
DS Roper spoke.
"Mrs Brenner, David will be in hospital for a few days. When he has recovered sufficiently, he will be charged." Roper stopped there to allow her to speak.

These were the facts and that is what he dealt with. She remained silent and continued to look first from one man to the other. Her eyes were dry but pitiful. There was a lot of pain in there and it had nowhere to go. There was no release. It would build upon itself, which made Roper worry. He had seen things like this before. He spoke softly this time, holding out his hand.
"Sit down Mrs. Brenner." She sat in the chair he was indicating. "Your son has brought this all on himself. We know about the court case in the past." She looked at the other officer who stood by the door. He nodded, he knew. "David had what you might call a second chance. He could have changed his life but he didn't. I can see you are a decent woman and will probably take the blame to yourself. Don't."

She sat there and let the words come to her as he continued to speak.
"There will probably be a great deal of press about this case, linking it to the other one and all, and the reporters will definitely come looking for you. My advice is to use these few days to get away, before he is

charged. Do you have family somewhere else in the country? Somewhere you could stay for a few weeks?"
She looked from one officer to the other before she spoke.

"Thank you Mr. ... Roper?" He nodded. "But I don't have anywhere to go. I don't take the blame for his actions, I take the blame for mine. I could have done so much more for him but as time passed by and he became more set in his ways, I left him to himself." She stood up and moved towards the door of her room, the room that contained the drawer concealing the album. At the door she turned and spoke to the two men in the room, they were both standing now.
"There is something you can do for me." This would be her last act to break the bond between her and her son. With the album in their hands, they would have a case against him and she could turn and walk away. That possibility of a new life attracted her. She was thinking of herself at last and on the heels of that thought was the terrifying ordeal *she* would have to go through if the album got to the police. There must be another way. She changed her mind.
"Can you take me to see David?"

The officers looked at each other. Their work here was done and they should go but something about the .... goodness.... of this woman touched them and DC Roper spoke for them both.

"That can be arranged, if you would like to come with us now, someone will bring you back later. He is still in casualty, under guard, and you won't be able to spend much time with him but I am sure it will be all right."

The officers put on their coats and waited for her to fetch hers. She walked them to the door and closing it behind her she took a deep breath. This was going to be very difficult for her but she had to find the strength. It had to be done and done tonight. He would not be coming home again, not to her home anyway.

The hospital was bright and lively. Corridors full of equipment and specialist people working with patients. The officers flanked her all the way through the maze and to an area where a uniformed policeman stood. The detectives gave him a knowing look and he moved to one side

and opened a door to a single room, one bed, one patient. DC Roper signalled for Mrs. Brenner to stop and then immediately caught the eye of the doctor on duty who finished his sentence with the nurse he was speaking to and then came to meet the newly arrived group. DC Roper opened the conversation.
"Doctor, this is Mrs. Brenner, his mother. Is it OK for her to see him?"

The doctor looked at her with sympathetic eyes but then switched to describing wounds, conditions and treatment of his patient.
"He has a severe concussion and he has lost a lot of blood. His jaw is broken and will be wired in the morning after some of the swelling has gone down. He won't be able to speak, I'm not sure if he is even conscious."

They all made their way towards the open door. David lay on his back but not completely flat, the bed was arranged in a slight sitting position. There was a drip in his arm and bandages all around his head held tight by a lace elastic net. He had handcuffs on his right wrist attached to the bed. A slight perceptible movement of this head towards the door was the only evidence that he was awake and aware of what was happening around him. His eyes were open.
Mrs. Brenner took a deep breath and said, "He doesn't need to speak doctor, I just want him to listen. I will only be five minutes." She turned and looked at the doctor, his lips tightened, he lowered his eyes and nodded his head. Mrs Brenner walked into the room.

Her son followed her movement into the room, with his eyes. Eyes that were full of shame, guilt, sorrow and fear. She walked up to the left side of the bed so the detectives outside the door could not hear what she had to say. She kept her back to them so they could not see the expression on her face. She came very close to David and took a look at him. Most of his face was bandaged but she could easily see her son. She also saw the little boy she once knew, she remembered the love she had for him, she remembered much that was good and wholesome, fine times in the past. But her strength returned forcing her to remember why she was there. She did not come to add support or to comfort. She was not there to forgive. She could never forgive.
"David?"

This was her start. It was the hardest thing she ever had to say. There would be no reply because she would continue to speak. She would say the words she had rehearsed in the car on the way over. Words that had been forming in her subconscious for some time but she was too afraid to give them substance.

"David, I am sorry, I have failed you. I should have been a better mother for you and I should have done something a long time ago. I should have done something to stop you turning out this way. For that I blame myself. But you have been heading this way for a long time. You had many chances to make changes but you didn't. I can see that there is some sort of devil in you that you like to have. You have failed yourself. You could have made the change but you didn't want to. This time there is a price to pay, you have gone too far and I can't help you. I don't think I can stand by and listen to my heart break either. You must face this alone."

Tears welled up in his eyes. She looked past his tears and continued. "I will go away. You will have to cope with whatever happens to you now. I can't help you. I want you to know that I will take certain things with me. I will take the things I found in the wardrobe."

The tears in David's eyes instantly dried. Now those eyes stared, searched her face for what she knew. They found that knowledge - and filled with fear! He moved his body and winced as he tried to speak. She closed her eyes and gently shushed him.

"I will take those things. How could you David? What makes you treat yourself this way? I don't know all the facts, I don't want to know. I want to have a life that is free of worry and pain." She was coming to the hardest part now and she called on that courage and determination she knew she would need to make the break.

"I am going now David, I won't see you again. I will try to forget these times. I will try to forget you and the pain that we have endured. I am so sorry." She stood up and took a last look at her son. It was done. A new strength was flooding through her. A bridge had been crossed and now she took the first steps of her new life.
"Goodbye David." These were her last words to him.

She stood up and turned towards the door. She never looked back. The detectives had to lengthen their stride to keep up with her as she retraced her steps to the hospital entrance. Walking into the cold night air brought her back to her senses. She was not relieved, she was destroyed. She was not looking forward to a new life free of pain and sorrow, she would always remember that she had abandoned her son, her flesh and blood, and the pain would sharpen and worm its way deep into that place where it hurts the most.

The detectives could only stand there, awkwardly, as she held her head in her hands and cried.

* * *

John knew that something was wrong as he entered the first of the alarmed doors. There was something different in the eyes of everyone he saw. It was as if they all had bad news but were too afraid to tell him. He met his companions and the story unfolded. The story was told in an economic way, there was no need for frills. The story was told by several different officers. As they each spoke, he stood and gave them his undivided attention. The way he listened, sent fear into every speaker, for it would not do to be unclear with the facts, and cause John to ask questions.

"They were mopping the east landing, second level. When they got to the sluice room at the end, Davies dragged Treevill inside and gave him a right going over."

John looked to another officer.

"Janson says that they seemed to be getting along alright, even joking and having a chat. It lasted less than a minute, the MO says that Treevill's skull was fractured, his neck was broken and three of his broken ribs had punctured his lung."

John looked for more information.

"The doc said that if he hadn't died he would probably be a vegetable for the rest of his life." This was all the information needed about the incident so the conversation stopped. The officers waited to see what John wanted next.

The wait was not long.

"Where is Davies now?"

Another speaker. It was Brooks.

"I had him taken back to his cell. The cell has been stripped of everything except his bed and bedding. I talked to the governor and he is making arrangements to have him transferred to Waverly because he would cause too much trouble here. He will be charged there and sent for trial."

John looked at Brooks and the two men understood each other. Brooks knew that Deverall must not get close to Davies, a meeting would only result in violence and this time Deverall might not be able to control himself. He had to keep these two men apart. He could see from his eyes that John wanted Davies now. Brooks had to control this situation. John broke his eye contact with Brooks and looked at the other men.

"OK, let's try to put a lid on this situation. The place will be full of rumour and fact. All of the cons will see this as one over on us and will be trying it on. Keep your wits about you today."

The conversation was ended. They all continued their preparations to go to work and they made their way to the briefing. As they made their way out of the door Brooks placed his hand on John's arm, stopping him and making him look into his eyes. The other officers continued down the corridor.

"I'd like to have a word with you John, after the briefing."

John looked at the hand on his arm and then into the eyes of the younger officer. He felt a need to get on the landing so without asking questions he nodded and agreed. They both continued to the briefing.

Unusually the governor was already there. He stood silently furthest from the door. They filed in and took up their places. No one sat. There was a grave silence about them. All of the prison guards took responsibility for the actions of the others. They felt a community guilt at what happened even though it was not on their shift. An incident like this could not have been prevented but they still felt responsible. When they were all present the governor spoke.

"Yesterday one of the inmates was killed. William Davies fatally attacked Drew Treevill on the landing during a work detail. There was no weapon or motive as far as we can tell." The governor looked up from the paper he was reading. He scanned the faces of the officers and went back to his text.

"Treevill was pronounced dead at the scene and Davies is in his cell without privileges." This brought a slight reaction from the men. Removing a prisoners personal possessions sounded like an unsuitable punishment for murder!

"He will be transferred to Waverly tomorrow before breakfast. I don't want him to have any contact with the other prisoners. If it is at all possible, I don't want any of you to have any contact either."

He looked directly into John's eyes but John fixed his stare on a spot on the wall beyond the governor.

"Do you hear me John?"

All of the other officers looked at him, they knew how he felt but they didn't know that the governor was aware of it as well. It was also a shock to John and suddenly the spot on the wall was no longer interesting. He felt the gaze of every man in the room but ignored them. He looked directly into the eyes of his superior and with calculated, measured words he replied.

"I hear you … Mr. Endersley!"

Somewhat embarrassed by speaking to his friend this way, the governor returned to his text for a moment but then tossed it on a table nearby.

"This shift is not going to be easy. Until we get rid of Davies, I want everyone to be extremely vigilant. This sort of thing makes the population a bit touchy and fear runs through the landings. Double up the manpower and cancel anything that could be a potential incident. I will deal with the press. Refer any news people to me should you meet them on the outside. Are there any questions?" There were none.

"OK then, let's go."

They filed out like they always did.

Brooks intercepted Deverall after the others went toward their duties.

"John, I know how you are feeling."

John stopped and slowly looked at Brooks but let him continue.

"We all know how you are feeling but we don't want you to ruin your career, your life, by doing something to Davies. Let the system do its job. In a day or two he will be gone and things will get back to normal around here."

John Deverall was a strong man. He was powerful physically and mentally but there appeared a little crack in his control. He felt it happening but he also had a need to let it go. It would make him feel better.

"What do you know about me Brooks? How can you know how I feel? Did you know that my life was ripped apart once and the system couldn't do a damn thing about it? I look around me every day and see the system failing the ordinary person in the street. I see the inmates in here being provided with almost everything they want while their victims on the outside continue to suffer. I see guys like Davies getting away with murder and not a hand is lifted against them because *they* know how to work the system. He is going to Waverly for the rest of *his* life and you can bet *your* life that this story will get there before he does. He will be treated like royalty. He will rule that house. Do you think that is fair? So, what if I were to go down there and pay him a little visit, like the last time, but this time finish the job? It wouldn't matter to me. My life doesn't matter to me. It would give me the greatest satisfaction and no tears would be shed outside."

Brooks stood there and endured the tightly bitten words directed at him. Deverall stopped speaking and also stood there waiting, poised as if to defend himself. He was waiting for Brooks to react, to speak, to defend his earlier comments. He was waiting for an apology but none came. Instead, Brooks leaned closer and looked deep into Johns eyes before he uttered the words that would change John's life.
"There is another way."

* * *

Six

Davies sat in his cell completely spent. All of the emotions and frustrations which had been building up inside him were out. The injustices were no longer there, he didn't feel them anyway, he just squatted there against the wall – empty. He was calm and still. His inner self no longer tormented his head for some sort of action. It would take a few days for it to start its slow inexorable climb towards the next violent climax but it was *this* time that his brain craved, these moments, a time to be still and have no thoughts at all.

On the landing outside the cell a prison guard was posted. All of the prisoners in the wing were confined to their cells. Unusually the landing was quiet. The inmates knew what was happening and what had happened. They too were breathing a collective sigh of relief. The sooner it was over the better it would be. Every inmate wanted to see the back of Davies and if that meant a lockdown, it was a small price to pay. A prisoner like Davies was the uncontrolled element every prison dreaded. He could be the spark or the instrument. Either way he was trouble and with a person like that around, you were always looking over your shoulder whether you were a screw or a con.

The rest of the prison was feeling the disturbance. The long-term prisoners had seen a lot before but this was new to them, they were shocked but they would never show it. It didn't do to show too much emotion in prison, especially fear or surprise. The prisoners on shorter sentences were wide eyed with amazement. They gathered in smaller groups and talked about the murder. It fed their own fear and caused them to cast suspicious glances at the men who were serving longer sentences. They soon realised just what a place a prison is. Take potentially dangerous men and lock them all up together and what do you get? It would take a great deal of time for this wave to settle, in this small pond.

The guards were affected too. Of course it was their responsibility to lock the prisoners up, to control their lives, to keep them safe. In order to do this, they had to have some sort of communication with them. They would never feel sorrow for their plight but understanding ... yes. A distance grew between them and the inmates, they would not be drawn into conversations. They gave no information - *that* would come from another quarter. They were not at ease and their body language was positively hostile. It was not a time for fraternising but instead it was a time to mind your own business and try to get back to normal – if there was such a thing inside this or any prison. The guards were vigilant and always mobile. They never became isolated, they moved about in twos and threes. The fear and control was in their eyes. It was the fear of a mob uprising which focused their thoughts first, swiftly followed by the realisation of the measure of control which would be needed, to gain the upper hand again, if the mob attempted to take over.

The crime had to be reported and the report was picked up by the media. They were set up outside talking to camera and trying to get interviews from anyone who worked in the prison. Everyone was instructed to say nothing to the press and a statement was issued.

"Today a prisoner attacked another inmate during a supervised work detail. That prisoner, as a result of his injuries, has died. His attacker has been isolated and will be charged with murder. He will be moved to another prison tomorrow and a trial date will be set in one week. Renkill Prison has one of the best care records in the country and this incident was not a failure in duty or procedure. It is regrettable and a full public review will take place in the near future. Thank You"

The press clamoured for more information.
"We understand that the attacker is Bill Davies can you confirm this?"
"It has been said that Drew Treevill was involved, was he the prisoner who was attacked?"

There was a brief futile barrage of questions but the messenger had turned and disappeared through the prison gate. There would be no more, but more was not necessary. The grapevine was working overtime and the press had all of the information within the hour. It went out starkly on the nine o'clock news.

"It is believed that William Davies, convicted armed robber, has attacked and killed a fellow inmate in Renkill prison. The two men were on a working detail inside the prison when Davies suddenly attacked the man. The prisoner, who died of his injuries is believed to be Andrew

Treevill who was serving a life sentence for the murder of schoolboy James Thomas at Eastleigh Towers last year. Davies has been charged and will be moved to another secure prison tomorrow."

Mr. and Mrs. Thomas were informed by the police as soon as Davies was charged. They were told only the starkest details, Treevill was dead, killed by another prisoner. The reason for being told was to prepare them for the press. The papers and the TV people would have all the facts about Treevill and would be looking for background information and it didn't take long. They arrived only one hour after the official statement. Mr. and Mrs. Thomas sat in their darkening house. They sat there and just held each other, so lights were not needed. The doorbell rang several times and they quietly roused themselves from their memories and sorrow. The wound from the loss of their son was still very raw and would now be picked at by the media.

"We better get this over with" he said softly as he stood up.

"What will you say?"

"I will tell them exactly what we have told each other for the past year. I will tell them how this makes us feel now. I will tell them and then they will go away because I will also tell them that we want to be left in peace. Let me tell them dear."

She stood and joined him in the middle of the lounge. She held his hand and they moved through the house to the front door. When it was opened a rush of reporters and camera men focused on them.

"Mr. Thomas, have you heard about the death of Drew Treevill?"

"Yes, we have, the police informed us earlier today."

"How does this make you feel Mrs. Thomas, now that the killer of your son is also dead?"

"My wife does not want to speak about this matter. I will tell you how we feel and then, when I am finished, I would like you to go and let us continue to live our lives."

Mr. Thomas stood on the threshold of his home, his wife stood behind him. He looked at the gathered press people and camera equipment and tried to engage each eye and lens, trying to personally speak to everyone there. He created an expectant hush and he received a collective respect from them.

"Our life revolved around James. When he didn't come home that afternoon our life stopped. Something had killed our life. That something was Drew Treevill. When he was convicted, we nearly went out of our minds because *he* was there in prison, living and breathing, while the mutilated body of our son lay in a box in the cemetery. Drew Treevill was given a life sentence but he could always look forward to being free. Not our son. He was gone forever. Our life was gone forever. Ever since that day, half of our emotions have been directed towards Drew Treevill. Not one day has gone by without us wishing, hoping and praying that he would suffer a painful and slow death."

The hush rippled but held. This was good stuff! The paper and TV people were lapping it up. It was raw uncovered emotion and it was being delivered slowly and precisely. No questions came from the huddled mass of reporters, there was no need.

"We can continue to remember our son, and perhaps the pain will lessen and we can rebuild our lives. James will never be forgotten, we still love him and we tell him that every day. We have our memories and we will dwell only on them now."

He had finished talking for the moment and the assembled listeners gave him this chance to pause. They would not interrupt with a question because their instinct told them that there was more to come. The appetiser was finished, the meat of the statement was about to be served. A change came over Mr. Thomas, he stood taller and looked more forceful. Mrs. Thomas took a slight step behind her husband. She knew what was coming from the way he stood. She knew that this was what he was building up to and he would be finished once he had said his piece. His voice changed and he became more forceful, he raised his voice slightly.

"What we will NOT do anymore, is give any thought to Drew Treevill. He has now been punished in a fitting manner for the crime he committed. We have prayed for this to happen. Drew Treevill now rots in hell where he belongs. Now it is over for us. Now I hope you will leave us alone."

The reporters uncharacteristically left it at that. They packed up their things and moved off the lawn. Within twenty minutes, apart from a few polystyrene cups, there was no sign of them.

* * *

"How long have you been stalking him Mr. Casey?"
Martin and Cheryl Casey were 'helping police with their enquiries' about the assault in the laundromat. Officially it had nothing to do with Mrs. Casey but she refused to be separated from her husband. Officially the police could have prevented her from being there but they were sympathetic and after all the Casey's HAD done them a favour. They all sat in the interview room and spoke to DC Roper. His last question was like a bolt from the blue and hung between them for only a moment. Up until now the questions were ordinary, what had happened, what did you see, what did you do? Now this was an accusation! Like the majority of guilty people, the Casey's reaction to the question was typical. Resentful indignation!
"What do you mean!? My husband is not a stalker!"

Mrs. Casey stood up and squeezed herself to her full height and vented her feelings.
"It was just an incredible coincidence and you should be grateful! If my husband hadn't been in the neighbourhood at that time that woman could be dead, or worse."

The burly policemen could hardly hold back their smiles at this performance. They endured the tirade while sending glances to each other across the room, finally resting their gaze on the lowered eyes of Mr. Casey. His wife continued.
"Most people would have just walked by and done nothing. You should be thanking him, not have him here … making accusations and asking all of these questions!"

DC Roper shifted his position and looked directly at Mrs. Casey and she stopped talking. He continued to stare until she sat and calmed herself down. The other policeman and Mr. Casey now felt the need to look at Roper and he began to speak.

"Mrs. Casey, your husband is not under arrest, he is not even being officially interviewed. There are no notes being taken and this conversation is not being recorded. It is true that the woman probably owes her health, probably her life, to you Mr Casey and it is also true that we are very grateful for what you did – however stupid it was."

Mrs. Casey bristled and took a deep breath ready to speak but the words died in her chest when Roper looked at her. He continued.
"I just want to know what has been happening. How long has this been going on?"

Everyone's attention was now directed towards Mr. Casey. He looked up first at his wife who had an expression on her face which was a mixture of pride and sympathy. He looked over at DC Roper who was looking straight back at him expectantly. He took a deep breath and reached out to take his wife's hand. He gave it a little reassuring squeeze and then gave in. It was all going to come out but he believed he had a friend in this burly policeman.

"After the trial, when Brenner walked free from the court, I just couldn't sit there and do nothing. I did have thoughts of killing him." This made the policemen shuffle in their chairs with the pretence of just having missed the last statement. "I decided…."
"We decided …" Mrs. Casey stepped in to take her share of the blame. Her husband gave the hand another little squeeze and used her words as his own."
"We … decided that I should make a note of his movements. I stood outside his flat every night and followed him when he went out. Most nights he just stayed in and I would wait until the lights went out and then I would go home. I don't know what I was going to do, I didn't have a plan, I always thought that something would happen. I didn't know what. I was just watching him. It was something to do. I just couldn't sit there and do nothing! We had to be doing something. For Gods sake he was responsible for the death of my daughter! I couldn't live with myself if I did nothing."

He looked up at each of the officers in turn. Looking for some expression of solidarity but there was none. They all remained steadfast in their attitude. They showed no disgust or accord. They were just listening.

"So … you were just waiting for a chance to do what?" DC Roper knew what the answer to that question was but the answer had to come from Casey. If he admitted it then the episode could be put behind them. Brenner was going to prison for a long time and this couple had to get back to their life, make the most of it, but they had to acknowledge what they had done, for their own sake.

The older couple were uneasy, they shifted in their chairs and the policemen waited. Mr. Casey took a deep breath and released the hand he was holding. He looked straight into the eyes of Roper. He was weighing up the consequences of the statement he was about to make. If he admitted his innermost intentions, he could be in serious trouble but something else flooded his emotions. It was time for him to stand up for Victoria. It was time to do something for the daughter that he felt he had failed. It was time to think about her and not himself. He looked directly into Ropers eyes and spoke clearly and with measured words.

"I followed him every time he left the flat. I made sure that I wasn't seen. I didn't specifically plan to do anything, like I said I always felt that something would happen. I was waiting for a moment when I could confront him with what he had done. It would have to be a moment when we could be totally alone, unseen and unheard. I wanted him to feel something of the loss we had suffered. I wanted to look him in the eyes when he realised what was about to happen to him. When the moment came, I would be sure it was the right one and make the move. I wanted to take his life away, make it fair, get justice for Victoria. That's what I wanted to do."

Mr. Casey broke eye contact with Roper and looked at his wife. He retook her hand and spoke towards her but it was meant for Roper. "My moment never came. He did all this to himself."

DC Roper sat back in his chair and led the feeling of relief for the interview room. It was out in the open now, everything was disclosed. He spoke to the other officer.

"I need a cup of tea, how about you Mrs. Casey? Mr. Casey? Get us all a tea will you Pete?" The officer took the cue and left the room. Roper continued.

"You have played a dangerous game Mr. Casey. Even on a bad day, Brenner could have sorted you out. It could be you in the intensive care ward now, or even worse. You have been very lucky. I must say that I do understand how you feel. Sometimes the police have to stand by and let guilty people walk away, our hands are tied by the system. I don't condone your actions but unofficially, every man in this station has a secret admiration for what you have done."

The weight fell from Mr. Casey's shoulders and he regained some of his fatherhood. He had done something for his daughter and it was right. This was confirmation. He was not alone, there were other right-minded people who felt the same way. Roper wasn't finished. He continued to speak to try and stem the feeling of pride he saw building inside Mr. Casey.

"Don't misunderstand me though, what you did was wrong. What you intended to do would put you in prison for the rest of your life! As things turned out we will be able to convict with the testimony of the lady who was attacked. I don't want you to be brought in to the case so, officially, you were just a passer-by, who helped a lady who was being attacked. You left the scene before the police arrived. I want you to go home and restart your lives. Let us take it from here and trust us to do the job properly this time."
He held out his hand. Mr. Casey shook it heartily as they all stood up.
"Here is my private card. If you have any problems or need to talk to someone you must give me a call. Remember, I have been understanding towards the way you feel and what you have done. Someone else finds out that you followed Brenner and then brained him with a fire extinguisher, regardless of the fact that he was committing a crime, they will not be so sympathetic. You could face serious criminal charges. Do you understand what I mean?"
"I understand … We … understand Mr. Roper."

Still holding Ropers hand Mr. Casey had one last thing to say.
"Do you have any children?"
Roper gave a slight sigh, he knew what was coming.
"No, I don't."
"Then, when you have children and love them so intensely that you just can't believe it, when their life means more to you than your own and then, that life is taken away, then, and only then, you will understand. Then you will know how it feels Mr Roper. Only then." They left the

interview room passing the officer who went out to make the tea. He carried no tray, no tea had been made. It was never his intention to do so.

*   *   *

Mrs. Brenner was dropped back at her flat as the morning light was just making a difference to the ink black night. She was not tired. She was busy. She went through the flat selecting belongings to take with her to her brother's home in the West Country. He didn't know it but he was about to be visited. The morning would bring people looking for information so she had to be quick. She packed some necessary clothes and documents, a few mementos … and the album! This item stopped her in her tracks. She sat down on the couch and opened it. The newspaper clippings were yellow with age and the corner of each page was grimy from being turned hundreds of times. She shuddered at the idea of David thumbing through these pages with some sense of pride. She did not know the man at all. The pictures and headlines told the stark tale of the murder of a young girl. She saw pictures of the parents. What must they have gone through when this happened. There was a picture of the little girl in a school photograph, in a rabbit outfit from the school play and another with her parents on holiday. The clippings spanned months of time, from the outrage of the event and gradually, becoming less and less. There were more newsworthy events to report until the murder went out of the public perception. The clippings ended, to be replaced by a small envelope stuck to the page. The outline of the contents could be seen through the paper before she even opened it. The pressure of the closed book, stashed away in the wardrobe for years made the distinct outline of a cross. She lifted it out of the envelope, held it eye height, and watched it spin in her hands.

Such an innocent little thing with such a terrible history. There was so much pain and terror attached to it. It was linked to destruction and mourning. Mrs. Brenner sat there and wondered what the parents of that little girl were doing now. What had happened to them? The light was becoming stronger outside and the shapes of buildings could be clearly seen through her window. She closed the album and closed her old life. Things would be different from now on. She stood up with a purpose. The album was placed into the top of the suitcase and the zipper terminated the packing.

She walked to the door carrying the suitcase. It was going to rain today so she put on her coat and wrapped a scarf over her head. She made sure that the lights were turned off in the flat and lastly, she turned to see this place that she had shared for so long with him. It was tidy, ready for the next owner. She would contact a firm to put everything into storage. The gas and electricity meters must be read and she would make arrangements to settle the bills. Later today she would contact an estate agent and start plans to sell the flat. First, she must phone her brother. These things had an order to them, they were practical things that had to be done and she surprised herself with the way she was putting things in order. She was stronger now, this life – this old life – was over. It was time to go so she turned, opened the door and walked into the corridor. She didn't look back and only knew that the door was closed by the sound that it had made. That sound had brought a sigh of relief from her a hundred times in the past as he went out of the flat. This time she gave a sigh of relief for a completely different reason.

*   *   *

When Brooks was finished speaking Deverall was lost for words. He looked closely at this young officer and saw a different person. He really didn't understand what was happening. What did he mean there was 'another way'?
"What do you mean there is another way?"

Brooks looked around and considered what he was going to say next. He was at the cross roads. His next statement would either be accepted or land him in an enormous trouble. When you spoke to John Deverall you could not be vague. He was a man who demanded straight talking, but Brooks yearned to be vague, not to put his cards on the table. He did not want to commit himself just in case the idea was rejected. If Deverall was interested it would be fine and they could discuss the proposition. If he didn't, if he was indignant, he could be violent and that would be bad for Brooks. Worse still, Deverall could have Brooks dismissed or even jailed. He was waiting and Brooks took a deep breath and continued.

"There is another way. Davies is down there in isolation. He is going to be shipped out to Waverly and what do you think is going to happen there? Well for a short time he will be sizing up the new situation. He will work his way back into the prison population. OK, the security will be tighter but he will find his time. Another scene in the cell like the one we had here. Have they got anyone there like you? It will be another poor screw like us who has to deal with it. He will end up in a pool of his own blood and have to go home to the wife with a jaw wired up for weeks. Remember what he did to Roxburg? He still bears the scars. Then there will be another inmate just doing his time and Davies will unload all over him too. Davies will do this over and over again. He brings pain to every place he goes but there is a way to stop him."

Brooks had been talking to the open space over the landing in a voice that only Deverall could hear. It was as if he was just thinking out loud and John was just in the right place to hear, but John's eyes never left the face of the younger officer. John wanted him to get to the point. "What are you getting at Brooks?"

Brooks now gripped the rail with his strong hands. He must be straight with this man or lose his respect. He turned his head to speak but was just not ready to tell everything. More reasons must be presented, he must show that the ground had been prepared.

"Waverly knows what is coming John. They are bracing themselves for it. They know exactly what is going to happen. One of *them* could get killed this time. Is Davies worth that? What is Davies worth? He would kill you or anybody in the blink of an eye and not show an ounce of remorse and he will go on doing the same thing until the law stops him, and the law can't! There is no justice as far as Davies is concerned, just us, the screws. We are the only ones who can contain him and that job is not worth dying for."
Brooks sensed that Deverall was taking an interest in the argument. There was no protest or denial. There was nothing that he disagreed with. There was a glimmer of agreement in his eyes so Brooks pressed on. "I know the guys at Waverly. They are planning to do something but it is all going to go wrong. Not one of them has the strength of character to do what is needed and then to walk away from it. They are going to bring the whole service into disrepute and make Davies look like the victim." Deverall started at this information. The thought of Davies as a figure to be pitied was revolting. He had heard enough for the moment. He had to speak.

"What do you know about me Brooks? What gives you the right to put such an idea out in front of me? I have been in this service a long time and in the military police before that. What gives you the right to offer me this …. thing? I have always stood for what is right. I have always followed the rules, it has been my job for Christ's sake! If you don't have laws, you have nothing to live by. You lose the ability to tell the difference between right and wrong. Where would we be then?" He looked over at the younger man.

"I know you John. It takes about ten seconds to know you. Men can tell instantly. You are a man with unshakeable values, they are clear and precise. You have a will. You get things done because people want to do things for you. You lead and are easy to follow. You are dangerous only to the unworthy. As a friend you are dependable in any situation. You would take the hurt, for a friend. That's who you are John. You are just, and will always seek justice. There is no justice here John. It is a time for you to make a difference for those who crave justice."

John Deverall looked at Brooks. He turned his body to be full square towards the younger man. It was a threat. Action was going to follow and Brooks also turned to face the older man, to take whatever would come.

John spoke.
"Brooks, I have been standing on this landing all by myself for the last half hour. You were not here, you did not speak. Nothing has been said so I didn't hear anything, there is nothing for me to report. I don't want you to say another word and never speak to me about this again. It didn't happen. Like I said I have been alone here all the time so when I turn around that is the way I want things to be."

Brooks gave the almost imperceptible movement of forming a word of protest but the stare from Deverall killed it instantly. Deverall turned around to stare down the body of the prison wing and listened to the retreating steps of his fellow officer.

*   *   *

Detective Sergeant Reynolds sat behind his desk and he looked closely at the untidy pile of papers that blocked his view. He was thinking of how things could have been and how they now were. Long ago he had the chance to look the other way but he didn't. It was not his way and he was not prepared to lower his standards. He had been called to the house of a prominent member of society because it had been burgled. Important documents had been stolen, along with a fair amount of money and some substantial antiques. He was on the scene very quickly and immediately he realised that something didn't quite look right. He was an experienced policeman and as such he possessed a keen instinct. Other officers didn't seem to be doing their work as diligently as they should. All around him there was incompetence and shoddy detection work. The case couldn't be solved but he kept gnawing away at it in his mind. Much later, when the contents of the documents that were stolen were leaked to the press, he thought he had a lead. As a result of the leak the victim of the burglary who held stock in various key companies, made a fortune overnight. So, Reynolds dug some more, he went over the transcripts, the facts and the photographs. When he found what he was looking for he took it to the Chief Constable.

Shattered glass from the broken window where the burglar had entered covered the table where an expensive vase had been standing prior to being stolen. He pointed out that the glass could not have occupied the same place as the vase, so the window must have been broken *after* the object had been moved.

The Chief was not impressed and suggested that there must be more important work that Reynolds could be doing but that was not the kind of policeman he was. He wouldn't let it go. He tried to encourage others to help on the case but there seemed to be little enthusiasm from his fellow officers. When all of the paperwork and photographs were destroyed in a freak shredding accident the case came to a halt. The burglary victim, along with his fortune gained on the stock market, was paid another huge sum by the insurance company, a fact that the public never found out about. This individual was also strategically placed in the government, to promote greater funds for the police.

The Chief Constable called Reynolds into his office some months later. "I was very impressed by the determination and attention to detail you showed in the delicate matter of the Minister's burglary recently. I want you to head up a small unit of hand-picked officers to deal with crimes that we have on the books and are, shall we say, stubbornly resisting closure."

Reynolds could see a career opportunity here and accepted immediately. He was given an office. It actually started life as a store room but was converted hastily to an office when the 'post' was created. He was given a case log. These were cases that stubbornly remained unsolved. They went nowhere, then stopped and stayed there.

His most recent case was on the top of the pile that he was staring at. The pile that never got smaller. Case 10622-SM was a tricky complicated one. Taking and driving away coupled with theft. He reached for it again, opened the manila folder and read the incident report.

It seems that a local milkman was enjoying the hospitality of one of his customers, a lady whose husband was on the late shift. He left his milk van parked outside the house. Unfortunately, the husband came home unexpectedly and upon entering the house he could hear the distinctive noises that such 'hospitality' could produce.

Most men in this situation would confront and perhaps get rough with the dairyman but not this one. He drove the van on to the nearest tower block housing estate and offered all of the produce aboard, to the tenants. In five minutes, it was all gone! Four hundred and eighty litres of milk, thirty loaves of bread, six dozen eggs and assorted yoghurt, creams, cheeses and buns! Once the tenants of the estate realised what was happening, they also took the wheels and the doors off the van. He raised his eyebrows and muttered.
"What could they want with the doors?"

The milkman, after hours of deliberation and insistence from his employer, finally contacted the police. Surprisingly there were no witness, no evidence, no description, no leads. It was a crime that could not be solved and it ended up on Reynolds' desk. He closed the folder and placed it back on the top of the pile.
It was still blocking his view.

* * *

Eileen Brenner pulled her raincoat tightly around her and bent her head to the weather. It pleased her that it was raining, it suited her mood and kept the people in the busy streets occupied with their own weather protection so they could not focus on her. Everyone walked purposefully towards their destinations and they bowed their heads to the task. She couldn't help looking into the faces of those she directly met. There seemed to be an accusation in every eye of every person she passed or met so she decided to keep her eyes fixed on the pavement. She moved through the streets to the station carrying her case like it was filled with stolen goods. Any moment she expected someone to stop her and ask to see the contents and when they found what they were looking for, what she dreaded them finding, they would give her a look of shame.

She didn't deserve this. It wasn't her fault but a little voice always told her that it was. A feeling grew in her that she would not be really free until she could dispose of the item that carried the guilt. It was not until the rhythm and motion of the train calmed her that she started to make her decision. Her journey put many miles between her and her old life but she reached inside her bag and pulled out the card that DC Roper had given her. Something had to be done, but not now. Now she must gain some strength. This card would bring her back, to shed the guilt and make things right. As she flipped it over and over between her fingers, she looked out at the blurring scenery and watched the rivers of rain slanting across the window.

*   *   *

Davies stayed in isolation for two days. It was impossible to allow him to return to the population of the prison and they couldn't transfer him without the proper paperwork. Paperwork always takes a long time because the people pushing the paper never work at the sharp edge. They sit, and push, paper. The greatest threat to them is a paper cut. People who handle Davies could be put into hospital or worse.

On the third day the t's were all crossed and the i's were dotted. He was to be shipped to Waverly prison and kept alone, in their high security wing. The transfer took place just after lock down so the community areas were deserted. All the inmates knew what was happening so they did not tarry as they usually do when the doors are closed. It was now time. The guards took no chance.

When the door swung open Davies was at the far end of the cell looking out of the slitted window into the gathering gloom. It was raining. He turned his head and looked over his left shoulder and smiled. He smiled because of the respect the guards were showing him. They had chosen the biggest of them to enter the cell first. Two huge men entered the cell one at a time because the doorway just wasn't big enough to enter side by side. Other guards entered behind them and still others made their presence felt out on the landing. Any thoughts Davies had of making a move on this lot died in his mind. This show of force went some way to slake the thirst that Davies had for respect. It galled the guards, but it was a small price to pay to get Davies out of their world. Every guard stood there expressionless. The first held out the rigid handcuffs and the second carried shackles. More respect. More smiles from Davies.

"Are we going somewhere boys?"

"Davies? You can walk or you can roll. What's it gonna be?"

Walk or be transported on a hospital trolley, it was a simple choice. Davies was getting what he wanted. He wanted respect, he was getting it. He wanted out and that was happening too. He was going to new pastures and for the time being, the demon in him was sated. That demon was full, asleep, dormant but not dead. It was just a matter of time before the demon woke again. He held out his hands and the officer took a pace into the cell, all of the others tensed. This was a crucial moment.

The cuffs went on without a hitch. They were squeezed a little too tight for Davies but he didn't complain, it was not the stage for that. He stood there staring and smiling into the face of the first officer while the second applied the shackles. When that was done, the shackles were connected to the cuffs. This brought the tension down. Davies, trussed up like this could now be handled and the men on the landing moved to the right side of the door. With a guard in front and one behind Davies left the cell. He stopped momentarily in the doorway and looked at the assembled officers positioned all the way to the gate. It was like a state occasion, and he was the royalty. More respect, a wider grin. His gaze landed on a smaller officer to the right across the canyon of the landing. Davies stopped and squinted and with recognition came his greeting.

"Hey Roxburg, why don't you come along for the ride buddy. We can go over old times yeah? I almost didn't recognise you. What happened to your face?"

Davies turned and started his shuffle towards the end of the landing. The whole prison listened to the roars of laughter coming from him. It was not done for effect. It was laughter that demanded huge lungsful of air. Davies threw his head back and let it all out. His eyes watered as he did so. Roxburg turned and walked away, the other officers stepped aside for him as he passed.

Up at the top of the landing a lone officer looked down at the scene. He gripped the railing hard and the knuckles on his hard hands shone white. His face displayed the concern that the others felt. Tight lipped, frowning, glaring down at the prisoner mocking them all. There was nothing he could do. It was the way thing were. He was offended by this. It wasn't right but there it is. The world is a shitty place and his job was to shovel it from here to there. Here he was in Renkill and the shit was being shovelled to there, Waverly. It wasn't right but it wasn't his job to think of such things – just grab the shovel and get in line. Letting out a strangled breath he relaxed his hands, lifting one to within his eyesight to look at it. It bore the marks of the iron he had been gripping. It was cold and white because the blood could not force its way beyond the vice like flexed muscles. He rubbed some life back into them and turned to make his way to the staff room. It was the end of his shift, time for John Deverall to go home.

There were two other onlookers surveying this scene. They stood in the shadow at the far end of the middle landing. It was not a good vantage point to watch Davies depart but Davies was not who they were interested in. They watched John Deverall. When John left, the Governor looked at Officer Brooks. There was something in the look, a transfer of orders, an encouragement, something that they both silently agreed upon. They also turned and left the landing. There was a brief flash of light in the prison, followed closely by its thunder and then the rain.

*   *   *

The rain was incredible. John never carried an umbrella and so became completely soaked during the short journey from the bus stop to his flat. He entered and went straight to the bathroom, shedding his sodden coat on the way. The towel took away the bulk of the water on his face and head. The rain had refreshed him and this robust rubbing brought some life back into his face and scalp. When he finished, he stood there and looked into the mirror over the sink. His hair was dishevelled and the streams of water from his head had created a dark 'V' of wet blue shirt under his chin. He looked deeply into his own eyes as he deftly removed his shirt and dropped it behind him on the floor. The eyes told him nothing. They were cold. He had not shrugged off the demeanour that he adopted every day at work. He had not shed the role of prison officer. The realisation that he rarely stepped out of this role showed in the face in the mirror.

John Deverall attempted quickly to sum up his life. Could he call it a life? Wake every day and go to work. He was surrounded by stern men doing a hard job with the scum of the earth. He finished work every day and went home, here, to what? There were times when he tried to go out but it didn't work. He felt such a fool, awkward, and it always made him twice as reluctant to attempt it again. He hid here in the plain flat surrounded by evidence of darkness, sadness, failure.

The face in the mirror looked back with eyes that were reddening, a tear was forming in each. His vision blurred slightly but he did not correct it. The tear welled and fell. John Deverall was aware of a new feeling. The feeling was one that he must have felt before because he consciously remembered it. It was not fresh like the hate, disgust and disappointment he felt every day. This feeling weakened him but here in the flat, he was safe so he didn't brace himself against it, he just let the feeling flow. It was pity and sorrow. He detached himself from the image in the mirror and felt sorry for him, pitied him.

Something inside gathered some strength and made his eyes close. The pitiful person in the mirror disappeared. He refused to rub his eyes, instead he closed them as tightly as he could to clear the tears. He dropped his head and reached to turn on the cold tap. The sound of the rushing water broke the silence and the trance. He let it run to get really cold then he filled cupped hands and pushed his face into the liquid. He was back, his strength returned. He turned off the light and left the room. His ordeal was not over yet.

Just before the dawn, John is visited again. It had been a while since the dream had returned. After the episode with Davies the dreams stopped for a while. During that time, he tried to change his life but failed. The dream is always intense as if it is being endured for the first time. It never diminishes and even though he has experienced it a thousand times it is always new, always filling him with terror and helplessness.

Helen is there in the grass on that sunny day. She is looking at him with helpless eyes. Her frail little body is being ravaged by the youth but she shows no pain on her face. She looks straight at her father who is standing there straining every muscle in his body to break free and help her but he can't, all he can do is speak, shout, scream!
"Fight girl, fight for your life!"
"Daddy."
This always wracks his soul. This little thing being destroyed in the grass on a sunny day while the granite hard figure of her father stands statue-like, and watches. She put so much faith in him. He was her champion and he failed her, he could do nothing. He was put on this earth to create this child, this little light and all he can do is watch it being snuffed out.

The deed is done and the man walks away leaving the broken body of the child in the long grass. Everything in the dream is crystal clear. The sound of the wind in the grass, the warmth of the sun and the laughter of the man walking away. There is a new focus. This laughter is different but not new. This laughter is familiar and John takes a step nearer to hear it more closely. The first step is ignored as he keened his hearing to listen to that shouted laughter the man was producing, but the second step took all of his attention. Never before had he been able to move, he looked at his feet and took the third step like a man who was only now learning to walk. He gathered his senses again and looked up to see the back of the laughing man. He was moving swiftly now and John was gathering speed too but he could not close the gap. Without breaking stride the man turned and what John saw made him stop instantly. It was the leering laughing face of Davies.
He heard a voice behind him which made him spin to face it.
"Daddy."

Helen lay in the grass with her hand outstretched towards her father. She only seemed to be a few feet away but he couldn't reach her. His movements had slowed and he was not strong enough to force more speed into his limbs. The ground clawed at his legs and the air was thick like water, resisting his progress.

"Daddy." She looked at him with lifeless eyes.

When he finally reached her, she was cold. He knew she was cold but not from touch. No matter how he tried he could not gather up the broken body of his child. If he could he might be able to give some of his strength, his life, to her. He would give it all to her if he could. What a release it would be for him. She was cold and troubled, there was a frown on her face, a face turned away from him. Her voice came again, through lips that pouted, just about to cry.

"Help me Daddy, I feel bad."

Tears came to his eyes and dripped noiselessly onto the grass. Once again, he was helpless. The power of movement was brief and was gone. He stood there and had to endure. Powerless.

"He's a bad man daddy. He hurt me daddy."

He looked up toward the route that Davies had taken and there, in the far distance, Davies stood with his hands on his hips, head thrown back, roaring with laughter.

He looked down at his broken child in complete astonishment. All of this was different, even more unendurable. He couldn't think, couldn't speak, all he could do was listen as Helen spoke again.

"Daddy, he will come back again. Don't let him do it again daddy."

John Deverall knelt on the ground next to her. He had never been this close before. She turned her head and looked at him with her lifeless eyes as if she was focusing on something in the distance.

"Help me daddy."

Tears come to his eyes and she goes out of focus. He does not rub his eyes, he just squeezes them as tightly as he can and as he does, he makes a promise to her.

"I'll deal with him Helen. I'll protect you."

His waking is not gentle. He sits bolt upright in bed. The bed shows the evidence of his predawn ordeal. The blankets are on the floor, the sheets are screwed into a ball and the bare covering of the mattress shows in the dawn light. The sweat covering his body and face is exactly like the rain that soaked him the day before. His breathing is laboured and his chest heaves to claw the air from the stuffy room into his lungs. His heart is beating in his ears.

John Deverall stares at the curtains. He doesn't see them. He doesn't see anything. He is trying to make some sense out of the vision he has just endured. The alarm clock starts to make its noise and he reaches out without looking and shuts it off. Recovering slightly, he stands up and moves toward the curtain and with a sweep of his arm he pulls it open. The sky is clear, the streets are wet and clean. The rain from the previous day has freshened the world. Last night was different. Today was going to be different too.

* * *

Seven

Last night was a distant memory for Mrs. Brenner. As she lay there in the morning the memories were leaving her, memories about arriving, being soaking wet and cold, being welcomed into her brother's house, children being shoo'd to bed, a hot drink and getting into bed. She did remember the whispering and the haunted looks full of sorrow, pity and fear. Now she waited in this strange bed while her memories left and when they were gone, she sat up.

Listening very carefully she could hear no sound in the house. No sound from the street. The lack of sound made its own noise – a humming in her ears. She was used to a city background noise and this silence disturbed her. Was it quiet like this because they too were listening for sounds she made? The conclusion she came to was that it was early, in the quiet countryside. That is why there was no sound within the house. It must be very early because the children always got up first with squealy noises and laughter. With her visit from out of the blue, in the middle of the night and at the height of a rainstorm the children were probably under orders to stay in bed until called. She looked to her suitcase on the chair nearest to the bed.

It was scarred by the life it had elsewhere. It bore the marks of a previous existence. It was old and she made a mental note to replace it and a thought darted across her mind. How could she do it? Give it away? Throw it into a pit? Burn it? Would she ever be able to get the picture of that case and what it held out of her mind? It was something that she took from the darkness of her old life into this lighted morning of her new one. It was a dingy case, moody and full of secrets. It held her dark secret that no one must find.

She curtailed these thoughts and dragged a dressing gown out of the middle of her hastily packed clothes. She stood and wrapped the garment around her. The window was now the focus of her attention. The curtains barred her view of the world and that is what she wanted to see. If she pushed the curtains back would this dream end? Would she be back in the dreadful place that she remembered. Did she ever want to venture out there again? She crossed the room slowly and mentally made a decision that her life would be different today, this day. This first day. It all depended on what she saw, if there was to be any reconciliation with herself it would depend on this day. She finally reached the curtain and she cursed herself. Why had she promised herself that the day would determine her life?

She had to go through with it now.
She felt ashamed that a chance event like the daily weather could make such a decision. A new thought entered her mind. She didn't *have* to keep her promise to herself. Those promises didn't count. Did they? Oh yes, they did, because if you ever broke a promise to yourself then you could never get away from the taunts of the person you let down.

She was at the curtain now, a heavy curtain which didn't give a clue as to what it was hiding. Oh this is silly she thought! Mrs Brenner reached out and grasped the cloth and pulled it to the side.

The streets of the housing estate were quiet, it was too early in the morning for any local traffic. Their surface, all surfaces, were wet from the torrent of the previous night. There was a slight breeze made evident by the movement of the young trees and bushes. The sky was a silver blue caught between the night and the morning. The sun was very low and very orange. It shone directly into the room straight into her eyes. It made her squint. An observer might have said there was a hint of a smile in the expression on her face. The observer would be right, this sunny morning had refreshed Mrs. Brenner and she allowed herself a little smile.

She enjoyed the feeling so she kept it there. Without taking her eyes away from the sun and the warmth it gave her she pushed the curtains back as far as they would go. The room flooded with light. She stood there basking in it, soaking up the warmth, taking all of the energy she could from that nearest star. Mrs. Brenner decided to be the last person to get up this morning so she got back into bed. She left the curtains open so the light could fill her eyes. She would listen for the noises of the house as it woke. There was her brother, his wife and their two boys. She would wait until she heard the toilet flush four times. Then she would start her new life. There was a smile on her face as she laid her head on the pillow.

*   *   *

It was a different story for Bill Davies.

He left Renkill Prison under a full escort. There was not going to be another incident like Roxburg. Oh the respect they gave him. He was cuffed and hobbled when he left his cell and shuffled down to the end of the landing where there were even more guards, poised to take action but it was never going to come. Davies was dumb but not stupid. As long as he didn't make any sudden moves or give them an excuse, he could say what he liked. So, he shouted and laughed in their faces. It was a lesson for all the con's who were listening. They don't have to live like shrews; they can make a difference to how they do their time. They can do it on their knees or with respect! He had won, they couldn't take it, or control him. Oh, the respect! It welled in his chest and drove out all other feelings. Not a chance of remorse for Treevillillll. He had it coming. If you couldn't look after yourself you had to take what came your way. The kid was a child killer anyway! Probably some pervert so the world was now a better place.

Davies tried to look into the eyes of every guard that he met. He wanted to make an imprint, leave something behind. He looked for some recognition but there was none. These men were carefully picked for this duty. Some worked a double shift so they could be here for this. These were the more experienced men. They were blank – gave nothing away. Each one would give a weeks pay to squarely smash Davies in the face. To rid themselves of the pent-up frustration each held in check. They did not show it though. To do that would be a result for Davies. He would get into your skull, somewhere right behind the eyes and it would never let you go. You would always be plagued by the look of victory on Davies' face and washed with a shame that you would never be able to shake. It is inside the skull. You can't scratch that kind of itch.

They took him to the security van that was to transport him to Waverly Prison. It had been brought in from the yard because if the rain. It was time to check out.
Two guards flanked him either side and he could feel the presence of another two behind him. A large cardboard box was set on a table in the

dispatch room. Behind the toughened glass stood the duty officer and Davies was made to face the glass.

"Davies, you are being transferred to Waverly tonight. These are your belongings. I have checked them and all is correct. You have to sign for them."

From under the glass, through a grill, came a sheaf of papers that Davies had to sign. Sitting on the top was a pencil, attached to a chain that disappeared into the inner office. Davies looked at the pencil and smiled. They certainly were taking no chances. He looked at the officers either side and reached with both hands to sign. He felt an electric tension at that moment. These men were ready.

"Shouldn't I check the contents?"

"Don't piss about Davies, what could any of us want with your pathetic stuff?

The officer was given a look by the men on the other side of the glass. Don't let the side down. Let's just get this over with. Keep him out of your skull.

The officer dropped his gaze, responded to the silent message and adopted the demeanour of the others. Davies also knew that this conversation was over so he leaned forward and signed the paper. Just as an act of defiance he pulled the pencil to the full extent of the chain but instantly felt hands on his arms. The moment passed when he let the chain go to swing on its own. He closed his eyes and laughed again. Boy was he in control! From his right he heard a voice.

"Let's go Davies" and with this he was pointed in the direction of the van.

Lightning was very close because it was almost instantly followed by thunder. It was the only sound that could drown out his laughter. Two guards got into the van and readied themselves. Davies was then urged into the vehicle, he had some difficulty negotiating the step with the chains on his feet. Once he was in and seated the other guards took up their positions beside him. The last guard shut the door and signalled to the driver who started the engine. The gates opened and then Davies was gone. This episode was over. The remaining guards relaxed but said nothing because there was nothing to say. Each felt the same. Glad to be rid of him. Ashamed for not being able to prevent what had happened. Angry that they couldn't do anything about it and sorrow for the staff at Waverly because their nightmare was just about to begin.

* * *

Davies stirred in his new cell. He threw back the covering blanket and let his bare feet touch the cold concrete floor. This wasn't bad, a cell to himself and a new beginning.

He was happy. He knew that his reputation would go before him and it would be interesting to see what the reaction would be today. He looked up at the heavily barred window. All he could see was the opposite block of the prison. The roof was slate and it was oily wet. Above that there was blue sky. The sun was still too low to shine into the cell but he knew it would be there later in the morning. This was good, a south facing aspect! Location, location, location!

He moved over to the stainless-steel toilet in the corner and urinated noisily. When he finished, he looked around the cell. None of his belongings were delivered yet. The walls were bare but bore the marks of previous owners. Scabs of adhesive and flaked paint where posters once lived. Everything was bolted down to the floor, walls and ceiling. This was a special cell. You couldn't rearrange the furniture here. This thought made him frown. His urination made it worse, made his memory of that moment become real. The one time at Renkill, the one memory that he couldn't get rid of. It would be with him always, in *his* skull. His submission and defeat. He wouldn't let that happen to him here.

There was nothing to do so he got back into his bed. He pulled the covers up to his chest and put both hands behind his head. He would wait. Let's see what the day brings. A smile played across his lips and he closed his eyes. The sun started to come into his cell.

* * *

This day was like all the rest for DS Reynolds. He woke gently from a dreamless sleep and opened his eyes. He could hear the measured breathing of his wife beside him and feel the warmth of her back against his side. He then took stock. It was Thursday and so he went over his Thursday routine in his head. It was the same as Wednesday and would be the same for tomorrow, Friday. He could look forward to the weekend. That always held some variety for him but it would come and go all too quickly, then it would be Monday again.

He carefully tipped himself out of bed and made his way to the kitchen where he filled the kettle. Standing there looking over the back garden he watched the birds. He wondered what *they* looked forward to in the day. Food, fear, fly, land, more fear. Fear everywhere! They still got through the day though, and they seemed happy enough. He caught himself wishing that he was a bird and he felt stupid. The bubbling kettle dragged him back to reality. He did this every morning, waking too early and making the tea. It was strange. Every workday he woke early. Every day that he wished he could shorten, he woke early. It just seemed to drag out the torment of not being in control. He made the tea and filled two cups.

The garden was wet from the torrential rain the night before and every plant seemed to react to the fresh water. They stood taller, greener, happier. This was too much. A happy plant? Before he started wishing _he_ was a plant he turned with the two cups of tea and started back to the bedroom. His wife was awake as he pushed the bedroom door open with his foot.
"Tea?"

She sat up in bed and arranged the covers around her and to welcome him to his side of the bed.
"Ummm, yes please!" He gave her the cup and inserted himself into the bedclothes. They both sat and sipped for a few moments. He thought about work for a moment and sighed. She picked it up immediately.
"I wish I could help."

They had talked about this subject so many times that each knew how the other felt. There was no need for words. He was stuck, there was no way out. He was proud and wouldn't give up. So many times they talked about moving to another part of the country where he could join another police force but his record would follow him. They talked about leaving the force but that would be defeat. He was too proud to do that.

"I know but there is nothing you can do." He held her free hand. "I just have to take every day as it comes. I have to take every dud case they send me. Keep them piling up. Maybe there will be a change in management, someone is bound to get promotion sooner or later and with a new broom, who knows?"

"I hate seeing you like this though. You are such a good man and they are wasting you. It preys on your mind all the time. I feel it even though you try to hide it."
He smiled. He thought he was much better at hiding his frustrations but she knew him inside out. Occasionally he would drop his guard to get the support and kind words that he needed. He didn't do it on purpose, it was his soul calling the shots. When it was over, he would be strong again. He got the assurance and praise he needed, it was a man thing.

He took another sip of his tea and stared towards the end of the bed at nothing in particular. "I am going to keep at it love. I will go in today with a new attitude, I think. I will turn the case load upside down and start with the oldest cases first. They are going to see me putting energy into every file. It really is the only thing I can do. What I can't stand is the smirk on the face of that pencil pusher, Wiltshire who drops the cases off at the office. He knows that they go nowhere and he has this look in his eye. It's hard to take." Reynolds put his tea cup on the side table and swung his legs out of bed. He stood at the window and turned to look at his wife.

"They can't keep me on this detail for long, something has to change soon. When it does, I will be ready." He looked out of the window at the landscape drenched in night rain and waiting for the sun. There was an expectant mood out there. He looked for longer than he wanted to, because he did not want his wife to see the despair on his face. Who was he kidding? There was absolutely no reason in the world why his 'superiors' should change the way they feel. They had him where they wanted him and he knew it. He would stay in the same job until he rotted or quit. They could wait forever. He didn't know what to do and it showed on his face so he stared out of the window.

"Let me make you some breakfast" he said to his wife as he left the room.

* * *

John Deverall had to take a shower. The sweat from his dream was cold on his body and he needed to warm up. Automatically he rolled from the bed, moved towards the bathroom and set the shower to run. He stripped off his soaking night clothes letting them just lay on the floor where they fell. He stepped into the shower.

He stood and let the hot stream of water hit his head while he focused on a cross of grouting between four tiles. The sound of the water hitting him slowly faded in his ears, the sting of the heat subsided and he became numb to it. His vision went beyond the wall into the open world. As he stood still, there in the shower, a landscape rushed by at break neck speed. He was oblivious to all around him but there was something telling him that if he wanted to stop, to return to reality, all he had to do was blink and concentrate on the shower. It was good to know but not what he wanted to do. He was fast approaching that field, that dreadful piece of grass where his daughter lay. He wanted to know why! The journey came to a halt and sitting there in the grass was a grown man. There was no sign of his daughter. The voice came again.

'All you have to do to stop this is just close your eyes and have your shower. Get on with the day.'
He stubbornly continued with his vision. The man was a stranger to him, he was bigger and more powerful than the other men in the dreams. He only offered his back so his face could not be seen. John concentrated and began to move to the side. He could hear a mumbling coming from the man.

The shower was hot but inside John felt a chill move from the centre of his being outward toward the tips of his fingers and toes. He began to recognise the man, he would not believe it fully until he could see the entire face but deep inside, he knew who it was. He recognised the voice and understood the words. Now he faced the man on the ground. He was looking straight in his eyes. Straight into his own eyes as they stood there chanting …
"I'll deal with him Helen. I'll protect you."

He closed his eyes and the pain of the scalding shower took over. It was a pain he could endure but the feeling of helplessness would not leave him.

He stepped from the shower and began the ritual of getting ready to go to work. He went through this ritual every day but today was different. He was now haunted by his own words. They ran through his mind over and over again but there was another feeling making its presence known. It was hope! Perhaps he could do something to relieve the torture that Helen felt every night. It was a thought that would not go away even as he pulled the door closed behind him and he made his way to the street.

Everything was wet and fresh. The sun was starting to shine meekly as if it was apologising for being late and letting all this rain happen. Everything was wet and looked new. John Deverall took a deep breath and spoke just before he stepped onto the pavement, "I'll deal with him Helen. I'll protect you."
He was determined to make a difference today.

*   *   *

Bill Davies had resigned himself to a life in prison. It was easily done. He knew he was not the type to escape. He never planned anything – things always just happened. Maybe if the opportunity to escape was suddenly available he would take it but he could not form an alliance of men to plan an escape. You needed friends to do that and he never had any. This brought a wicked smile to his face because he never needed friends. He could manage by himself. He never entertained the thought that what he had managed so far, was multiple life sentences, in the most secure prisons in the land and there was no light at the end of the tunnel. He would never get out of prison. He knew there were two ways to do your time, keep your nose clean and cause as little trouble as possible or stake your claim and rule the roost. The decision was already made and this little subconscious conversation had no purpose. It was time to let everyone know that Bill Davies needed respect. It was time to send a message to everyone in this house. A horn sounded outside the landing, it was time for breakfast, it was time to send his message.

The food hall was a cavernous place. Tables and benches were fixed to the floor in row upon row. Each table held four prisoners in pairs facing each other. At the end of the hall, along the entire wall, the food was offered by a selection of prisoners who proved themselves worthy of such a responsible position. The guards spaced themselves equally around the tables and they were always on the move. At the door a group of guards recorded the number of each prisoner as he entered and would do the same when they left. The hall was already one quarter full as Davies entered the doorway where he was stopped by one of the guards. They looked each other in the eyes and Davies saw what he wanted. Fear. It was almost imperceptible but it was there all the same. The gaze of the guard dropped to Davies' number and he spoke to his colleague.

"Red 20696"

The other officer recorded the number and looked up. They had all been told about Red 20696 and he thought he would have a look. Davies saw it again and he smiled when he was told to move along. He looked around the hall. The noise level had gone down ever so slightly, there were more inmates turning their heads than usual and some of the guards stopped their wanderings to take in the new situation. They also felt something different in the hall but it brought no smiles to their faces.

Davies moved toward the hatch and offered his tray. The young inmate serving the cereal held out a portion sized box of flakes. Davies refused and moved on. He lifted a plate towards the inmate serving the eggs.

"Scrambled or fried?"
"Oh I think I will have fried eggs this morning."
One fried egg was deposited on his plate.
"I always have more than one egg in the morning chief."
The middle-aged inmate slid another egg on to the plate but Davies still stood his ground. The other prisoners in the line had moved on and the rest were backing up because of this hold up. One hungry prisoner further down the line raised his voice.
"Come on! What's the hold up down there?"

Davies turned, still holding the plate out towards the hotplate, and looked straight at the complaining man who quickly returned to the line and decided that it would be better to be quiet and wait. Davies turned back to the man with the eggs.
"Another."

The server looked at the inmate in charge of the kitchen who gave a slight nod. Another egg was delivered.

"And another"

Sweat was now apparent on the brow of the man with the eggs. Other prisoners in the line were backing slightly away and the guards started to move towards the hatch. The smile was growing on Davies's face. The guards were moving closer one was assuming responsibility and approaching directly. Davies had his man.

"You've got three eggs Davies, that's more than anyone else now move along the line."

The distance between the two men was closing and when it was just right Davies turned and thrust the plate into the face of the guard. The speed of the guard, added to the speed and force from Davies, lifted the guard off the floor and he landed on his back. All the time he fell he screamed as the scalding eggs entered his eyes and nostrils. He landed flat at Davies's feet who was perfectly prepared for the event. Davies took one short step forward with his left foot and planted his right into the chest of the guard. The screaming stopped to be replaced by the sound of breaking ribs. All this happened in a split second but it seemed like an eternity. The other guards were stuck to the floor. They all knew that something like this would happen but couldn't believe that it had! When they could move, they did. So did the other prisoners at the hatch. The traffic was in both directions, uniforms going towards Davies and the rest, anywhere else!

Davies stood with his back to the hotplate still holding his tray. The first officer rushed in head first and took the full force of the tray edge across the nose. It opened up to the bone and blood sprayed through the air as he hit the floor. Whistles were being blown and more officers were rushing through the door. Two guards had their sticks out and were advancing towards Davies. He picked one and stepped forward to meet him. As the stick swung towards his head Davies moved under the arm, twisted and pushed. The arm released the stick as the elbow joint shattered and the man went down to the floor. Davies picked up the stick, turned and parried the blow from the second officer and brought his new weapon down on the man's head.

In a matter of twenty seconds Davies had laid out three guards.

Now there was a lull.

The remaining officers stopped. Evidence of what might happen to them was there on the floor and no one wished to end up like that but they had to do something! All of them had drawn their sticks and formed a semi-circle around Davies. They were collectively on the point of making up their minds to rush him at once when there was a shout from the rear. "Stand back all of you!"

It was a voice they instantly recognised. It was the prison governor. He was flanked by two officers each carrying a shotgun. They made their way through the ring of guards. The governor looked at the situation. Three of his men were laying on the ground, only one was moving. There was blood all over the place and it was forming a pool on the floor. His gaze moved from his stricken guards to Davies who was standing at the hotplate breathing heavily, splattered with blood. Davies had a smile on his face. The two men looked at each other. Davies saw no fear just frustration in his eyes. The governor looked at Davies and spoke very clearly.
"Davies you are going into isolation. That's a fact. How you get there is up to you."
The flanking officers cocked the shotguns.

"I haven't had my breakfast yet guv."
"You'll get what's coming to you Davies, that is also a fact."
"I hope you don't think any of these boys can do it guv, they just don't have the stuff."

He dropped the stick and it bounced away from him. He surrendered himself to the guards and they pushed and pulled him into a secure standing position where he was chained hand and foot. He was led out of the hall. As he shuffled past the guards he smiled. As he shuffled past the other inmates, he added something to his grin. They got the message. When he reached the door, he stopped and spoke.
"Red 20696."

They shoved him through the door and he started to laugh. He laughed all the way to the isolation cell deep within the bowels of the prison.

* * *

Renkill had settled down again. The disturbing wave of violence that Davies had brought and delivered had subsided. It was still a violent place but the guards were on top of it. What was disturbing were the stories coming out of Waverly.

John Deverall listened to them and they hit him hard. He had Davies under control and just one lapse let him off the leash. He blamed himself for not being there when Davies made his move. He listened to the stories but no one ever told them directly to his face. They were all overheard and quickly halted when he came into earshot. He knew the gist of the episode but not the details and he wanted to know. It would not be right for him to make an official enquiry so he had to wait. Sooner or later, it would all be explained and the time came sooner rather than later. It was the morning briefing with the governor.

They were all assembled and waiting for the information. They wanted the details so they didn't need to talk about it anymore. There was some good in knowing but that was all. He had passed through, made all their lives worse and now he was somebody else's problem. There was a community guilt when this thought passed through their minds. The poor bastards at Waverly had a problem now that nobody wanted but these men were pleased it wasn't them.

The governor came in and the burly men shuffled into a standing position which showed some respect but was not attention. The talking stopped and all eyes looked at him. He shot a glance at Brooks and it was returned. Each man felt that the look they exchanged was discreet but another pair of eyes from the back of the room had seen it too. John Deverall stood where he could survey the entire room and judge the reaction of all the men as the news was given out. He looked at Brooks until Brooks looked at him. The voice of the governor broke the contact.

"Our friend Davies didn't take long to cause mayhem at Waverly. I am sure that you have all heard some of the stories and before it gets to the inmates here, I want you all to know exactly what happened. We don't want Davies to become some sort of hero here and give anyone any ideas. If the prisoners ask let them know the truth. If rumours get out of hand, I want you to put things straight.

It was thought that with a change of scenery Davies might calm down. Waverly staff didn't want to alienate him early by overzealous control. It was thought by the psychiatric results that more freedom might affect Davies positively …"

There was an audible moan and sounds of disgust from the men. They knew all too well about psychiatrists, they gave loads of advice but are never there when the shit hits the fan. Endersley was a doctor of psychiatry and when he stopped speaking the room followed. He slowly looked at each of his men from the right side of the room to the left. He looked at his notes and after skipping further down the page he continued.

"Davies caused a disturbance in the breakfast line yesterday. The first officer he attacked was left with a gashed, broken nose, serious burns to the face and eyes when Davies threw a plate of fried eggs at him. When the officer fell, he suffered a concussion and while he was down Davies broke three of his ribs with a kick that punctured his lung. That officer will be off work for three months." Endersley looked up. These men were too hard to show much dismay.

"A second officer, coming to the aid of the first, suffered a severe hyper extension of the elbow joint and will be in plaster for four months and physiotherapy for six."
The governor looked up again to gauge the reaction from his men. There was none. Deverall was also in a position to see the reaction from the men but he didn't need to. He knew these men and what made them tick. He was one of them and he didn't feel the urge to react to what he was hearing, so why should they?

"The third officer was severely clubbed in the head and is in a coma. That third officer is now fighting for his life in intensive care and will not work again. It was Ricky Beer." The governor looked up.

This name caused an unsuppressed wave of dismay amongst the guards. Last year 'Boozer' had been transferred to Waverly from Renkill. He was a friend to them all. He was a face they knew. They knew his wife and children. He was a brother and now he was laid low. This added embarrassment added a sense of failure to their feelings. They looked at each other and shook their heads. Anger and futility were rising in them and the governor sensed it too.

"Gentlemen we have a job to do. I don't want this episode at Waverly, to affect the prisoners here. Davies will be dealt with."

"How?"

It was a question from the back of the room. It came from Deverall. No head turned to look at him because every man knew who had spoken. Every man knew that there was only one guard who would dare to ask the question and the question made the governor uncomfortable. The governor looked around the room again to gauge the feeling of his men and he sensed that they all wanted an answer. He had to give one.

"Davies has been put into isolation where he will stay until he is charged and the episode investigated. If he is found guilty...."

The men openly moaned and grunted and only by raising his voice could he continue. "... **and *when* he is found guilty,** his sentence will be increased and he will probably be moved to Marshview."

The guards settled down again.

There was nothing else so the men started to file out and talk amongst themselves. Deverall remained at the back of the room and he noticed again that glance from the governor to Brooks. The two men were the last to leave the room. Brooks turned to look at Deverall for a moment and then he too turned and left the room leaving Deverall there by himself to ponder what exactly had just occurred.

* * *

John Deverall walked the landing looking for trouble that morning. He wanted to put somebody straight. He needed to gain the upper hand again. He felt that every eye had an accusation in it. If he had not been interrupted during the confrontation with Davies maybe things would be different. The killing of Treevillillll was no loss. He had it coming, it was justice, nobody cared and most were happy that he was gone. He had no problem with that but these other officers were good men. 'Boozer' was a good man and didn't deserve to be a victim of scum like Davies. Deverall looked for trouble but it didn't come. The fact that he was ready for a confrontation preceded and followed him like a smell and everyone got out of his way. Even the guards were wary of him and one in particular avoided him like the plague.

Brooks wasn't afraid of Deverall, he had no need to be. He actually *wanted* to talk to him but not at this moment. He would give him some time to think and when the time was right, he would have his chat. The time was right in the mid afternoon and Brooks made himself available on the top landing of the prison block. He made himself available by just standing still next to the railing. At this place he could be seen by every guard on every landing. It took about fifteen minutes for Deverall to take the bait.

"John?"

"Brooks, I want to have a word."

The two men turned to survey the cathedral-like proportions of the main wing of the prison. Deverall could not see it but there was a hint of a smile on the face of Phil Brooks. He spoke into the void.

"John, you know that Davies is going to do the same thing at Marshside. It will take a little more time than usual but you know it will happen again. There is no way that the system can stop him. I don't mind if he tears the heads off of the scum he lives with but those officers are good men. Remember 'Boozer'?

John stood up straight but still didn't look at his colleague.

"Of course I remember him!"

Phil Brooks had the first reaction he needed. John Deverall talking.

"Well, 'Boozer' is in the hospital and he might not make it. Davies will get isolation for some time, he will endure the system as the charges are pressed and he is further convicted and more time is heaped on his sentence. What is the point? 'Boozer' is worth more than that. He doesn't deserve that John, he doesn't deserve to be clubbed by vermin like Davies. And then there are the others. Every person who Davies comes into contact with will be a potential victim. It is going to happen over and over again."

Deverall stood there and dwelt on the words. 'Over and over again.' Just like his recurring dream. Brooks continued.

"You and me John, we are the ones who stand between the public and the garbage like Davies. There is a Davies in almost every nick in the country and all we do is hold the line. We bite our lips. We hold our tongues."

Both men continued to look into the body of the prison. Brooks sensed that he needed to deliver more but he was treading on dangerous ground. He still hadn't committed himself but he had to have Deveralls acknowledgement before he could do that. So he waited and it was a sign for John to take up the conversation. He turned to look at Brooks and spoke.

"I was sorting out vermin like Davies when you were still in short pants Brooks. I have rubbed shoulders with men that thought they could make a difference by themselves and they didn't last long. It is something that can't be done by one person. One person never makes a difference. One person puts his neck on the line and as soon as the weak link in the chain is found the neck breaks. The sight of a man who has his dream taken away is a terrible sight to see. He can be a very dangerous man. He becomes bitter and will seek to punish those who betrayed his trust." Brooks inwardly sighed with relief. He knew this was a small step toward acceptance. It was also a warning.

"I understand what you are saying John, but this is not the dawning of an idea. This conversation with you is the final step. If it goes well then everything will fall into place. If we can't reach an agreement then we will both walk away as if we never had the conversation."

John was taken aback by these remarks. In order for them to be true then every guard in the prison would know the subject of this conversation so he turned to look again into the body of the prison. He looked again, but with different eyes. He looked for the guards on their rounds and every one of them stole glances towards the high walkway where the two men stood. They would exchange words with each other, look up and then move about their business. They all knew what was going on. They were all waiting to see what John would do. It gave him a thrill and it also disgusted him. He was thrilled to know how much faith these men had in him, they would put their professional lives on the line.

But that was all they risked. He was disgusted that none of them had the courage to do it themselves, they were prepared to let him take the ultimate risk. These were indeed brave men but they only followed a lead. He looked at them closely and felt something else. There was a pleading in their eyes. They needed help. They needed him to lead and they *would* follow and he knew that they would be firm when the shit storm followed. Helen needed help and he wasn't there to give it to her. He remembered her words and the dream came back to him in his waking state.

'Daddy, he will come back again. Don't let him do it again daddy.'

He promised her that he would make a difference and inside, at that moment, the resistance was over. He finally admitted to himself that his life was over and he didn't have the strength to resist the torment any more. Let things happen as they will from now on. It seemed that his day was a living nightmare and his night was no better. He turned to look at Brooks.

Phil Brooks inwardly sighed – with relief. The pressure was off and the fear was over. He could now talk to this man.

"Every man here supports this effort John. I have spoken to them all and outlined what can happen and what length they must play to take a part."

John turned to look at Brooks and waited for him to finish talking.

"The guards at Waverly are one hundred percent behind it too." This caused Deverall's eyebrows to raise, this plan was truly in the final stage. It caused him to interrupt.

"Just what did you have in mind Phil?"

This was the moment.

"We are going to get someone inside Waverly prison, into Davies' cell and ….."

It was hard to actually put his mouth around the words. His tongue refused to act properly. Once the words come out, they would not be able to be recalled. The words, when spoken would make him as evil as those around him locked away from society.

He had to start again.

"We are going to execute Bill Davies."

There, it was out, and said like this it wasn't so bad, but it was still the same.

John Deverall followed this with a question.
"We?"

* * *

Eileen Brenner waited for the toilet to flush for the fourth time and she got out of bed. She made herself move quickly and with purpose, she picked up her washing things and went to the bathroom. The room was filled with the things a family with small children use to wash and play while bathing and this time of the morning it was in a chaotic state but it made her smile all the same. She smiled and caught herself doing it. It shamed her for a moment but she pushed it back and defiantly smiled some more.

Undressed she confronted herself in the mirror. She was not a wasted life, she still had a great deal to offer. Looking at herself objectively she realised that she had nothing to be ashamed of. That life was over and a new one was beginning. The sun made her feel like that. The rain too was a good sign. She washed, brushed her teeth and combed her hair. It was welling up inside her, the guilt was coming up like gorge. It had to come, to purge itself from the system and these first times were the testing times. If she could resist now then every time after this it would be easier until it was forgotten alltogether. Finished with her morning ritual she looked again in the mirror to confront herself. This was the test, could she pass?

"You're damned right I will!"

She smiled a determined smile and left to return to the bedroom.
The first thing she did was to go to her bag, then her purse then that little secret place behind her credit card. There was a small rectangle of card there and she took it out and placed it on the dressing table against the mirror. Now she could look at the card and watch herself get dressed as well. She focused on the words printed on the card. At this distance she couldn't read what it said but she knew. It was the card that DS Roper had given her if she needed to call him. To talk. She promised that she wouldn't but this last thing had to be shed in order for her to start over. It must be cast out but if it was just discarded, she would always feel like an accomplice.

There was a knock on the door.

"Eileen?" It was her brother. Calmly she went to the dressing table and put the card into the palm of her hand and turned to face the door as it was being opened.
"Good morning sis! Want to join us for breakfast?"
"Oh yes please Chris … and Chris, I can't thank you enough for letting me stay. I promise you I won't get in the way. In fact, I will only be staying for a few days and when I get a few things sorted I will be on my way."
"You are welcome to stay for as long as you like sis!"
They kissed each other and went down the stairs to breakfast.

*   *   *

David Brenner was not so fortunate. He was still taking all of his food through a straw and since the bandages round his head came off, he had to cope with horrified reactions from everyone he saw. His eyes were deep black purple and his jaw was still swollen up. Speech was impossible but not necessary. He didn't have any reason to talk to anybody and if he could he probably wouldn't anyway. His mind raced in all directions at once about several different subjects. The court case coming up was going to be bad. There was no way he could get off this one. They would drag up his past and it would not be good.

His past! What was going to happen about that? His mother. What was she going to do? She promised, that was a relief, but she took it with her. He had to get to the flat but was in no shape to go anywhere and if he could there was always a guard posted outside the ward doors. He needed a drink. There would be no drinks for a long time. He could only sit and suck at whatever they gave him. Sit and suck and think. He needed to get out of his head. What was he going to do? He closed his eyes when he realised that there was nothing that he *could* do. Now his life was in the hands of everyone else but himself. What was she going to do?

*   *   *

"We?"

"No John, you. It's you because of your determination and ability. It's you because of the way you feel and the convictions that you hold. It's you because of the backup that you need and that backup will come from these men." Brooks waved outwardly towards the landings. "These men would only do this for one man and that's you."

John Deverall looked again at the men on the landings.

"What about the men at Waverly?"

"Every one of the men at Waverly is behind this. They are as reliable as the men here. This thing John, has been growing for a long time. If I hadn't asked some questions someone else would have done it instead. We all feel the same, something has to be done."

"This is all coming from you Phil?"

"Everyone feels the same John, I am just the person who has put a voice to those feelings and let others know that they are not alone. Every time I get the same reaction, disgust with the system and the need to do something about it. When I tell them that they are not alone with these thoughts, they show surprise. For some time, we have become aware that we all felt the same but there has never been a man who could do something about it. I saw you that day John."

John turned to look at Brooks.

"In the cell with Davies. It was there on your face and through every fibre of your body. I saw you that day and I knew that I had to have this conversation, it was only a matter of time and skilful manoeuvring."

John didn't turn his gaze away from Brooks. He just started to speak like he was confessing to a crime, that he knew was no longer necessary to lie and deny the facts. He was looking at Brooks but he wasn't seeing him. He just spoke.

"I didn't go into the cell to confront Davies, I always knew that it might happen and I suppose I was ready for it but I thought he might have backed down. When it started, I couldn't feel a thing. He hit me twice and I didn't feel it at all. Time seemed to stand still and movement stopped too, it was just Davies on the end of my arm. It was as if I had all of the evil things in the world there on the end of my arm. I had the power to rid the world of evil so I squeezed. I watched as he crumpled but I didn't care. I didn't care for him or for myself. I didn't think of police charging me with a crime or the reputation of the prison service.

There was no sound, no pain, no thought. I could see him slowly dying and just knew that I had to keep squeezing until it was over but something got through to me, your voice. If you hadn't struggled to stop me then I would have killed Davies and probably started on you. Your calm voice got through to me and brought me back." John focused on Brooks' face. Looked at him inquisitively, trying to find something special, unseen. "It was you wasn't it Brooks?"

Phil Brooks nodded.
Deverall looked away.

"Ever since that day I have been .... concerned ... with some of the things going on in my life. There have been times when I didn't think that anything was worth anything at all and if I was to just detach myself, it would be best." He looked again at Brooks.
"But now I can make a difference and you say I would have the backing of everyone here and at Waverly?"
"We are in control of everything John."
"OK, I suppose we better start making plans on how to do this."
"There is no need, it doesn't matter where or when just how it is done."

John could scarcely disguise his amazement. Plans were already made and in place? The method had been decided? He was the last piece of the jigsaw to fall into place and he never felt any sign from his men? Brooks could feel thoughts going around in Deverall's head so he continued to speak.   .
"There are no plans John, this thing just has to … happen. It has to happen quick and then our ranks close up. Too much planning gives people time to think and have second thoughts. Everyone is committed and I have to have an answer from you. I don't want you to have second thoughts John. I need to know if you are with us. We are ready now John and this thing must be done. Are you with us?"

Davies had clubbed many lives. He had touched very few. John felt that if he had strangled the man when he had the chance then that inmate Treevill would be alive and the prison officers from Waverly would still be fit and healthy. Instead, there was a death and good friends were in pain, which could last them for the rest of their lives.
There was only one answer.

"Yes."

Brooks offered his hand and the men shook. There were no smiles or congratulations. They were making a bond. What happened next took John Deverall completely by surprise.

Brooks stopped shaking his hand and spoke.

"Be ready to move tomorrow."

* * *

Eight

David Brenner spent a week in hospital. He couldn't speak or open his jaw and only the medicine kept the dreadful pain in his broken skull from wracking his body in agony. That pain was gradually creeping into his nervous system because the doctors were weaning him off his medication. It was at the request of the police because they wanted him out of hospital and in front of a judge as soon as possible.

The black, blue and yellow hue to the skin around his eyes was diminishing and the swelling relented. His eyes were active though. They darted to and fro all the time. They questioned everyone who came into their view. They were the eyes of a trapped animal inside looking for an escape. This was not missed by the police who always kept a high profile in the hospital. He suffered physical pain but this was not his greatest concern.

He continually looked at the door to the ward hoping that she would come back. He couldn't talk but he had to communicate with her. She held his life in her hands. It was too late to make things right between them, but he was her son! He would promise, swear to change, ask to be given another chance. He would do anything just to make this thing right. It wasn't him, he found the necklace and just had a morbid curiosity about the case. That's why he collected the clippings.

What was she *thinking!* How could she do this to her son, her flesh and blood?
Why didn't she come back? If only she would walk through those doors, he could convince her that what she was thinking was unthinkable, their life would change, they would move away. He would get a job and they could live happily together. He would look after her.

His eyes would close and reality behind the lids would display itself. She wouldn't come back, that's what she said. The least that would happen to him was a conviction for the assault.

It might not be so bad. Look at him! Who came out worse! He could get the sympathy of the judge and maybe even cast some doubt on the woman in the laundry. She beckoned him in. She has to take some of the blame. He would offer mitigating circumstances, no father, a mother who has deserted him, he has an alcohol problem, a drug problem, no job, no money.

He was starting to feel a little better. Things didn't look so bad, it wasn't entirely his fault. But there was that man. The man who clubbed him over the head. What had he seen? What was HE doing there? Suddenly a shadow was cast over the sunny picture of his defence. The thought of a setback like this allowed his pain to creep through and he winced. The wince caused more pain so he relaxed and forced himself to think positively again. He would get off, maybe even bring charges against his attacker! That was something to consider and he made a mental note to mention it to his defence lawyer. On the other hand, he might be convicted. It would only be a short sentence when they take into consideration how he had suffered. It could be a long sentence, more pain crept through. Released or convicted there was something he had to do when he got out. He would find her. He would get his property back and destroy it. What a fool he was for keeping it in the first place. He would never be free until that was done.

* * *

Eileen Brenner spent a similar week in silent thought. She was a changed woman. Now she had something to look forward to - a life of her own! Her brother and his family were real. They were a family showing signs that she didn't recognise because she had never experienced them for herself. She looked at the love in their eyes for each other and the amount they cared. At first, she felt like an outsider, guilty. She felt a sorrow and question in their stares but during the week it she changed. She interpreted them differently. It was normal the way they felt. She grew to accept it. There were times she would break her silence and have long talks with her brother late at night.

"You have such a lovely family Chris."
"Yeah, the kids are a handful but they are a good bunch."
"I can't remember David being like that. It seems that all of the recent years have blotted the good times out. I wish I could have done more."
"Eileen, sometimes there is just nothing you can do. Things just turn out the way they do because that is the way it is and nothing can change that.

Everything that David has done he did because he wanted to. He has only himself to blame. What you have to do now is start again and sort a life out for yourself. Try to be happy. I can help you if you will let me."

"I couldn't really ….." She said this and turned away. She was a proud woman.

"Eileen, I have to confess something to you. We have watched for some years now, what you have been going through and we didn't do anything. I feel really guilty about that."

"Chris …."

He waved her mild protest away and continued.

"No, I mean it. I could have done so much more but I thought it would be meddling, none of my business, so I didn't do anything. I think things could have been a little different if I had. So, I want to do something now."

He moved closer to her and gently took her hand. She looked at her younger brother and felt that foreign feeling again. She let him speak. He spoke as a person does who has thought things out. It was delivered with precision, a point at a time.

"My firm has offices all over the country. Every office needs staff of all descriptions all of the time. All you have to do is tell me where you would like to live and I will find a job for you. I have some money put to one side and when you decide what you want to do we can set you up in your own flat and you can close this part of your life."

"I couldn't really Chris."

He was ready for this too.

"Why not? Arranging the job is easy. My firm would be happier with you working for us than someone we don't know. The property? That will be an investment for me. You will just be looking after my investment. After a while you will be able to afford to buy your own property and I will split my profits with you."

She was warming to this idea, it was carrying her away and he sensed it.

"It is a fantastic opportunity Eileen, we will visit regularly with the kids. You can come here whenever you like. What do you say?"

She looked at him with hope in her eyes and as he looked at them, he knew he had won but at the last moment they closed. They closed to hide her despair and the realisation of the futility of it all. This was just a dream born from a nightmare. Only the nightmare was real. Her brother knew what was holding her back so he moved to the more serious topic that he hoped he would not have to open.

"Who are you going to live for Eileen?" He squeezed her hand and spoke gently to her closed eyes.

"Think of David as if he has moved away. He made the decision to move and is not coming back. You can't do anything for him. All that can happen is you will become more broken hearted and you don't deserve that. He is in another world now and other people will look after him. It is out of your hands. There is nothing for you but pain if you insist on standing by him."

There were tears welling up in her eyes but they were not tears of sorrow. This man, her brother, was the first person in years to show her any kind of love and she couldn't cope with it. A tear rolled down her face and she opened her eyes. He reached out and touched it away. She looked at him and knew that he had meant everything he said. He wanted to help her. Again, that feeling, that foreign feeling came to her. This is what life could be like and she craved it. Her eyes were open now, physically and mentally. She didn't know what to do but she knew that she must do something!

"Oh Chris, I can't give you an answer now but I will give it serious thought."

"You take your time sis, take as much time as you need." He had the feeling back again, that feeling of success. He knew that his sister would say yes, she just needed the time to compose herself and decide *how* to accept his offer. The sensible thing to do now was to back off and give her some space.

The next day she called DS Roper.

*   *   *

"Tomorrow??"

Brooks looked around to see if the louder than normal outburst had alerted anyone. It was very rare for John to raise his voice.

"Come to work as usual tomorrow and take the transport to Waverly."

The two men were looking straight at each other now. Brooks was giving instructions in event order and Deverall was looking for a flaw in the plan. When Brooks was finished there was silence. It was broken by Deverall.

"You seem to have thought of everything Brooks. This …. thing …. depends on a lot of people. Where is the weak link in the chain? It's my life on the line, my freedom. You know what happens to people like us when we become part of this population? I am taking the ultimate risk here. How sure are you of these men?"

"I know all the men at Waverly and all of the men here at Renkill. Every one of them is behind this. Every one is behind you. You can't fault it can you or you would have bailed out after you heard the plan?"

What he had heard was good, it was true. There seemed to be no faults but then again, this prison was full of men who planned, had sure fire plans, that had all gone wrong. He knew Brooks and he believed him. There was only one decision to make – take the opportunity or refuse it. Refusing meant terror all round but to accept meant justice, but there was more … there was his dream relationship with Helen to consider. He stood up straight and looked Brooks right in the eyes.

"Tomorrow then."

Brooks fought back the smile that Deverall was looking for. This was a grim business not a business deal. This was men making serious consequential decisions. Instead of smiling he held out his hand, which Deverall took. Their shake was firm and held for longer than usual. That contact meant a bond. Through the contact Deverall felt the strength of the conviction, total support and loyalty. What Brooks felt was totally different. He felt pure strength. He felt the strength to carry out the plan or to deal with anyone who put his life in jeopardy.

* * *

DS Reynolds arrived at work. He had to make his way through the outer offices where real policemen and women were doing real police work. He kept his gaze to the front because he knew that others looked at him and he didn't want to meet their eyes. Some looked with pity and some with a smile. He didn't care. He just didn't want to have to deal with that. When he entered his office, he always gave the same reaction. Nothing ever changed!

It was always the same way he left it. The last file he looked at was still on the top of the 'in' pile. The 'out' tray was always empty. It would take about an hour before the outer office could gather the 'going nowhere' cases to drop on him. The coffee cup he drained before going home last night was still on the shelf by the door. The cleaners didn't even come in here. With a sigh he rounded his desk and put down his bag and coat. He opened the window because the office was not part of the open plan where his brother officers worked and overnight it always filled with an odour given off by the stacks of musty old paper in the boxes of files.

He took his cup out to the outer office and washed it amongst the others. He went to the machine and poured himself a coffee and taking care not to spill it he made his way back to the office, again avoiding the glances from the others. His first case came before he finished half his drink. The door opened and in walked a very young officer, one he hadn't seen before.

"Good morning sir!"
"Son, I am Detective SERGEANT Reynolds, you don't call me 'sir', you call me 'sergeant'. What do I call you? What do you want?"
"I am PC Preece sir, er sergeant. I was told to give you this."
He handed over a manila folder with oversized felt tip scrawled across it. Reynolds always wondered why police files were never good to look at. They always had untidy writing always written in black felt tip. Hadn't anyone ever heard of a sticky label? He read the scrawl.

'Case 23445, Kingsnorth Fire – ongoing'

He opened the file and saw that the case was three months old and already there had been six officers previously involved. He looked up and the young constable was still standing there.
"Is there anything else Preece?"
"No Sergeant."
"That will be all then."
"I have been assigned to your office Sergeant, I will be working with you."

Reynolds sat back in his chair and looked at the boy. He had two choices. He could either find out what dreadful thing the constable had done to deserve this or he could just accept the fact and move on. It wasn't worth it so he kept quiet. He would probably find out in due course anyway. "Pull up a chair and let's see what we have got. Kingsnorth Fire." He turned more pages in the open folder. "It seems that a fire broke out in a tyre warehouse in Kingsnorth three months ago. By the time the fire brigade arrived the place was well alight and none of the 500 tyres could be saved. The fire brigade suspect arson but couldn't pinpoint the seat of the fire."

He flipped over a few more pages.

"The owner has been questioned, he was on holiday at the time of the fire, that rules him out. There seem to be no other suspects. How do you fancy a trip to the scene Preece?"

They arrived to find the building still boarded up and showing the signs of a huge conflagration. The owner was present.

"Mr Woods?"

"Yes?"

"I'm DS Reynolds and this is PC Preece. Could we ask you a few questions?"

The owner looked puzzled, "Where are the other police who were asking questions?"

"I am part of a 'Special Police Investigation Unit' Mr. Woods" casting a glance at the still smiling Preece, "we are handling the case now. Can you tell me what happened?"

Impatiently and without masking his frustration with going over the story again Woods started at the top. The story was very short. The top was nearer the bottom than most.

"I was on holiday and when I came back" he waved at his burnt-out property "this is what I found!"

DS Reynolds looked up and down the street. It contained the usual for this type of area. Industrial units, car part spares, sign writers, engineering premises. He took special note of one particular unit at the end of the lane.

"Is that a tyre dump at the end down there?"

Mr. Woods followed the gaze of Reynolds and said "Yeah, that's Beckley's place."

"Thanks Mr. Woods." Reynolds started to walk. Preece followed.

When they arrived at the end of the lane, they came to the tyre dump. It was a large open area where old tyres could be dumped for recycling. There was an office and they went in.

"Mr Beckley?"

The man sitting on the chair lowered his paper.

"Yeah, I'm Beckley, what can I do for you?"

After the introductions the questions followed.

"Do you know anything about the fire down the lane a few months ago?"

Beckley put the paper down and stood up to move behind his counter. "It was a big fire, took all night to put out. Why are you asking me?"

"We are making the usual enquiries. This is a tyre dump, right?"

Beckley looked out of the window at the few tyres stacked on his land.

"Yes, this is a tyre reclamation business."

Reynolds persisted. "You don't seem to have many tyres here, is business bad at the moment?"

"No, it's just that we had a big collection a couple of months ago and what you see now is what has come in since then."

Reynolds looked at Preece and then back at Beckley.

"Thanks for your time Mr. Beckley." Then he walked out of the door. He walked to the car and waited for Preece to join him. This was another going nowhere, case. PC Preece got into the car and immediately summed up the situation.

"It's going to be hard to prove this one."

The comment made Reynolds take notice. "What makes you say that?"

"Well it's obvious, you saw it straight away. The used tyres were swapped for the new ones and then set alight. We could look through his books but they are probably all over the place, it's the way these guys do business."

"Look Preece, I have to tell you something, these are the sort of cases I always get, the ones that can't be solved. Sometime I'll tell you about it but you could be with me for a long time!"

Preece smiled, "I know, that is why I wanted to work with you. I volunteered for the job."

"You WHAT?"

"It's a great challenge. Never mind that, look out there and tell me what you see Sergeant."

Reynolds dragged his stare from the young officer and looked out on the lane. It was filled with industrial units, rubbish bins, a few trucks and an assortment of cars. He shrugged his shoulders.

"Look at the vehicles Sergeant."

Reynolds looked again with keener eyes and then he saw them. Almost every vehicle was sporting a brand-new set of tyres. All matching, all expensive.

"Well, I'll be damned!"

"We would have to check every owner, look at every receipt IF they had them which I would bet they don't. And there is one other thing."

"What's that?"

"Don't call him 'Mr. Beckley' any more. That's not his name."

"Not his name?

"Well not *MR*. Beckley anyway. His *first* name is Beckley, his last name is Woods."

Each man smiled as they got out of the car.

*   *   *

A smile was a foreign object to Bill Davies. He spent almost all of his time in a sparse cell on the 'singles only' (isolation) landing in the prison. Every morning started with a rough thump on the iron door followed by a key deliberately rattled in the hole. The bolt would be thrown back and the door opened. These actions took enough time for him to throw his legs out of his bunk and stand in the far corner of the cell to watch the door swing open. Outside there were always three guards waiting for him. They would come into the cell and search it quickly constantly keeping a weather eye on Davies standing in the corner. After the search they would retreat to the landing and allow him to wash in the tiny sink fitted to the corner of the cell. After the wash they would watch him dress and present himself in the doorway of the cell ready for breakfast. All the time there is never a word spoken or a glance away from his direction. The guards back off and allow Davies to turn left down the landing and they follow at a discreet and safe distance. The walk takes about three minutes until they enter a small dining room where the chairs and tables are bolted to the floor. On the table is a tray with his breakfast on it. It is cold cereal served in a paper picnic bowl. There is a banana and a polystyrene cup of orange juice. The only dangerous implement is the plastic spoon but it is of such poor calibre that it becomes deformed if used to stir hot tea. There is nothing here that Davies can use to cause harm.

No chances are being taken. The guards take up strategic positions and do not relax for a moment. Davies sits and eats in silence. It is pointless to speak for he knows he will get no reply. He is no fool and knew that he would come off second best if he did try to start something. He would get through this, it can't be kept up forever. He had his rights after all! All in good time. The meal finished he stands up and faces the door and the whole ritual would take place in reverse until he was back in his cell standing in the corner again.

That part of the ritual was the most galling for him – to be made to stand in the corner. He would remember that, for a time in the future! When the door shut and the keys rattled again, he would relax and his long monotonous day would progress. On the other side of the door the officers relaxed also. They had been pumped up for action, waiting for a cause, any excuse to vent their anger and frustration. Now they had unused energy to spare and they felt like puppies wanting to play and be clumsy in the garden.

They were held together by a bond created when men face danger together and come through it in one piece. They didn't waste any smiles on Davies but now they lavished them on each other! Their duty was done. It would be a while before it came up again. They walked without speaking because that was the rule – no sounds on this landing. Other officers would be back for the lunch ritual at one o'clock and again in the afternoon for his 'hour of light' when they would watch Davies walk the empty tennis court at four. Last meal of the day for Davies was at seven o'clock precisely and the lights went out at nine. It was a rigid timetable and every officer in the prison knew it by heart.

* * *

"DS Roper?"

This was a moment she had not planned. All the time she knew what she wanted to do, what she must do, but it was all still just thoughts and intentions. Now she heard the familiar voice of the policeman on the other end of the line suddenly everything became real and action was needed. There was also something else, what she had done up to now was easy because she had been in control of all the actions but her next move would put things into the public domain. She couldn't guarantee the reaction of others. She must not let it get out of control but how? The name was offered again on the phone.

"This is DS Roper, hello, is anyone there?"
"Hello Mr. Roper, it's me Mrs Brenner."
"Mrs. Brenner?" he had not forgotten but was just puzzled why she would call him. They all do it, the officers dealing with the public. They give their cards and say 'call me if you remember anything or you need me' but nobody ever calls back! Once the case is closed the detectives move on to the next, leaving the ordinary people in their wake. He realised that he may have given the wrong impression with the tone of his voice so he quickly followed it with a question.

"Oh Hi Mrs. Brenner … It's good to hear you, how are you?"
"I am fine Mr. Roper." She thought about stalling, continuing with some idle chit chat but her determination, this new ally, came to her aid. She looked into the distance, eyes fixed, and continued to speak. "I need to see you Mr. Roper, I want to discuss something with you and I just can't do it over the phone."

Roper also looked into the distance but his eyes darted from side to side. He was thinking fast. There was something here. The years spent questioning and interviewing people gave him the skill to detect when someone was lying or telling the truth. He could tell when someone was speaking but saying nothing as well as when half a sentence spoke volumes! It was his turn to speak.

"OK Mrs. Brenner, where are you?" He picked up a pencil and poised to scrawl something on his note pad.
"It doesn't matter where I am Mr. Roper, I would like to meet you sometime later in the week." She was making decisions but nothing committed yet. "Do you know where West Park is?" Where had that come from? She seemed to be running on autopilot now, a new woman, someone else was making the decisions and it thrilled her! "Could you meet me there say, noon on Friday?"

He wrote down and repeated the place and time but couldn't resist pressing for more.

"Can you tell me what this is about Mrs. Brenner?"

"No Mr. Roper, I really can't, I need to speak to you in person. I need to speak to you face to face." She stopped, she would not be drawn.

"OK then, I'll see you noon on Friday."

"Come alone Mr. Roper. Goodbye." She hung up.

His 'Goodbye' was to a deaf receiver but he did not hang it up. He looked at it as if it had offended him. 'Come alone' that got him going. He opened his diary and wrote B-R-E-N-N-E-R in large letters on the Friday leaf. He continued with A-L-O-N-E and underlined it. He looked at his handiwork and gave a little chuckle and went back to what he was doing.

Eileen Brenner put the phone down like it was red hot. She stood there staring at it while holding both hands to her mouth. Her breathing was heavy and her eyes wide. What was she THINKING? She must call him back immediately and cancel the appointed meeting. The thought lasted only a second. She closed her eyes and moved her hands to her sides and took a deep breath. When she opened her eyes, she was composed again. In control. Determined. Life could only start when she finished this.

* * *

John Deverall spent a fitful, sleepless night.

For the last hour of the day shift he talked with Brooks about the arrangements for the morning. He occasionally asked a question and was always pleased with the answer. It was obvious that a great deal of thought had gone into the organisation and if everyone did what they were supposed to do it would go like clockwork.

The sleep he did manage to catch was full of her dream, but it was different.

He saw her there in the grass with the bright sun shining on her. She sat there alone just looking at him with a faint smile on her face. It could have been a picture because nothing seemed to move but occasionally the breeze caused her hair to fall across her face. The dream came several times and always the same. Whenever he fell asleep, he had the dream. No sweat, no pain. She was waiting. She was happy.

When the alarm went off, he was already awake, lying still in the bed and staring at the ceiling. He turned it off as he rose to his feet and headed for the shower. He went through his routine, it was important to do so. It was key to the success. Shower, dress, eat and walk to the bus. First break in routine – he must talk to someone.

He argued about this with Brooks, it was foolish, he was always noticed by the fact that he *didn't* talk to people but Brooks insisted.

"Good Morning." This was aimed at the old lady who regularly boarded his bus. This most innocent greeting had the completely opposite effect. The woman was startled and took a step back from him. She looked to see if he was talking to someone else. She was worried and wondered why she had been singled out for this attention. In fact, she had always wanted this man to talk to her or anyone in the line. The other regular travellers often discussed him and they all felt that he was a troubled person and to talk to him might help. She often practiced what she would say on such an occasion but this, right out of the blue, it took her off guard. She didn't know what to say and embarrassment at reacting like she did, was creeping into her complexion.

"What? Who me? I…" was all she could mutter.
"It's a good morning," John said again this time with a smile. He hoped that this forced expression wasn't too obvious. The lady seemed somewhat distressed but was recovering quickly.
"Yes it IS a good morning, how are you?" She was ready for him now but the timing was wrong, the bus was about to arrive.

John Deverall sensed that she was about to engage him in conversation so when he boarded the bus, he sat several seats to her rear. There would be no more conversation, he had done enough.

He arrived at his normal time and signed in. Ted greeted him in the usual way.

"Morning Sarge." But there was something different. Something added. "Always on time," and when he looked at the clipboard, "John Deverall, signed in at 08:32, thanks John."

John looked at the man and was given a knowing smile. He turned and went into the bowels of the prison.

The changing room was more quiet than usual but everyone went out of their way to greet him. The briefing was the same but John found that the only place in the room to stand was at the front, all the other places were taken. When it was over, the governor left the room and the men went about their business. The only officer remaining was Brooks.

"They are waiting for you down in dispatch."
The two men looked at each other again. Deep into each other. This was a serious business and if there was even a glimmer of doubt on either side then it had to be called off. There was none so he turned and made his way to dispatch.

There were two prisoners to be taken to Waverly today and the transport was ready and waiting for them. Deverall walked into the dispatch office and sat down in the back room. From his chair he could not be seen by anyone in the outer office or the corridor beyond. The first prisoner for transport arrived and was halted to go through the transfer ritual, forms to sign and belongings to transfer. The dispatcher assigned him cubicle one, the first on the left inside the security van. The second prisoner was dealt with in the exact same way and was allocated cubicle three, the second on the left inside the van. When they were locked away in the van the dispatcher put his head around the office door and quietly spoke. "Cubicle six John."

This was clever. The prisoners had a very small but secure window in their cubicle and they could, if they wished, see outside on their side of the van. They were in cells on the opposite side to John's so would not see him board. The officers in the corridor and the drivers seemed to be distracted as he boarded. He made his way to the cell and the doors closed, the engine started and the van left the prison.
John Deverall sat down and made himself as comfortable as possible because the journey would last two hours.

* * *

Reynolds and Preece didn't take long to break the case. A few words with the Woods brothers, requesting invoices and stock numbers with a view to cross checking them with the receipts and paperwork for every vehicle in the street soon had the culprits pointing fingers at each other. They took them down to the station and the news that Reynolds was down in 'booking' caused a stir right through the building. Even the Chief Superintendent Maxwell came down.

Reynolds and Preece stood there and related the reasons for arresting and detaining the Woods brothers. They did it loud for all to hear and the volume did not go unnoticed by the Chief. He was not pleased.

"Reynolds, I want a full list of all the officers who have had anything to do with this case, anyone who passed this case on. Have it for me right away please."
"Yes sir, I will get right on it as soon as I am finished here."
The Chief went to push his way through the swing doors and halfway he stopped and forced some words through his teeth.

"Well done Preece."
"It wasn't me sir, Sergeant Reynolds saw straight through the scam right away – I only helped with the leg work."
The Chief looked at Reynolds and nodded, "That list, right away," and he went through the doors.

Much later in their very small office in the back of the police station, Preece and Reynolds were filling out forms and writing up the case so far. Soon they would get the brothers out one at a time and interview them – all on tape. They were feeling good. Reynolds could hardly contain himself and were it not for the presence of the younger officer he would have strutted around the room punching the air! They were interrupted by a knock on the door, as it immediately swung open.

Two detectives entered the room, they did not seem to be that happy. Their names were the last two names on the list of officers who had passed the case on. Reynolds knew them.
"Come in gentlemen, make yourself at home."

"Just give us the case file Reynolds." said the taller of the two as he outstretched his hand.

This information made Reynolds sit up and pay even more attention. "Why, what's going on?"

"The chief wants us to pick up this case and finish it. He says we knocked it back too soon and … well he just wants you to hand it over and we will take it from here. Just finish your notes, give us the file and we will get on with it. Sorry."

Reynolds looked at Preece who was still smiling.

Twenty minutes later the case was gone and they were left staring at each other and occasionally at the pile of old cases.

Reynolds gave out a long deliberate tedious sigh as he leaned over the desk to pick up the next file on the top.

*   *   *

Caution prevented Roper from just arriving at the predetermined meeting in the park. Instead, he arrived half an hour early and so he could place himself in a position where he could see everyone going in to the park and not be seen himself. To his delight he found a café which commanded a full view of the park gates. He ordered a tea.

It was a big park and Mrs. Brenner didn't say exactly where to meet so this was the best way. He had almost forgotten the meeting because of his current workload, police officers tend to move on from successful cases quickly but they never forget the unsolved ones. It is what a being a policeman is all about. His tea arrived.

The lunch time trade was starting, and sitting there with only a cup of tea made Roper seem out of place, but he had a look for that. People looking for a place to sit and have their lunch would look his way and facially say – 'Why are you taking up all that space with just a cup of tea?' and he would give the look – the look that all police have – the look that said – 'Go away, I don't care what you think, stay and there could be trouble.'

He saw her when his tea was half finished. If he had not been trained over time to be observant, he may have missed her. He was going on the height, build and the colouring he remembered but much had changed.

Her clothes were more expressive and her hair had a body to it. She seemed to be taller than he remembered but that could be because she stood up straighter now. She walked with a purpose. She used her right hand to hold her coat closed at the front and her left held a shopping bag that seemed to contain very little. He watched her walk down the street to the park gates where she stopped. She looked around as she stood beside one of the huge pillars which made up the entrance to the park. She was reluctant to proceed because now she realised, like Roper, that they had not planned a particular place to meet in the park, She, was now looking, for him. She stood there among the lunch time hustle and bustle. He finished his tea and stood up. By now the café was full and his departure raised some eyebrows from the diners and relief from those looking for a seat.

Roper left the café and stood on the pavement. He looked for a gap in the traffic and crossed the road. He walked right up to her before he was spotted.

"Mrs. Brenner?"
The woman nearly jumped. She was so intent on seeing him first that she had no time to compose herself for their meeting.
"Mr. Roper! You startled me!"
"I'm sorry, I got here a little early to *catch* you before you went in the park." Inside he chuckled. Police officers were fond of that little joke – *catch you later* - especially when they had to let a villain go because of lack of evidence. They were invariably right. Roper could afford this little meander of attention because he had nothing to focus on yet. He was anxious to solve the mystery for this noon meeting in the park, he was also anxious to get back to work!

She composed herself and became very serious. She looked straight into his eyes.
"Can we find a place where we can sit and talk?"
He looked back at the café but she derailed that train of thought.
"Somewhere in the park where we can't be overheard?"
He looked through the gates. She was calling the shots so he might as well tag along. He stuck out his bottom lip, tilted his head and waved his hand at the park. She walked through the gates and he followed. She no longer held the shopping bag at her side. She clutched it to her chest.

They walked almost into the centre of the park and found a bench. She always kept one step in front of the police officer and neither of them spoke a word. He never spoke because it seemed inappropriate to discuss the weather or what she had been doing since the trial. He remembered that she did not attend the trial. It was not surprising, no-one likes to see their son sent down for fifteen years for grievous assault and robbery. It was a good result for Roper, cut and dried. The trial lasted only a week and Brenner was banged up in prison, a job well done. He was musing on these thoughts when she suddenly stopped and sat down. He joined her and waited. She still clutched the shopping bag to her chest and suddenly becoming aware of it she released her grip and put it on the bench between them. She raised her eyes and looked at him, and spoke.

"Mr. Roper, my son is in prison now. He was once a good boy and I will always try to remember him like that. I am going to forget what he became but there is still something from the past that I have to deal with. I hope that you can help me."

Roper knew this was going to be embarrassing. She was going to ask him to do something for that son of hers and he would have to refuse. He didn't have any kids but he did know how parents just can't see the bad side of their children. He steeled himself to say no, to make an apology and get back to work. He was formulating a few soothing sentences for her when he realised that she was talking about him!

"I feel that you are a compassionate man Mr. Roper. I believe that you are an honest and honourable man. I know that if you make a promise to me, you would keep it. It is for these reasons that I have come to you. I have decided to start a new life and put all of this dreadful past behind me. I have a new job, a new place to live and more importantly I have new friends. There is still something from the past that I must deal with. I can't do it alone, indeed I don't think I can deal with it at all, that is why I need your help, but there is much I must know first. You must convince me that you are the person who can help me."

This was different. The conversation was going in a completely different direction from expectations. It made him pay greater attention. He didn't speak but shifted his body position and its new language said 'Go on'.

I want to tell you something. I want to give you something. Before I do, I must have a promise from you. I don't want any more court cases, no more papers, reporters, radio or television."

Roper looked at the bag.

"If you make these promises to me, I will also make a promise to you. I will never tell a soul about this meeting or this conversation. That way we will each have a hold over the other. I don't want to say any more unless you are prepared to listen."

Roper thought for a moment but the decision was easily made.
"Mrs. Brenner, I can't make promises like that. I don't know what it is you are going to say, or give to me." He looked at the bag again. "You have to tell me more."

It was starting to fall apart. This is not what she expected. She couldn't just get up and walk away, he could follow her, arrest her and search the bag. She should have made other plans. What was she doing!?
"Mr. Roper, I want to give you evidence to solve a crime." That wasn't too much of a giveaway. He was interested, she could tell by the way he shifted his position. Now it was his turn.

"What crime Mrs. Brenner?"
"Mr. Roper, this crime took place many years ago. It is out of the public memory now but it is linked to me, to …. David." She was giving away too much and getting nothing in return so she waited.
"Mrs. Brenner, I am a police officer, I can't make a promise to you like that no matter what the crime is. Believe me you will feel much better if you just tell me everything."
"Mr. Roper, I believe you are a compassionate man. That night when I cried and you offered me help, I felt it in your voice. I could see it in your eyes. I trust those feelings so I am going to take a risk. It could be the end of my life, that is how dangerous this information is to me." She reached over to the shopping bag and gripped it tightly. "I want to give you this. I want you to take it and I don't ever want to hear about it again. I want you to deal with it. I can't go through the misery it will create if it gets to the public. I just can't."

He looked at her, she was shivering in spite of the warmth of the day. Her eyes were filling with tears slightly masking the terror he could see. She never took her gaze from his but he felt the bag being pushed across the bench towards him.

He sat there for five minutes looking through the printed matter from the album. He didn't need to ask where it came from or what it was all about. He remembered the case. He remembered it very well, but this was just a scrap book that anyone could have put together and he had to say so.
"Mrs. Brenner, this doesn't mean anything. It is just a collection of clippings. It shows that David had an interest in the news at the time." He closed the book and put it back in the bag. "I'm sorry."

"That is not all Mr. Roper." She never stopped looking at him, reading him. She had gone too far now to back out. It was now or never so she reached into her pocket and brought out the paper envelope. "This was at the back of the album."

He took the envelope and looked from it to her and back again. He felt that it was not empty but heavy. When he tilted the envelope, the contents fell into his opposite hand.He looked closely at the necklace in his hand. It was a small thing, made for a small child. His eyes were not focused on the chain but what hung from it. It was a pure silver, delicately rounded letter. It was an 'H'. There was no need to look any longer.

This was the evidence that was needed but she was waiting for him to comment. She was waiting but he couldn't rush this. She spoke about the end of her life but had just offered him the end of his! He knew what he should do but completely abandoned it. The decision was made and he looked up at her. She was on the edge, waiting to see if her balance would bring her back or if he would give her a push and make everything collapse. Roper put the necklace back into the envelope and the envelope into his pocket. He reached over and took the shopping bag and put it under his arm in a manly way. They both stood up, she followed his lead trying desperately to get an answer. He broke the silence.
"Go and continue your life Mrs. Brenner. I assure you I will take care of this. You just take care of yourself, you deserve it."

She closed her eyes slowly and let out her held breath. After several seconds she opened her eyes again to see Roper striding down the path towards the entrance to the park. Her strength was gone so she sat down on the bench again. It was over now, it was done. As she sat on the bench, she lost some of her new straightness and her hands came up to support her head. The tears that had been threatening were finally released and flowed freely as her body shook from the uncontrolled sobbing.

* * *

Inside the cubicle John found a small paper bag containing prison clothes. He started to disrobe. It was like trying on a complete wardrobe at the clothing store. He folded up his prison uniform and shoes and placed them into the bag and placed the bag where he found it. The van was making its way through town traffic now, stopping and starting at junctions and lights. The journey ended with the grating sound of the outer gate of Waverly Prison opening and then closing after the van entered. Keys could be heard opening the outer door and then the cubicle doors inside and voices coaxing the other prisoners out and away. John sat there in silence what seemed to be hours, but was in fact only minutes. Then movement. Someone was climbing into the vehicle. Keys rattled and his door opened.
"Please follow me."

John followed. He walked down an empty corridor and into a room filled with sheets, pillows and blankets. There was an officer standing behind a counter with a small pile of bed linen in front of him.

"Take these."
John took them and continued to follow the first officer. They walked down empty corridors and any officers they met seemed to ignore them. Finally, the officer in the front stopped and turned around. There was no need to speak because the cell door on the landing was open. This was the destination. John entered the cell and waited.

* * *

Davies was having his lunch. He was sitting, as usual, in an empty canteen eating off of paper plates and drinking out of a plastic cup. Life had been like this for the past couple of weeks. He didn't have the urge in him to cause trouble. It was OK like this but he would have to start planning his next demonstration. While he was finishing his ice cream an extra officer entered the room and had a brief discussion with the officer in charge. A feeling was generated which migrated to the other officers in the room. Davies felt that something was about to happen, these were the signs, he had seen them all before.

"Finished Davies?"

Davies pushed forward the empty bowl and dropped his plastic spoon into it. He stood up and faced the door. Routine.

He was flanked by officers left and right, front and back as they walked the landing to the cell. Davies was expecting something but as the distance to his cell shortened, he felt safer. They wouldn't start anything now surely? The lead officer rattled his keys in the lock and pushed the door open, into the cell. Davies walked to the far end of the cell and faced the wall until he heard the door close again and the keys throw the lock. He relaxed and turned to see John Deverall standing in front of him.

For more than one second Bill Davies was scared. He was petrified. It was the longest he had ever felt like this in his life.

Deverall couldn't do anything either. What stopped him was his last sense of fair play. He just couldn't attack this man no matter what he had done. His hesitation lasted exactly the same length of time it took for Davies to shake off his fear. Silently, simultaneously, both men went for each other. There were no punches thrown but like wrestlers they swayed there in the middle of the cell each reaching, thrusting to find a hand hold or grip. The table was dislodged, turned over and the contents covered the floor as the men changed places in the cell. This was a trial of strength. Davies was fighting for his life and that gave him the edge. Twisting he managed to gain the upper hand pinning Deverall to the wall and wrapping his arm around his neck. This gave him the courage needed to speak and through breathless gasps spoke to John.

.

"What you come here for screw? Think you going to get the best of me twice? Think again screw … it just aint going to happen! What are they going to say when they find your dead carcase in here eh?"

Deverall felt his head being slowly twisted towards snapping point. All he had to do was let go, relax, and everything would be over. His torment would be gone, he wouldn't have to see his daughter in his nightmare anymore. She couldn't be saved, it was over. This was a mistake, but it was too late to change things.

In the end it was his daughter who saved him.

He saw her there again, her hand outstretched 'Fight Daddy', he closed his eyes and stood up to his full height. Davies left the floor and lost his leverage. Deverall turned quickly and broke free from the grip. For an instant the men faced each other again. Davies was the first to move, he rushed forward arms seeking another hold, but Deverall was faster. His arm shot out and gripped Davies by the throat. He stepped in under his arm and lifted the prisoner from the floor. All Davies could do now was flail at the hold and gasp for breath. Deverall swung his man to the wall and continued to squeeze. This was it, this was the end. John spoke.

"Go now Davies, it's over. No one sheds a tear for you. The world is a better place now that you are gone."

Davies couldn't hear. He couldn't think, he couldn't breathe. He couldn't do anything to get out of this grip. All he had left was the expression on his face. He tried to appeal to this man, his eyes pleaded, showed that he was sorry.
His life raced.

He got angry because nothing worked. His body gave a last, almost superhuman spasm, in an attempt to break free but it was no use. Deverall was ready for that. He tried to move his limbs but they didn't respond. Lung's bursting. There was pain and light in his eyes. He felt the grip tighten.

This was the moment he gave up.
Then he left.

John Deverall stood there for some minutes unable to move. He couldn't believe what he had done. He couldn't believe how he felt and how close he had come to being killed himself.

He let go. The lifeless body of Davies fell to the floor. Deverall sat on the bed taking deep breaths. He heard the view plate on the door being moved and then the rattle of the keys in the lock. The guard who escorted him from the van appeared in the door, from under his coat he produces a bag containing John's uniform.
"Here are your clothes. Dress, then knock on the door."

John slowly dressed and knocked and waited. Something must have gone wrong, he waited at least ten minutes until the officer returned and looked through the spy hole. The door was thrown open and several officers burst into the cell. They treated John as if he was invisible. More guards arrived and others left in a hurry. One took John's arm and motioned him to follow. He retraced his steps to the loading bay. Once again, they met no-one. The officer stopped at the back of the van, turned to John and spoke.
"Thank you, goodbye."

They looked at each other for a moment until John got into the van. The door closed and the vehicle started to move. When the door opened again John was back in Renkill prison.
When he returned to the landing it was late afternoon. He did his final rounds and made preparations to leave. All of his men went about their business as if he had been there all day. On the way out he met Ted again.
"See you tomorrow Sarge." But again, he added something different as he made a recording of the time on the clipboard, "John Deverall, signed in at 08:32, signed out 17:15."

John looked at the man and was again given that knowing smile. He turned and started his journey home.

* * *

Nine

Reynolds and Preece were enjoying an unusual series of successes in their cases. Preece was proving to be an asset to Reynolds as another pair of eyes to look at crimes differently. Between them they had started new lines of enquiry on six cases from the books in the past three weeks.

Their latest was particularly pleasing.

The file stated that during a burglary at his home the owner had lost a great deal of valuable coins from his collection and all his video equipment. The owner had confronted the burglar and had received a large bump on the head for his efforts. Because there was an actual assault during the crime the scene was photographed by the forensic team. There being no prints or suspects or leads of any kind the file found its way to Reynolds' desk. Preece picked it up first and started to read very carefully passing the individual papers to Reynolds as he finished them. When the last page was read Reynolds put it back in the folder.

"Another dud. I can't see anything to go on."
"You're right Sarge but there is one thing that I am not happy with."

Whenever this happened Reynolds always felt a tingle, he was getting better at concealing this enthusiasm now. Reynolds liked working with Preece but he didn't want the lad to get too cocky and treat him like an idiot! They worked well together and if the young constable would only give him a short insight to his thinking, they would usually arrive at the finish together.
He frowned in a studious way and spoke.
"Oh yeah, what was that?"
"Look at picture labelled AW21 – is there anything strange about it?"

It was a photograph of the shelf under the television set. It should have contained the video cassette recorder but that had been nicked. The shelf was dusty and covered in glass from the shattered window. There were four circles in the dust where the feet of the machine had once stood.

Reynolds looked hard but for the life of him he couldn't see anything out of the ordinary – the video was gone and this is where it should have been – it was the scene of the crime that's all.

"You will have to give me a bit more son …."

Preece liked working with Reynolds and he didn't want to spoil the relationship by being too much of a smart arse, so he always led the older man a half step at a time.

"OK – look at the picture and *imagine* that the video cassette recorder is still there!"

"Uh huh"

"Now imagine the window is suddenly smashed and glass is sprayed all over it."

Reynolds joined in with the thinking.

"The glass would be on top of the VCR."

Preece continued, "And when the machine is removed it should leave the shelf clear of glass. In fact, you can just see trails in the dust where the glass has scattered from the force of the smashed window."

Reynolds sat there for a moment, he had seen something like this before – a long time ago and it was the cause for his predicament at the moment. Not wanting to share THAT moment with Preece he just softly replied. "Preece! The window was smashed after the VCR was taken!"

Reynolds covered the disappointment with himself well. It had been such a long time since he had been given quality work to do, that he was less the detective he once was. This type of evidence spotting got him where he was today – oh how ironic!

The case was reassigned to the original detectives who followed it to a successful conclusion.

It was while the two were poring over their unsolved caseload that the door opened and their latest case was deposited on the pile. There was a title to this one just like all the rest but at that time it didn't have the importance that it would later command. It would change their lives. It simply stated "Case 23565, Waverly Suicide – ongoing"

* * *

John Deverall did not sleep well that night. There were no nightmares. He was now *living* in a nightmare of his own. He couldn't keep a thought in his head for more than a second at a time before another from left field, pushed it out. He couldn't come to a conclusion or make up his mind what to do. Some things were definite though. He would control this situation. He would not let it get out of hand. Going to prison was NOT an option and he didn't want to think about what the alternative would be.

He made a mental appointment to see Brooks, to see them all, and let them know that he was not happy about what they knew. Let them know what would happen if they were careless. These thoughts were always pushed out by the reality of his situation. He was not in control anymore – they were. Now he was right back at square one though. He didn't want to start all over again; it was too depressing, so he got up and headed for the shower.

John Deverall did not break his routine and he went to work the same as he did every day but now there was something different. He was now outside of the law. Up until now he held the high ground with the prison population, but now, he was no better than them. Looking at it another way he was responsible for their well being while they served their sentence. He had to keep them safe from harm even if they were the scum of the earth and deleting Davies from the population may have saved someone from being killed.

This was a better train of thought. He could talk his way through this one, it made him feel good, vindicated, less guilty. The thoughts kept coming until he was walking through the gates of Renkill Prison. On the way in he met Ted again.
"Good morning Sarge."

He looked at the elderly man like it was the first time he had ever seen him. He wanted to say something to him so he stopped and stood for a moment. They were alone in the small room looking at each other for that moment.
"Ted?"
"Yes Sarge?"

They looked at each other and at that moment John Deverall knew there was no need to spell it out for this man. It was there in his eyes – they were innocent – they did not hold any secrets. His eyes said that he was on the same side and his duty was to keep quiet, as if nothing out of the ordinary had happened. John need say nothing. He just looked into the eyes.

"Nothing, see you later."

Everything from that moment seemed normal, *was* normal. He met the men and they exchanged the usual pleasantries and discussed the job in the usual way.

He met Brooks in the briefing room.

"Morning Sarge."

Deverall was about to speak when Doctor Endersley entered the room. The Chief gave John a fleeting glance and a nod but moved straight to his briefing without waiting for a return. Something was different.

"Gentlemen I have some news for you. Yesterday William Davies died at Waverly Prison." The Prison Chief stopped speaking to answer the anonymous unspoken question that he heard. "Yes, he *died* in his cell. He strangled himself by using strips of cloth tied to his window. There was no indication that he was suicidal. There will of course be an enquiry and I expect that the verdict will be suicide, anyway the whole matter has been handed over to the police. We have to create a profile of the man while he was here." This generated moans from the men which stopped very soon after the Chief stopped talking. He continued by looking straight at Deverall.

"John?"

Deverall felt cold and hot, he was aware of sweat on his brow and upper lip, he felt the men looking at him – all eyes were on him, he couldn't speak but he didn't need to. The Chief just kept on talking.

"Davies was a troublesome inmate, you know that better than most, I have some profile requirements that need to be filled out, please do that for me this morning will you?"

"Yes sir." That was all that he could squeeze out. It was a relief, the moment had passed but it made him more aware that he should be on guard for other moments to come. He was also aware that he was making it difficult for himself. Act naturally for goodness sake, everyone else is! He had to speak to Brooks, but the men were filing out now and Brooks was gone. It was after lunch before he found him.

Brooks was standing on the top landing looking out over the void of the centre of the prison. He stood with his hands on the railing as if he were the captain of a ship looking out to sea. He stood looking out over the prison but he felt the presence of Deverall behind him. He knew John was looking for him, he knew what he wanted to say and had prepared his reply. It was John who spoke first.
"You're very cool I must say!"

Brooks turned and spoke lightly.
"John … I was hoping that we might have a chat today."
"This is serious Brooks ……" but Brooks cut him off in mid sentence.

"John, you have to relax. Waverly are going to take the heat and every one of the staff there have a concrete alibi as to where they were at the time Davies killed himself. They covered themselves long before you got there and as for you, you were here all the time. Logged and confirmed. Nothing is coming our way. Just get on with your routine here and let things happen. The police will not put too much effort into the case and tomorrow the newspapers will be used to wrap fish and chips."

Deverall stood there trying to think of something to say. All of his questions were answered so he stayed silent. Brooks, sensing there was nothing left to say, continued.

"It's over John, let's just get back into the routine. I have to go and supervise exercise changeover now, might see you when we clock off?"

John did not acknowledge the question – he just watched Brooks retreat into the body of the prison. For the rest of the day, he did just what he always did.

That night getting to sleep was effortless. His body clock was over wound and as soon as his head touched the pillow he was gone. He found himself sitting on a park bench on a glorious summer day. He could feel the heat of the sun on his face. There was a slight breeze blowing and somewhere somebody was mowing grass. He could hear the mower and smell the grass! In front of him was a little girl playing with tufts of grass. Her yellow dress glowed in the sunshine and there seemed to be an aura all around her. She looked up and smiled as she spoke. It was Helen. "Daddy."

He dare not speak for speaking could destroy the dream, but his silence caused concern, he could see it on her face. She stood up and walked towards him.
"Daddy?"
He had to take the chance, he had to speak.
"Hello Helen." This brought back her smile. The dream continued.
"Daddy you are worried about that man. He was a bad man so don't worry about him."
"How are you my sweetheart?"
"I am fine Daddy, now that you are here to play with me."
"Don't you hear me when I call, don't you hear me when I … shout to you.?

The expression on her face changed. She looked puzzled and concerned at the tone of his voice.
"You don't shout at me daddy."
"Yes I do! I tell you to run, I tell you to fight." He was slightly raising his voice now and she began to back away. "I want you to run when he comes, I want you to kick and scream and FIGHT!"
Tears started to fill her eyes and her lip curled with the onset of crying.
"I can't Daddy, only you can do that for me, you have to do that for me, why won't you help me?"

He reached out for her and for an instant they touched and, in that instant, he was awake in his bed. Sweat covered his body but there was no pain, no nausea, no aching bones. It was useless to try to get back to sleep and recapture the dream. The alarm went off and he stopped it with his hand. He sat there on the side of the bed and tried to recall the extraordinary events of his dream. If he closed his eyes he could see her again, he could hear her. He sat there for some minutes, motionless, filling his senses with her sight and sounds.

* * *

"Case 23565, Waverly Suicide – ongoing"

The case was a new case.

Preece and Reynolds remained motionless until the constable who delivered the file left the room, then they pounced. In this case, seniority demanded that Reynolds browse the file first so Preece looked on over the shoulder. When he had finished Reynolds sat back in his chair and asked a question, he offered the question to the room not particularly at Preece.

"Why have they given me... er ... *us* a fresh case?"

Preece picked it up. "Probably because you have done so well on the last few cases you handled." This brought Reynolds out of his absent muse. "I don't know lad, I am very suspicious about this. There is not a lot to go on here and maybe they just want it to end up on the pile forever. I think we should get over to Waverly and have a look. What do you say?"

The smile on the young constable's face was his answer.

They did not inform the prison that they were coming but the staff there seemed to be expecting them. There would be no surprises here. They were shown to the cell where Davies had resided. It was tidy now and did not resemble the mess that was discovered on that day. Reynolds spoke to the guard.

"What is your name?"

"Walker sir."

"Well Walker, were you on duty the day Davies ... died?"

"Yes sir, I was responsible for supervising his midday meal. Myself and three other guards."

"Did Davies give any indication that he was depressed or feeling suicidal?"

"No sir, he never expressed any feeling out loud, except hatred. He was a very hard man sir. Very troubled. Only recently he attacked some of the guards. That's why he ate alone and we supervise his meals together."

Preece began his questioning. "What happened when Davies finished his meal?"

"We escorted him back to his cell. Two guards in front and two behind. He went into his cell and we locked the door behind him."

Preece continued. "There were no other prisoners on the landing?"

"No sir, we have been given specific orders that Davies was not to mix with the general population. Just recently Davies attacked some of the ...... "

Reynolds re-entered the conversation "Yes we know Walker." This made Walker stop speaking and adopt a surly stance outside the cell.

Preece entered the cell and looked around then turned his attention to Walker again.

"It was this window that Davies attached his makeshift rope to was it Walker?"

"Yes sir."

"I believe that the contents of that table there by the door were disturbed, all over the floor weren't they?"

Walker looked at the table and answered. "Davies must have kicked about in his last dying moments, I suppose he kicked the table over."

Preece continued "And he was about six feet tall, wasn't he?"

Reynolds was beginning to get that tingling feeling again. Walker answered.

"He was a tall man, yes sir."

Reynolds was on it in a flash but kept his cool. He looked at Preece who gave way so Reynolds continued the conversation.

"Walker, this table is at least eight feet away from the window and Davies was only six feet tall. Do you not find that strange?"

Both police officers looked at Walker. Walker looked into the distance as he spoke.

"I was asked to show you the cell and answer your questions. It is up to you to do the detective work. If you have any more ... *questions* ... you can deliver them to the governor. He is waiting for you in his office. Now if you will follow me gentlemen *that* is where we are going now."

The detectives looked at each other and smiled as they followed the guard down the landing.

* * *

DS Roper sat in his bathroom at home. The door was locked. It was the only way he could assure privacy. If he were caught by his wife looking at this material there would be questions and he did not like to lie to her, he did not want her to know. He sat on the toilet trying to make the biggest decision of his life.

In a plastic carrier bag at his feet there was a scrap album. It contained the newspaper clippings over several months from two crimes. One was the rape of Victoria Casey, the original press report, the appeal from the papers, the arrest of David Brenner and the report of the trial. There were harrowing pictures of the parents leaving the court and a school photograph of Victoria. There was a picture of a man with a coat on his head leaving the court and running away from the press. The legend on the printed page named David. There was more to follow. The largest story of all was about Victoria's suicide. Her terminal leap from the hospital window. More harrowing pictures of the parents and something else about how the social services had let her down.

Roper sat and read every word and felt the case. He had seen it all before on similar cases. It was obvious that Brenner did the deed but with a good brief and a little doubt cast on the circumstances of the victim, the scum walked. It was evident here. These days you have to catch the criminals in the act, on film and with an unsolicited confession before you can bang them up.

Roper turned to the front of the album. It was an act that he had been dreading and even now he had to force himself to do it. Here there were more clippings of a crime, a murder. The pages were old, dog-eared and fragile and seemed to have been read many many times. The clippings came from several papers and contained the similar information. Roper read every word. He wouldn't be able to make up his mind unless he had all of the facts and was certain beyond all reasonable doubt. He had to *feel* that what he must do - was right!

The girl was taken from school and found dead in the local woods. She had been sexually abused, tortured then strangled.

His wife was downstairs pregnant with their first child, a girl.

Roper closed his eyes.

All of the information was there. Not many photographs but names and places were printed. The little girls picture was printed, again another school photo.

Her name was Helen Deverall, the daughter of John and Naomi Deverall. It's possible that David Brenner just had some morbid curiosity in the case and collected all of the newspaper clippings but this flew in the face of the reason for collecting the other cuttings. He was involved in both cases.

Roper had to get up and look at himself in the mirror. He needed somebody to talk to. He placed the album on the floor and walked to the sink.

"What do YOU think?"

He looked deep into his own eyes trying to find something which would give him strength of conviction. He was torn between what he should do and what he wanted to do. Each decision had repercussions. On the one hand he could sidestep the responsibility, absolve himself and let others take over but would justice be done? It would mean more people would be drawn in to the mess and more hurt dealt out. On the other hand, he could get involved himself but that meant putting everything on the line, his job, his reputation, family and friends ... his freedom! It was not an easy decision to make. There was no answer in his eyes so he ran the cold water and splashed some on his face and buried his head in a towel.

When he pulled the towel down from his eyes they landed on the album on the floor. He walked over to it and placed it into the carrier bag as he sat back on the toilet. His hands squeezed the plastic at the top of the bag in an effort to seal it, to deny what else was in there but he knew what it was. Something inside told him to have another look and his grip slowly relaxed, the bag unfolded and his hand knowingly felt for the envelope. He pulled it out with his right hand and held it at eye level as he lowered the bag to the floor with his left. Originally it was a white envelope but the years had given it a yellowness. Pinching the sides made the top open like the begging beak of a chick in the nest and his fingers entered like its feeding parent. Thumb and forefinger pinched and held the contents. As he raised his hand the light caught the glimmering sheen of a silver chain. The hand continued to rise until the ornament hanging from the chain was revealed.

It was a silver letter 'H'.

His mind was made up. He replaced the chain and envelope in the bag. He stood up and flushed the toilet. Tomorrow he would do something about it.

* * *

Back at the office, Reynolds and Preece were having a brainstorming session and going over all of the information they had gathered from their trip to Waverly.
"There were no others on the landing and he was the only occupant of the cell. All of the guards have the same story and timesheets and corroborating accounts have been made by independent witnesses. It just has to be suicide. He probably trashed his cell before he tied himself up."

Preece listened to and agreed with Reynolds. He looked at the folder and ceremoniously closed it.
"When you're right, you're right Sarge."
"Ok then, our recommendation for this verdict is that Davies took his own life. The reason? That's one for the shrinks to figure out. I will send this up to the Superintendent in the morning."
"I believe that he is coming here today Sarge, you could make your recommendation in person. That would be good, wouldn't it?" Preece said this with a wide smile on his face.
"How do you know that? Why don't I know that?"

The questions had no time to be answered because there was a knock on the door and the young WPC from the front office popped her head around and frantically spoke.
"Superintendent Rivers is on his way up to see you Sarge!"

Reynolds looked at Preece who had not lost the smile. Both men stood up, Reynolds started to adjust his tie and had only just finished when the door opened.

There couldn't have been a more police-like policeman. He stood there, hat under arm and gloves squeezed in other hand. His shoulders were broad and needed to be, with the amount of silver attached there. There was not the slightest hint of a wrinkle in the deep blue uniform and the whole room was mirrored in the reflection of his shoes. His face was remarkably shaved as if he performed that operation every hour.

"DS Reynolds?"

"Sir!"

"What have you got on the Davies case?"

"We are in the final process of making our recommendation," at the '*we*' the officer looked at the still smiling Preece and made a grunting acknowledgement of his presence, "which will most likely be that Davies took his own life. That is what we will write in the report."

The tension of the entry and the abrupt questioning was over and the senior officer relaxed.

"Good. It's a nasty business when an inmate at His Majesty's Pleasure takes his own life. Well never mind." He turned to Preece. "And how are you William? Police work agreeing with you?"

"Yes sir." Said still smiling.

"How's my sister?"

"Mother is fine too … sir."

Reynolds looked from one to the other and back again until they felt his gaze.

The mood changed again and Superintendent Rivers straightened his uniform and adopted a more detached air.

"OK gentlemen, thank you for seeing me at such short notice. I will convey your report to the Chief Constable at my meeting with him today." He put on his hat and continued.

"I am very pleased with the reports I am getting on this department," he said glancing towards Preece who was *not* looking at either officer, "and I hope you will keep up the good work."

"Thank you sir." Came from both officers

With that he was gone and shortly after Preece tried to follow.

"Come back here and sit yourself down … *William!*."

* * *

The days came easier after his visit to Waverly. The incident wasn't widely reported, there wasn't a family that would openly mourn for

Davies and the official enquiry found that he had committed suicide. Case closed. Slip back into the routine of life and work. That was a problem for John Deverall. His routine was one of nightmare, torture, pain, remorse and helplessness. All that had changed now. Since Waverly his dreams had gone from ecstasy where he had been able to talk and be with his daughter to agony again. This was doubly painful because he felt that there must be something that he could do to rid her of this nightly torment but he was too weak or dim to understand what it was. There was a thought that often gnawed away at his mind and he pushed it away with less and less force. His actions and her torture were linked. When he confronted Davies at Renkill she spoke to him. After the visit to Waverly he spent dream time with her again. It was madness and he pushed the thought away again but he knew that it wouldn't stay away for long. Something deep inside him also wanted it to come back. That was the way he was feeling on that day when he had another deep conversation with Phil Brooks.

"How is it going John?"

"I am fine Brooks. What's the problem?"

"There is no problem, John, I just wanted to have a little conversation with you, that's all."

It didn't need an answer, just a listening ear, so John stood and kept quiet and listened. Brooks continued.

"There is a family in Hartknoll who are living in grief. Their house was set alight one night when someone poured gasoline through their mailbox and struck a match. The flames took hold of the house really quickly but there was just enough time to get the family out – well almost."

"Why are you telling me this Phil?" John was perplexed. He couldn't possibly see any reason for the story but Brooks didn't answer, he just paused for a moment and then continued.

"There were twin boys still upstairs. In the confusion, people leaving the house from the back and the front, they were overlooked. They were burned to death. They were only seven years old." Brooks stopped speaking and waited for Deverall to make a reply. He stifled the reply by continuing the story.

"There was a dispute between the father of the twins and a local thug, something about a second-hand car sale, something trivial but the thug threatened to burn the guy out of town. He went around telling everyone what he was going to do - he was that sort of guy. He has a long history of assaults, wounding, brawling, robbery and burglary. We would like to add murder to the list."

Deverall was interested in the story for no other reason than he knew it wouldn't end until it was completely told. He let Brooks continue. "The guy was arrested but nothing could pin him to the crime. He sat in the interviews and just laughed at the detectives. None of the public would say what he had told them he would do – not on the record anyway – so he was freed. Just when they managed to shake up a witness who would swear that the guy had threatened to torch the house something strange happened. He confessed. The strange part about the confession is that it was for a different crime – a break in that took place fifty miles away on the same night at the same time as the fire. There were already two men in custody and they swore that he was with them even though there is no evidence on the CCTV."

Now John knew how the story had meaning for him. He wanted Brooks to make his moves, to tell his story, to purge himself of this task. Brooks looked at Deverall with unblinking eyes and continued to tell the story but now there was a frustration and angry tone to his words.
"This guy burned down a house while the family were asleep inside. Two little boys didn't make it out and died a horrible death. The guy killed those boys and ruined the life of the family because he didn't get a great deal on a used car. He bragged about what he was going to do and when he did it the community were too scared to testify. To cover his tracks, he puts his hands up to a crime he didn't commit. He is going to do a little time but he will walk away from the murder. The police will never be able to get him."

Brooks was finished and he turned away. He left a vacuum between them that could only be filled by a question from Deverall.

John looked at the other officer for a moment and weighed up the situation. He had been told this story for a specific reason. Something inside him wanted to know what, but there was a stronger urge that pushed it away. It was pushed away for the last time. It would never be strong enough again – but it would always be there. Inside he sighed, the struggle was over. He had made a decision and although it would have been abhorrent to the public at large it pleased him. He could now let it take him, make his decisions for him. He didn't need to think all he had to do was act. He looked out over the prison in the same direction as Brooks.

Phil Brooks could hear the blood pounding in his ears. He had to congratulate himself on a job well done. He did it well because he believed in it. The anger and frustration weren't feigned, they were real. The sweat on his brow was from the heat of his anger but also from fear. He was taking a chance with Deverall, a small chance because he knew the man, but a chance all the same. They were in this together now and this moment of waiting for John to speak was the crucial one. John didn't let him down.

"Where is he now?"

Brooks sensed that this was a step taken. He turned to Deverall and maintained the angry frustrated stare. It was that stare that sometimes men share before they do outstanding things. It tells each everything. It says 'I am in this with you to the end.' It says 'You can depend on me.' The eye contact didn't waver from either man. They both understood.

"He is at Walton Farm."

"Minimum security?"

"He was convicted for breaking and entering remember, and as he was not on the video so he got off with a light sentence. He terrorised the families of the real criminals so they would say he was with them during the break in. There is no other way for justice to be done."

John looked at Brooks sideways – it was something that all prison officers joked about – how justice was never properly dealt out to the worst of criminals. He took the glance back and continued to listen as Brooks spoke but the words were not going in. He thought of Helen and how he could get closer to her. Whenever he crossed the line – that first time with Davies – his contact with his daughter was better. The second fateful time his contact was almost real. He weighed things up. It was true that the crime would go unpunished, he could remedy that. Righting this wrong may be a way to stop the torment of his dreams and spend time with Helen.

What was he thinking? Where was reality?

He fell instantly back into the conversation with Brooks and he turned indignantly towards him and stopped him speaking with a stare.

"What makes you ask me to do this? I had history with Davies I know, but what do you take me for? This puts me right back inside with the scum we lock up. Is that what you think of me Brooks? Is that what all the others think of me?"

Brooks stood there for a moment with a half astonished look on his face. He measured his words and waited until he could look right in to John's eyes.

"You couldn't be more wrong my friend. You have a sense of justice and fair play that is written all over you. All the men respect that. Every man in the prison service considers it almost an honour to stand beside you in this place – they all want to be part of your team. They trust you and will follow you without question. They know there are no ulterior motives – no politics about you. They all believe in the action too. They can't all be there at the time but they are with you in spirit. Each one is prepared to do whatever he can. They trust you John, they trust your spirit and your strength."

John's protest was cosmetic; it was something that he had to do. It was part of a game that everyone plays when they have subconsciously given in. He had given in but just didn't know it. All of these plaudits coming from Brooks would make it seem that he was doing this for the men, for justice, to rid the world of truly evil men. But something was coming from deep down inside of him, it was rising towards the surface and he was confronting it for the first time. It would normally be an unspeakable admission, something to be ashamed of, something to haunt you in quiet thoughtful moments. It rose to the surface like an animal coming up through deep water. It started as a shadow and then a form. Now it had features and at last all of the details could be clearly seen. This was his last chance to push it back where it came from. His last chance to summon inner strength to force it down again and forget about it. He could have done it but it was easier to let it surface, give in to the inevitable. The last thought John had before the monster broke the surface was that he wanted it this way anyway. His last emotion before his life changed forever – was relief!

His monster was the fact that he enjoyed what he had done.

Now came all of the reasons why this course of action was good. It was justice. Hey – if he didn't do it nobody would. They were scum and deserved it. He had the backing of the men. They wanted it. He couldn't disappoint them. The reasons went on and on and became stronger. He felt relief, like making a confession, getting it off his chest.

There was something new in the face of John Deverall when he turned to speak to Brooks. There was also something new in the junior officers' face too. For John it was defeat and he waited to be given instructions and for Phil it was possession. He needn't persuade any longer, John Deverall was there to coax, urge and command.

"What do you want me to do?"

* * *

DS Roper had made his decision and he was a man who stuck to decisions. He entered the station the next day clutching a sports bag with all of the zips closed. He was a fit man and to be seen with such a bag was not unusual but he felt that all eyes were on him. He felt that people could see through the bag to the contents within. The distance between him and his locker seemed it increase with every step he took. He waited for somebody to ask what he had in the bag, he was ready with an answer but he feared there would be a tremor in his voice that would cause suspicion. When he got to the locker, he opened the door and deposited the bag on the floor, closed and locked the door and went to his desk. He felt like he had just run a marathon.

One more thing to do before he could get on with his caseload.

He reached for the phone and punched in the number at the same time taking care to make sure others couldn't overhear his conversation. He gave out a short gust of a laugh because the last thing he was going to have on the phone was a conversation. No, this needed something a little more covert.

The connection was made and there was a voice on the other end.

He cleared his throat.

"Hello, I would like to speak to Officer Phil Brooks please."

* * *

Preece had been elevated in Reynolds' mind but not in the reality of the day-to-day routine in the office. In fact, the experienced officer treated his apprentice with slightly more disregard since he was discovered to be the Super's nephew. Preece expected it and accepted it. He knew that the fact he had a high-ranking relative was better kept secret and he hoped that his work would speak for his ability. Nevertheless, there was a conversation he was waiting for and it soon came.

"Preece why the hell didn't you tell me that the Super is your Uncle?"

"It has nothing to do with the work we are doing here so I didn't think it was something people needed to know. Anyway, I was afraid that I would be treated differently if everyone knew."

Reynolds thought about that for a moment and continued.

"You know what this place is. It is where all the shit cases come that can't be solved, well it *was,* until **you** came, but that is beside the point. If I had people in high places, I certainly would have them pull strings to get me a better job than this!

What's the matter, doesn't your uncle like you?"

Preece gave one of his energetic smiles and answered.

"I already did that Sarge. I got him to pull strings to assign me to this job."

Reynolds coughed into the coffee that he was about to drink.

"THIS job? What on earth would you want to do that for? I told you how I got this job. I stepped on too many toes, and it doesn't look like I will ever get out of here. You must be mad!"

The smile came back to the face of the young detective.

"You are always thinking about things from the wrong angle Sarge, you have to look on this as an opportunity. If we do well in this job, they have to take notice! And we have been doing well have we not?"

Reynolds wiped coffee from his chin with his handkerchief and agreed with the lad. Preece changed his smile from cheeky to wry. "I have been thinking about the Davies thing." Reynolds stopped mopping up and sat down. "I noticed that there were CCTV cameras on the landing. Do you think we should have a look at the footage before we put the recommendations in the report?"

* * *

Every 'perfect' crime has a flaw, something overlooked or it comes from outside the comprehension of the perpetrators – so how are they supposed to know? Sometimes it is just a glaring simple mistake that humans are likely to make and regret afterwards.

Nobody thought to doctor the closed-circuit television security tape.

Reynolds and Preece arrived unannounced again and it didn't cause much concern. They asked to see the cell and were promptly shown the way. On the landing outside the cell, they stopped and looked up. There, some thirty feet in the distance, was the CCTV camera. It pointed slightly to their left but it would record the comings and goings of people entering the wing. They turned to their escort and Reynolds stood silently and gave the nod to Preece.
"We would like a copy of the CCTV tape for the day that Davies … died."
There was an almost imperceptible draining of blood from the prison officers' face.

The policemen insisted on being present during the recovery of the tape and as a result they soon found themselves sitting in front of a monitor watching the traffic of people entering and leaving the landing. The position of the camera was too far away and too high to make out individual details of people and it didn't have a view of the cell door but it was a record they could work with.

The tape started with total stillness. Just the occasional officer making his rounds. The prison was still asleep. The morning progressed and prisoners went off to breakfast and came back again. More officers on the rounds and then lunch. Both times Davies could be seen as he was escorted to and from his own private meal sitting. It was just as Walker had said – two guards in front and two guards behind. There followed more sporadic traffic then officers running on to the landing – then more officers – enter – exit – then the body of Davies is carried from the scene.

"So, what have we here Preece? Screws and cons coming and going. What is that going to tell us? We have watched this from morning until an hour after the event and unless we can see into the cell, we have nothing."

Preece didn't answer, he was totally engrossed in the small grey figures moving back and forth on the monitor. His finger repeatedly pressed the rewind and play buttons in that order.

"Preece?"
"Sarge?"
"It's a dead end Preece, there is nothing here."
"Sarge. You see that door? That door is the only way on to that wing if you are going to Davies' cell. To approach from the other direction would mean an extra five-minute walk and a diversion from the other side of the prison. Prisoners could come through that door and move to their cell and possibly not appear on the tape again. They will be in their cell longer than the duration of the tape, but the guards, they have a pattern of going over the same ground over and over again."

Reynolds sat up and tried to continue the train of thought.

"So, we can check the movements of the guards against their statements."
Preece appreciated the attempt.
"That's true but we really can't see who is who on this tape. But what we can do is simple primary school arithmetic."

Reynolds train of thought, now derailed, was abandoned and he sat listening to the young officer. Preece rewound the tape and depressed the fast review button.
"Here we are, first thing in the morning, two guards enter, two guards exit. Now the traffic picks up a bit, new prisoners and escorts enter and escorts exit." Preece paused the tape. "Every officer that enters this wing should also exit soon after. We should add one then subtract one."
"I get you." Reynolds took much greater interest. This was something he could do!
The tape continued the policemen calculated. Guards did their rounds and nothing seemed out of the ordinary. Suddenly Preece switched off the fast review because the traffic on the tape had increased. Davies had just been discovered hanging from his window. Preece depressed the slow review to make his calculations. The two men sat as Preece kept up

the running tally of officers entering the landing and officers leaving. When he was finished the score was minus one.

Fewer prisoners had departed than had arrived and more officers had left than had entered.

Preece did not have a smile on his face anymore. Each of them knew that this was different from anything they had done before. A suspicion that something was not right about the case had spurred them on but this was not what they had expected and at this precise moment they didn't know what to do!

* * *

Walton Farm, a minimum-security prison was half a day's journey from Renkill. It was not going to be a simple matter of covering for him. He would have to be away for the whole day. John decided not to worry about it. He would see what they prepared for him. He would let them make all of the decisions. It was a new feeling.

It was minimum security so the inmates would have open privileges. They would be able to wear their own clothes and move about in the estate as well. There were opportunities to work and mingle with other inmates. There would be few opportunities to target an inmate and get him alone. Suicide was not an option either because all of the inmates were near release and didn't have to do hard time anyway.

Brooks had all of the answers.

"His name is Cliff Culmer and he has already started trouble among the other inmates. There have been a couple of beatings that the staff can't prove but are sure are down to him. He is going to be on a working detail this Thursday in a flat in South Walton."

"Working detail?"

"Yeah, it is some government scheme to get cons to put something back in to the community – well it just so happens that our Clifford is an ace paper hanger and he is helping to decorate a flat as part of the working party."

They both paused for questions or answers, Brooks continued.

"I will get you a bus ticket to Walton and you find this address." He gave a piece of paper to Deverall. "Go in the front door and go up to the empty room at the back on the third floor. It will be the only unlocked room." Brooks paused again.

"Just wait for him he will come to you. Don't stab or strangle him. Leave him in the room and walk out of the building. We will do the rest.

"We?"

"You are not in this alone John." John kept quiet.

"When it is over, leave the building and go back to the bus stop. You will be given a ticket to get you back home. Go home and stay there. Come to work on Friday."

Deverall had a question.

"I will be missed this time. What if the warden does rounds?"

"The warden and the doctor have been called to central office for a conference on that day. They won't be here. We will take care of all the paperwork."

"What's going to happen?"

"John, you, like everybody else who wasn't there, will have to read about it in the papers on Friday."

* * *

D C Roper sat on the park bench wishing that he had never chosen the park bench as a place to meet. Everybody who walks by looks at you as if you are having a secret meeting with a spy from the Russian Embassy! It is impossible to look innocent either. He felt like telling everyone that he wasn't having a secret meeting but that of course would just confirm that he was! No, he would just have to put up with their looks and make a note not to do it again. To his astonishment there came a voice behind him. Speaking loud English in a Russian accent!

"Comrade Roper, the custard on my pyjamas comes from the tractor factory. Where did you get yours?"

Roper rolled his eyes and turned around and saw his old friend Phil Brooks who continued to speak in a Russian accent.

"Meester Ropesky, vie are you dressed in dat coat and hat, you look like spy from the KGB. Come let us go and drink some Wodka!"

They both laughed and shook hands.

Roper suggested coffee and they walked toward a nearby vendor. Brooks tried to put his friend at ease as they walked.

"So Ropes, how is that woman of yours."

"She's fine Phil, as big as a house though, I'm going to be a dad in two months."

"My God you have been busy, I haven't seen you in …"

"Two years Phil."

"I am sorry Ropes, the prison service takes up the time you know. One day you are at the police academy like we were, then the next day you are old with nothing but memories. Look, I promise to get round to yours for some nosh in the near future. Now you have to tell me what all this cloak and dagger stuff is about."

DC Roper gripped the bag at his side a little tighter. He gave it a sideways glance which Brooks did not miss.

"What's in the bag?" He was the very first person to ask that question. Roper took his coffee from the stand and motioned to a bench out in the open park.

When they sat down and had a good look around DC Roper put the bag on the ground between them and started to tell his tale. First there had to be some ground rules.

"What I am about to tell you is from me to you. What you do after that is your affair. What I am about to give you is for you. I do not want it back nor do I want to see it ever again. In fact, if I ever see or hear anything about this meeting or conversation ever again, I will swear that it never took place."

Brooks lost the childish aire with his friend. He had never seen him like this before. He assured the policeman.

"Another thing, I promised that whatever happens this must not bust out into a national court case. Believe me I have my reasons."

"That's OK Roper … you have my word."

That was good enough.

He passed the bag to Brooks along the ground. Brooks looked at it and then at his friend. This was scary. He expected to find a severed head or worse in the bag. He looked back at the bag and reached down to pick it up. It wasn't a head – too light. In fact, it just felt like a bag. The weight inside was almost imperceptible. He opened the zip and saw the scrap books and bundles of papers.

"What is all this Roper?"

"I'll go and get some more coffee, give you a little time to look at the contents of the bag. I will be back when you are done." He walked away towards the refreshment stand.

Brooks took out the contents and laid them carefully on his knee. He started to turn the pages.

Roper stood by the refreshment stand and waited. He watched his friend go through the documents one at a time piecing the information together until he came to a small envelope. Even from the distance between them he could see a little sparkle in the sunshine and the reaction that shook Brooks' body. He turned to the vendor and asked for two more coffees.

When he returned to the bench Brooks was just staring into space with an expressionless face. He didn't need to speak, he just looked up and took the coffee.

"Nobody knows about this stuff Phil. After today I won't know about it either. But the man responsible for this is living right under your nose."

"Who is he?"

"His name is David Brenner, he is an inmate at Renkill prison. You and John Deverall have been making sure that he has been tucked up safe and sound every night for the past two years!"

*　*　*

Ten

John Deverall looked at the house from across the street from a convenient bus stop. He stood there because it wouldn't cause anyone to wonder why he just stood and stared. It was a four-storey building with evidence in the front garden that building works were going on. There were some yellow buckets, half-filled bags of rubble and some wooden planks. The ground floor windows that were not broken and boarded were whitewashed. The front door was situated at the top of a small wide set of solid stone steps. It was a house just like twenty others along the street. The front door was neglected, scratched and poorly painted. From his position he could see that there was a gap between door handle and frame.

The door was open.

He stood and looked at the building for about ten minutes waiting for something to happen, something that would make him move, something to set this *thing* in motion. Up until now he had just taken the bus like thousands of others. Moving into that house would be like passing the point of no return. It was a big step and he was loathe to take it. It was something simple that made him decide. A bus was approaching – he had to either get on it or cross the street.

He stepped into the road.

He didn't look to left or right, he just crossed the road and calmly climbed the steps of the building and without slowing he pushed open the door. The ground floor entrance hall was empty except for some buckets and paint brushes. He could smell the odours of paint, putty and plaster. Everything was neatly stacked in the hallway, the workers had not arrived yet. That was the way it was planned. He looked at his watch, they would be here in half an hour.

He climbed the stairs.

The rooms on the first floor were open and all in a semi-finished state of decoration. Without pausing he turned and went up the stairs. The second floor was different. All of the doors were closed with external Yale locks on each. These were the front doors of bedsits. There was no sign of work being done here. He passed on to the third floor and found the room that Brooks had told him about. It was the only open door – the rest were padlocked from the outside. Uninhabited storage rooms. This door was half open and he went in.

This was another store room, there were boxes of decorating materials still in their wrappings. Tins of paint unopened and full bags of fresh plaster stacked beside the wall. There was a single window at the back of the room looking out to the rear gardens. All the other gardens in the terrace were neatly groomed but this one only contained weeds and a skip half full of brick rubble and broken glass from shattered windows. He had seen enough. He turned and went back to the landing. There was a window at the bottom of the half flight of stairs that gave him a view of the road below. He could do nothing else but watch and wait.

*　*　*

Reynolds and Preece decided not to let anyone at the prison know about their discovery on the CCTV tape. The officer on duty called the warden when he heard their request to remove it from the prison. When he arrived, he was the first to break the silence between the police officers and the assembled prison guards.
"What is on the tape that you are so interested in sergeant?"

Reynolds being the senior officer and with age on his side answered all of the questions. Preece was smart enough not to act like an over excited school boy so he kept silent and showed no emotion.

"It is a record of the comings and goings on the prison landing for the time duration when Davies killed himself sir, it is a long tape and we need more time to look at it. I just want to take it back to the station, make a copy, and return the original to you .. say … this afternoon?"

The warden looked at his guards. It was a look that said 'I *have* to do this … why didn't somebody think of this in the first place?' but his mood changed as soon as he spoke.

"Of course Sergeant Reynolds, by all means. Please return the original as soon as possible. I will need it for my records if there is an enquiry. You don't mind signing a receipt for it do you?"

With the receipt signed and the tape sealed in a bright orange padded envelope Reynolds and Preece made their way out of the office.

* * *

They workers from the Walton Farm were exactly on time. Their van pulled up in front of the house and four workmen got out of the back. The driver was obviously a guard from the open prison. It must be something in the way they walk, or carry themselves, or the way they always try to have a clear view of any situation but you could always pick out a screw. It had to be him because the others just couldn't possibly be in charge. Three spotty kids and a middle aged man. The man looked right out of place. He looked bigger than the rest and from his vantage point at the top of the stairs John Deverall started to weigh him up.

Cliff Culmer could look after himself at the best of times and in his present situation he had no bother climbing to the top of the food chain. Apex predator. Alfa male. This little prison stretch would be easy to do. The fact that he systematically terrorised all of the other inmates at the farm made it easier still. John looked at him and tried to see the little children he had killed. He tried to focus on the reason for his presence there waiting at the top of the stairs. His imagination was too good. He turned away from it and thought of Helen. He wanted to see her again. He wanted all of this to be over. He turned away, walked in to the room and waited.

It didn't take long.

When they entered the building, a radio was turned on and their voices, which were at best muffled, now could not be heard at all. The work for the day was planned, they would start with plastering the front room, Cliff was sent to get a fresh bag of plaster. He resigned to do this heavy task because the others were just not up to it. Giving them a few choice, vulgar words, he started slowly up the stairs.

John could hear a new sound coming through the music on the radio. It was the sound of heavy boots coming towards him. They were close, he didn't have much time so he stepped behind the door just as it opened.

Cliff Culmer walked into the room and moved towards the low stack of bags. He reached down and grabbed a corner and swung it into an upright position. Before he could lift it, John had clasped his hand in an iron grip. For a second, Culmer was shocked. He leapt away like he had been bitten by a cobra but it didn't break the grip. He was still reeling from the first action when John drove the arm right up his back and with his other arm reached around and covered the mouth. Now Culmer could not move or make a sound. His thoughts were reeling. Nothing like this had ever happened to him before. He was always the one dishing out this kind of treatment, it was a new spike on his learning curve, but he learned fast! He realised that no matter what was going on he had to do something!

He spread his legs and planted his feet firmly on the wooden floor. He wore steel tipped working boots and they gripped the dusty surface. Bending forward and twisting his body towards his excruciating arm he lifted his attacker off balance and spun him into the wall.

John had the grip that he wanted. No noise. Lots of pain. He wanted to hold this man in a position where he was helpless. When he was lifted from the floor the advantage went to his victim. He was thrown into the wall but never lost his grip. When they both recovered from that thrust John drove the arm up the mans back until it parted at the elbow. There was a muffled scream and John felt mucous and saliva cover his hand, it made it much harder to cover the mouth. Holding the man even closer he pulled back on the head and made him lean backwards to lose the grip on the floor.

Cliff could hardly breathe, there was a searing pain in his elbow and he couldn't feel his hand at all. There was only one course of action and that was to relax, see what happens, pick his moment. If this guy was going to rob him, he was in for a shock. He was in for a bigger shock when the prison guard called for backup!

John felt him relax.

Both men were breathing very hard. The room was full of plaster dust kicked up by their short exertions. John breathed heavily through his nose and held his grip until he trusted himself to speak. When he did it was very slowly and just above a whisper. He spoke almost directly into the ear of Culmer.

"Culmer?"

Culmer just swivelled his eyes toward the sound of the voice.

"Good, good. I didn't want to get the wrong guy."

Culmer waited, there was little else he could do.

"I wanted to meet the man who gets so upset over a second-hand car, that he torches a house with the family still inside."

Culmer now realised he needed a plan.

"Think of two little kids asleep in their beds. Their whole life ahead of them. Think of the way they died, flames blistering the paint on their door. Think of them screaming for their mother. I wonder what it was like for them huddled under their bed when the flames started coming through the floorboards."

Culmer had used the time to make some sort of recovery. He knew that this was a life-or-death situation. That alone gave him the strength he needed. Ignoring the pain in his shattered arm he pushed again and caught John off guard. Their heads clashed and John was stunned but he didn't let go. Both men fell into the corner of the room Culmer on top. John had no room to manoeuvre but didn't allow his man to turn. Culmer's only weapons were his feet and he brought the heels down heavily on John shins. He wanted to cry out but he just took the pain. He brought his legs behind him and the two men rolled on to their sides. John now experienced a new feeling. He felt that he was losing his strength. He was not in as much control as he would have liked. Breathing heavily again but wasting no time John continued to speak.

"This world would have been a better place with them in it, Culmer," he tightened his grip, "and will be a much better place without you."

Culmer started to thrash about as best he could but he couldn't loosen the grip on his neck. His head was slowly being turned by a massive strength. He resisted wildly but it was hopeless. He could feel the tendons stretch and hear the grinding of the bones in his neck. He heard an almost imperceptible pop in his neck and his pain was gone.

All feeling in his body ceased and he was allowed to slump to the floor. He had no control over his body but his eyes could still move he could still see. He watched John Deverall stand up and look down at him. He watched him wipe his hand on his chest. He watched him leave the room. He was left staring at the ceiling. He couldn't breathe. He made a conscious effort to draw breath but there was nothing there. As he slowly suffocated, the last thing he did see, was another man entering the room, cross to the window and open it wide.

* * *

Roper came back to the bench with the two plastic cups of coffee. Brooks was just sitting, staring into the body of the park. His gloved hand tightly gripped his jaw and pursed his lips. Roper sat down and offered his friend the coffee and that seemed to bring him back to the present.
"Brenner is in for aggravated assault and attempted rape. We didn't know anything about this." He pointed to the carrier bag.
Roper inhaled a sip from his coffee and looked away as he spoke. "How were you to know? His history is there in that bag not on his criminal record."
"Why did you give this to me Ropes? Why didn't you just sort this out yourself? You could have just dropped it on to somebody's desk and let them make the enquiry. Where did you get it anyway?"

It was Roper's turn to look away. There were a lot of questions to answer and he had to be sure that answering them didn't land him into more trouble. After a few moments he turned again and looked at his friend. "Never mind where I got the stuff from, just believe that it is from an impeccable source. Hand it over to someone else? – what then? These things have a habit of getting away from you. People lose interest. Cases are too old. Evidence is too circumstantial. Lawyers are too clever by half and juries are just too dumb. I chose you because you are my friend and I like to think that we think alike. I chose you because I can trust you. I chose you because you work with John and he needs to know. I chose you because I couldn't tell him. I wouldn't have the heart. I don't have the courage. I couldn't do that to him."

"Oh, and I *could*?" Brooks said sitting up straight and downing his coffee.

Roper looked away. "It's not like that."

Brooks had an almost imperceptible smile on his face. If Roper had turned and looked, he was detective enough to have seen it – but he didn't. Brooks composed himself and reached out to his friend's shoulder and turned him so they could look at each other face to face. He looked deep into his eyes and then spoke.

"Who knows about this?"

"Just you and me and the … person who gave it to me. They gave it to me with the same instructions that I gave to you. David Brenner knows about it too but he does not know that I have it."

"Alright then, I have this thing now. You never did. You are not involved. This meeting never happened. I don't know what I am going to do but I will think of something. The right thing. Whatever happens you must be assured that it was for the best. In a way I am pleased that you came to me with it. So, for that I thank you, but please, let's never speak of it again!"

The relief could be seen in Ropers eyes. A huge weight had been lifted from his life. He looked at the smile on his friends face and then to the outstretched hand. He took it and shook it firmly.

"It has been good to see you again Ropes." Their grips relaxed and hands fell away. Brooks picked up the bag and strode down the path leading into the park. Walking briskly and carrying the bag by his side he looked like a man on his way home with the shopping.

Roper's knees couldn't take it anymore and he had to sit down on the park bench. His breath was coming slightly faster than normal and was creating clouds in the cold air. He watched Brooks disappear around the bend behind some trees and then he got up from the bench and decided to go home early. He would go home, kiss his wife and tell her that he loved her. Tonight, he would tell her just that … many times.

* * *

The evidence was there on the tape – there were more guards on the landing than there should have been and there was a lost prisoner! There was no answer to the riddle. They sat there and wore puzzled faces. Reynolds was actually not thinking at all – he was just pretending. What he was actually doing was waiting for Preece to pick up the scent that he would then follow. This is what had been happening over the last few months and it was successful. This time Preece was not forthcoming but he was the first to speak.

"Sarge?"

"Hmmm?"

"I can't get away from a thought that I have. It is not the only explanation but it seems the obvious and the evidence points to it."

"What is it?"

"Well, we can see the landing and the door to the landing. If we assume that the word went out about Davies by word of mouth then that information would have passed through the wing through that door. If that is so, then it would have been odd for a guard to come from the other side of the wing to join in the commotion. That part of the wing – at that time – would not have known."

Reynolds could vaguely agree so he nodded his head. Preece continued. "Now we have counted all of the guards and prisoners coming and going and we find that the number is one more, both ways, foe each."

More nods.

"That means that there was a prisoner on the landing before Davies got back to his cell and an extra guard on the landing after he killed himself. "

No more nods – Reynolds was starting to get a whiff of the scent. "So a prisoner has disappeared and a new guard has suddenly appeared! What do you make of that? It looks like ..."

Reynolds had found the scent. He had also found his voice. He stood up and stared out of the window and finished his colleague's sentence ... "one of the guards killed Davies."

Preece sat there like a punished schoolboy. There was a look of sorrow on his face, not like the glee he couldn't contain when he started to break a case. Reynolds turned around from the window to look at his partner.

"What's the matter Preece? I happen to think you are right!"

"It can't be right Sarge … not a guard."

"Listen boy, it all fits. There was a scuffle in the cell – Davies didn't hang himself! Davies has been a handful at every prison that ever banged him up. He attacked one of these guards not long ago, another one at his last prison, he killed an inmate there too! He even assaulted a guard escorting him from the court. Davies has been bad news for all the guards." Reynolds was putting it all together now, walking around the room and punctuating his sentences with his finger.

"They got someone to do a number on Davies, smuggled him in to the cell to wait for him to return. No, it HAD to be a guard. They couldn't trust anyone from outside. It had to be one that they could trust, one of their own. Then when Davies is dead, a guard 'discovers' his body while doing a routine check and runs for help. More guards arrive and, in the commotion, the killer blends in to the crowd – the crowd of guards! They all enter the cell and tie a rope around Davies' neck and stretch him out like he hung himself."

Reynolds sat down on the corner of the desk and looked down at Preece. Preece looked up at Reynolds and spoke.

"What are we going to do about this?"

"We are going to write this up and present our evidence as well as our findings. The problem is who do we give it to?" With that both men went towards the pile of forms and the typewriter.

*　*　*

John Deverall left the building just as he entered it, through the front door and unnoticed. The other workers were busy with the guard at the back of the property. The music from the radio covered the sound of his tread on the stairs. He walked to the bus stop across the street. The adrenaline in his blood pushed the feeling of exhaustion from his body. The pain in his shins where the heavy boots struck, was absent. The damaged skin and bone caused no pain now but would take their toll later. For ten minutes he stood and stared at the house with the open door. He prayed for a bus to come soon to take him away from this place. At the moment he caught sight of a bus coming in the distance it was shared by the sound of screams coming from the house he had just left.

A young girl dressed in what could only be described as pyjamas ran out into the street screaming and clutching her body. The urge to run started to build up behind him.

She continued to scream and gather people around her. Cars stopped in the street and people dialled emergency services on their mobile phones. The bus was never going to get through the traffic so John turned and walked away from the scene. He was the only person going in the opposite direction.

He found another street and boarded a different bus.

He felt the eyes of every passenger on him. He mused about how he felt before he entered the house. His determination. His conviction. The knowledge that what he was doing was right, justice by another route. All these feelings were gone now and replaced by an inner fear of these innocent public citizens. How they would be disgusted if they knew. How they would shun him. How low he would be in their eyes.

He closed his eyes. He didn't care about them. He only cared about how tired he was, how his legs hurt and how long it would be before he could get home. How long it would be before his next dream. He wanted to see her very badly right now.

Getting home was like a nightmare.

Every step was an agony of exhaustion and pain but he didn't let it show. He walked through the pain and tried to put it from his mind but pain won't be denied. It waits until you think you are safe and then comes in a rush. His waiting pain was triggered by the sound behind him of the latch on his front door closing. The pain came in a rush and he fell to his knees and rolled forward on to his shoulder. He lay there for several minutes and let the pain do its worst. The training never leaves you. When it was over, he climbed to his feet and went to the bathroom and ran the shower. As he undressed, he noticed that his socks were full of blood from the gashes on his shins. His trousers stuck to the wounds and disrobing opened them and renewed the flow of blood. There was a bruise on his forehead and his back was terribly scratched from something he had fallen on in the scuffle. His face was darkened and drawn. He was a sight!

When he was showered and patched up, he joined her.

She was there in the light and she was playing. He could smell the grass and feel the sun on his face as he smiled at her. He sat there just drinking in these sensations. He just wanted to feel the surroundings and watch her. To speak would break this spell. She would play and look at him and smile then play some more. In the end her curiosity got the better of her. "Why are you so quiet daddy?"

Her voice was like an electric shock to his system. It brought him from his muse and instantly made him alert.
"I am just happy to be here with you darling."
Everything that starts has to have an end. John was aware that this conversation was a start of the end of his dream. How long it would last? He didn't know, but he knew it would end. She was talking again.
"Don't be sad daddy. He was a terrible man. Just think of those little boys. Just think of the people that he won't hurt now." She frowned and pushed a dolly away from her. She stood up and walked over to him. She got very close. She was close enough for him to feel the change of breeze that her presence caused. She stood close but still seemed far away..
"Don't be sad daddy."
"I'm not sad darling. As long as I am with you here, I will never be sad."
Helen looked down at the ground and a slight chill ran through his body. The sun lost a little of its warmth and the light seemed to dim slightly. She continued to speak.
"I have to go now."

On the hill in the distance, a figure of a man appeared. The distance was great but there was a feeling that he was right there with them, communicating with them.
"Don't go darling," he reached out his hand but she pulled back. "Stay with me a little longer."

"I have to go daddy." She started to move away from him. Walking backwards towards the figure on the hill, walking slowly but covering the distance quickly.
John Deverall stood up from the park bench and cupped his hands to his mouth. He needed to shout because she was now with him and very far away. He needed to shout because the wind had gotten up and was

starting to howl. He needed to shout because the darkness was closing in on them all.

"Fight Helen .... FIGHT!"

In a cold sweat. Again. John Deverall woke up.

* * *

Brooks sat in his flat looking at the television. He was only looking – nothing was going in. He sat there still wearing his coat and the shopping bag at his feet. He was thinking. The evening had drawn in and the street lights were illuminating the flat behind him. The light from the television cast strange and mobile shadows on the walls. Brooks was thinking. He was thinking about how things happen. He was thinking about divine intervention and how there seemed to be a plan out there that rules us all. He thought about the things that he had encouraged John to do and now, as if a higher power was behind it all. The thought appalled him, how could God be brought in to something as unholy as this. New thought, new fear, how was he going to bring this to the attention of Deverall. New thought, new worry, how would he control him? This was likely to push him right over the edge and then everybody would be right in it up to the neck! Something to do with the darkness and the TV being the only source of light in the flat, made him snap out of his deep thought. He stood up and switched on the lights, took off his coat and went towards the window to draw the curtains. A name spoken by the TV presenter stopped him. It got his full and undivided attention.

"Clifford Culmer was serving a sentence for burglary at Walton Farm Minimum Security Prison. He was part of a government initiative to refurbish flats in the city. This morning, he attempted to rape a young woman in the building where he was working. She managed to fight him off and escape into Valverde Road where she was helped by motorists and passers by. Evidently Culmer entered a part of the building that was off limits to the working party. He went into the room of the young woman resident and pinned her to the bed where she was sleeping. A struggle took place and when she managed to get free, she ran screaming into the street. Culmer tried to make his escape by climbing out of an upstairs window but he fell onto building rubble stacked in a skip three floors below. He was pronounced dead at the scene. The

young woman, whose identity is being withheld, will be spending time with her parents abroad until the inquest next week where it is thought that a verdict of death by misadventure is liable to be issued. Now there are new questions being asked about the scheme to use convicted criminals in the community. Should it be continued, is it being properly managed and are we safe? These questions were put to ..."

Brooks finished closing the curtains and breathed a sigh of relief.

* * *

The video tape with the results of interviews and an outline of their recommendations filled the large padded yellow envelope. Everything was typed out and labelled. The flap was folded over and the small metal clip was bent to hold it down. Both policemen looked at each other with confirmation that meant 'That's it – we are in this together' but it was Reynolds who spoke.
"Who do you suggest that we give this to?"

Preece knew what the answer was but he was being forced to say the words.
"Leave it to me Sarge and I will see that Superintendent Rivers gets it. I will give it to him personally."

The older policeman suddenly felt an uncomfortable emotion. He tried very hard to suppress it but the fact that it was even there surprised him. In the past he had trusted people to do the right thing and look where it got him. There was a little nagging, fleeting moment of distrust. He covered the momentary pause before it could be properly interpreted. "Look son, we leave it in the drawer overnight, that way it will give us time to think about it. We have to be sure about this." With that he put the envelope in the steel cabinet drawer and turned the key. He put the key in his pocket and gave it a pat. There was nothing left to do so they moved to the door and turned out the lights.

* * *

It took a superhuman effort to get out of bed. His whole body ached, his legs were severely bruised and cut. He had a splitting headache and his muscles seemed to have seized up. It was not an option to call work and cry off for the day. It would be a coincidence and too many of them could start people diverting attention towards him. After wrapping plastic bags around his wounds, he took the hottest shower he could stand. This eased the pain in his muscles. Tablets had to take care of the inner pain. The walk to the bus stop and from the bus to the prison limbered him up a little but his conversation with Ted at the prison office took away all sensation of pain.

"Morning Sarge"

"Morning Ted"

"That young girl must have been terrified!"

It made him stop. He looked at Ted who just went on speaking with his head down. He was actually reading the local paper. John moved closer. "This guy from Walton Farm tried to rape her. He was on a working party – I ask you!" Ted took the paper and turned it around so John could read the text but he kept on talking just the same. "Yeah, he went right into her room while she was sleeping. She started to scream and broke loose. He tried to escape from a third-floor window and fell into a skip full of bricks. Ended up in the right place if you ask me!"

John was engrossed in the text and the pictures. There was Culmer, a rather younger man in the picture. There was the picture of the house, the skip and the open window on the fourth floor. Ted kept on talking. "Good thing about it is that it is an open and shut case, no need for cops, courts or council." Ted reached across and reclaimed his paper. He turned the page and started to read something else. "Have a good day Sarge."

John stood there and stared for a moment still unsure of what he had just read. He started to feel the pain in his body again. He was coming back to reality.

"Yeah, you too Ted."

He walked down the corridor and through the gates. He used the time to take stock of the situation. He used the routine to get back into character. He mustn't let his men or the inmates see any change in him. The changing room was empty which was odd but a relief. There was a definite chance that someone might see his bruises or his damaged shins so he wore his working trousers and shirt to work. When he got to the briefing room the others were already assembled, his arrival meant that the briefing could start. A more determined mood took over the room. The warden entered.

"Good morning gentlemen." The warden continued to speak about the routine of the week but John was not listening.

He stood at the far right of the room, near the door, and he searched the room for Brooks. He found him at the back on the far left. Their eyes did not meet. Brooks was deliberately looking straight at the warden. John kept up his stare and Brooks soon felt his gaze and gave in. He made eye contact but broke it off very soon. John's message was clear. 'I want to talk to you' the message was received but Brooks didn't look comfortable about it. It would be almost mid-afternoon when they met high on the top landing walkway.

"Hello John." Brooks said with a cheery air. Almost as if he hadn't a care in the world. They were like two good friends meeting in the week ready to talk about family, friends, jobs, sport.
"What the hell is going on Brooks? How many people are in this theatre company? Where the hell did the girl come from, how far does this thing go? You told me that there were only a few involved!"

Brooks looked around because John's voice was a little loud. They were alone but others knew they were there and what was going on. They all had an idea of what was being said. Brooks knew that it was best to let John speak first, get all the questions out then calmly provide the answers, allay the fears. He forced a smile and took over the conversation.
"There is nothing to worry about John, everything has been covered and the less you know the better. Anyway, it is all over now. You don't have to do that anymore. There will be no comeback from the Davies thing and the Culmer case is as cold as he is."

"Who is the girl? Who else was there? She couldn't have tossed him out the window."
"John, you don't need to know. I don't even know." Brooks winced but it was too late.

Deverall's eyes widened. "I thought this was between us, you me and the guys at Waverly and the Farm, but its bigger than that isn't it? I am at the bottom of a long chain. I am being dangled on that chain!" Deverall turned away and stared out over the landing. This thing couldn't be controlled because he had no control.

"You said it's all over now?" He clung to the chance that it was over, that life could carry on somehow, someway.

Brooks found his smile again and he hastily put it on to cover his feelings.

"Yes, that's it. We can get back to work and I guarantee that you won't be contacted again." Brooks waited for an answer.

"So you are some part of this 'organisation' are you? You can make that sort of statement and keep to it? Was it something that you were told to say to me.? Who is pulling *your* strings Brooks?"

There was some anger in the words and the conversation was becoming dangerous and Phil knew that he must do something to diffuse it. He took a step towards John and his smile was gone. Deverall also met the step and the two men came close together. John had the strength and held no fear of Brooks but Brooks had knowledge and conviction. They were evenly matched. It was Brooks who spoke.

"You have been magnificent. You have risked your own life for a better society, inside and outside these walls. Many people have made it possible for you to be undetected because of your risk. They also took risks. I am telling you, from me, from them, it is over."

John sighed. He took a long look at his colleague and the anger went out of his body. It was replaced with the pain that had been ignored for the past five minutes.

Brooks looked at the man in front of him now. He seemed to weaken, get smaller, grow darker and hunched. John was in no shape to take any more news. It was a relief to put it off until another day.

* * *

Both Reynolds and Preece arrived at work early the next day and coincidently at the same time. Neither made a comment about it. They busied themselves with some trivia until the full squad was in the outer office until they found themselves alone and ready to make their decision.

Seniority demanded that Reynolds speak first.

"Well?"

There was no time for an answer. There was a knock on the door and DC Wiltshire popped his head in.

"Heads up lads, Chief Superintendent Rivers is on his way to see you again."

Preece, shaking his head, looked pleadingly at Reynolds.

"I haven't said a thing, honest!"

Rivers walked into the room smelling of fresh shirts and aftershave. He wore a large smile, carried a briefcase and as he entered the room, he took off his hat and put it under his arm.

"Good morning gentlemen!

"Good morning sir," came in unison from both.

"Lets all sit down, shall we?" When they were all seated, he continued, "Sorry to bust in on you like this but good news shouldn't be held up and I thought I would like to deliver it myself."

Reynolds and Preece looked at each other to confirm that each had no idea what he was talking about so they just kept quiet. Rivers continued.

"You two have done some excellent work here and it is time for you to share your skills with others on the force. You sergeant have been chosen to lead the Burglary team in Southampton. I am sure that very soon promotion to Detective Inspector could be on the cards."

Reynolds turned his head and looked directly at the smiling Preece.

"You too William have been reassigned. You will be working as a Detective Constable with the Robbery squad in Newcastle. Promotion may be a little further in your future but I see a good career for you in the force. You will also be closer to your mother. She will like that."

He stopped talking and looked at each man in turn. The smile never left his face. After leaving a 'sinking in' moment he stood up and became more business like.

"Now you will need to be at your new posts on Monday. That only gives you a week to get squared away. You will go now and make all the family arrangements that are necessary. What are you working on at the moment?"

Preece looked at Reynolds and the sergeant spoke.
"It's the Davies suicide at Waverly sir."

"What have you got?"
Reynolds moved over to the steel cabinet and used his key to open the door. He pulled out the yellow envelope and handed it to the officer. At that moment there was a knock on the door which immediately opened. DC Wiltshire stood there with a small stack of case files to deliver.

The smile was gone from Rivers' face.
"Who are you and what do you want?"
"I'm DC Wiltshire sir, I am just delivering more cases for DS Reynolds."
The Chief Superintendent looked straight at Reynolds as he spoke.
"DS Reynolds doesn't work here anymore."

The surprise on Wiltshire's face couldn't be contained neither could his tongue.
"Then who should I give these files to?"
Everyone looked at the Chief Superintendent.
The Chief looked at Reynolds and then to Wiltshire.
"Wiltshire, this is now *your* job. This is now *your* office. That makes these case files *your* case files. That will be all."

When the door closed there was a silent pause between all three officers but Rivers was in control.
"What are you waiting for? You have lots of plans to make, travelling arrangements, movers, accommodation to organise. You are released immediately. Off you go."

He said this with a sweep of the arm towards the door. The officers awkwardly left the room. Chief Superintendent Rivers put his hat on and set it firmly on his head. He watched the men leave the room and walk out through the squad room. Everyone was watching them. That is why no one saw him put the yellow envelope into his briefcase and snap it shut.

* * *

Brooks spent the rest of the week agonising over what he should do. If he approached John now there was no telling how he would react. If he left it too long, he might not even have the courage to talk to John about it. It had to be now, there was momentum, there was inertia. He decided to have a meeting in the morning. The morning came very quickly.

Both men met in the briefing room. He wanted to have a word in a place where there were others around that way he could count on John's reaction.
"John, can we have a quiet word sometime today?"
John Deverall closed his eyes. Here it comes, he thought, he would never be free, they had something over him and he could be reeled in whenever they wanted. He knew this would happen. He wasn't surprised. He was surprised with Brooks though. Phil was a man of his word and it was hard to believe that he would allow others to go back on their word. Perhaps they had a grip on him too. He didn't have any words to say. Saying nothing was actually an answer in itself. They would meet. Brooks would see to that. Later in the day John would look up and he would be there.

The smell of a prison changes throughout the day. At night it is quiet and smells of sweat and soap from the showers. In the morning you can get the trace of breakfast but it is mainly of bodily waste and disinfectant. Prisoners are shaving and shitting. During the rest of the day, it is body odour, disinfectant and tobacco. There is always disinfectant because there is always somebody mopping down corridors. You can always hear the metal handle rapping against a metal bucket. Tobacco is a mild escape and is popular with everyone. There is always smoke in the prison.

John stood on the top landing. He was trying to get the feel of the place, the sounds and the smells. He was straining to hear, see or smell

something out of the ordinary, something that would tell him that Brooks was near. He never got it. The first thing he heard was the voice.
"Hello John."

John almost smiled. He turned to see his friend standing not more that two meters away and he decided that he was not going to say anything. He was going to let things unfold, let Brooks sweat.
"John, I just wanted to talk to you, see how you are, see how *things* are."

When Deverall didn't speak Brooks continued.
"John look, it's not what you think. I haven't come here to involve you with anything. I just want to see how you are doing. Since …well you know. It's just that I am worried for you. I know what you have gone through in the past. You never talk about it. I just thought …"
"You are way out of line Brooks."
Phil Brooks went against all of the instincts that told him to shut up. He continued just as if he had heard the warning.
"I just thought that if you talked about those times, then things could be better for you. Believe it or not I am your friend and I want to help." He stopped. He waited.
"You don't have the right to talk to me about that. You can talk to me about work, about inmates, about other staff, but never about that. That is something that I keep to myself."
"You are wrong John, it affects me too. I see you quiet and haggard and I can't imagine what you are going through, what you must have gone through. We all see that from time to time and we keep our mouths shut and carry on. We feel that if we mention it things will only get worse so we act like nothing has happened. If there was only something I could do."
"There isn't, so just let it go."
Brooks had him talking now. John was a man of action and talking always kept him off guard. If you could keep him talking, you could slip up behind him and take him by surprise. He kept him talking.

"If there was something I could do, perhaps we could go out for a beer sometime, that might take your mind off it. Hey what about a weekend match when the team is in town? Golf, do you play golf? It's good exercise and we could talk things through."

Deverall was annoyed that the conversation was so trivial. To think that a few beers with a friend could relieve the agony and endless torment of having his daughter ripped from his life.

"Brooks you don't know what you are talking about. You can do nothing, absolutely nothing, that could make that even the slightest bit better."

Brooks had arrived at the moment.

"Not even if I were to give you the man who killed your daughter?"

* * *

It took a conscious effort from him to breathe. He couldn't speak because his vocal cords had gone into spasm. He could only hear a shrill whine in his ears. His peripheral vision had gone and his sight was filled just by the man in front of him. He was rooted to the spot and couldn't make up his mind what to do next. No one is prepared for such a moment. John Deverall's first reaction was to beat the information from this man but caution demanded he pause. It's not like reaching into a pocket and taking it. It could be withheld. What if he would never tell? Brooks had something that was more precious than anything in the world and John had to have it, but in trying to get it, he mustn't lose it.

"What?" was all that he could manage to say. He was starting to feel nauseous.

Brooks had taken a very big chance and he was counting himself lucky for getting away with the clumsy way he blurted out the information. He still felt as if he was in great danger and he needed to reassure John that he was going to tell him everything.

At a distance you could see the two men on the high landing. One talked and moved his arms and head to animate his story. The other just stood there, shoulders hunched and head lowered. Then the talking man stopped and the hunching man stood up straight. The first man reached into his pocket and pulled out a small envelope and gave it to the second who gently took it. He examined it and the contents. A small piece of jewellery on a chain. He bowed over and held it to his forehead. The first man respectfully takes several steps away as his friend convulses with grief.

* * *

Life for David Brenner in prison was uneventful. He seemed to be blessed with the ability to blend in, avoid attention. He wanted nothing and nobody wanted anything from him. He kept his mouth shut and did what he was told. The fact that he still had residual pain from the operation to restructure his jaw after the attack in the laundromat was part of the reason he didn't have long conversations!

He now had a routine and that took over his life. There was no need to think just follow the routine. It had been good to him up until now. He had just finished his lunch and was making his way back to his cell. He would lay on his bed for half an hour to let the food go down and then he would get some of the magazines out that he had hidden in between the mattresses. Shortly after that he would sleep. Usual routine for a weekday. As he walked through the door all plans were cancelled.

John Deverall was sitting at the table in the cell.
David stopped, momentarily shocked, and stepped back.
For a long moment the two men sized each other up. David searched his memory for a reason for the guard to be there. Why was he sitting there waiting for him and why was he alone. It was an irregularity for a prison guard to conduct a search alone. Was this a search? He was just sitting there, waiting.
John had prepared for this moment. He knew that he would have to restrain himself, haul back the urge to squeeze the life out of the prisoner. He knew that even then, killing wouldn't be enough, he had thoughts of dismembering and feeding the remains to vermin …. But he knew that he had to be sure first, and this was the first part of his plan.
"David Brenner?"

The question wasn't unusual. He knew only a few guards and other inmates. He wasn't familiar with this one so he wouldn't know his name. He just gave his usual one-word reply.
"Yeah."

John reached down into a sports bag that was sitting on the floor beside his foot. He pulled out a sheaf of papers and a pen and placed them on the table.
"Please sit down David."

Please? What was this? His habit of doing everything he was told to do and his curiosity moved his legs towards the chair opposite the guard who continued to speak.

"I have been looking at your record for the time you have been here, you have been a model prisoner and taking into account the nature of your offence and the time you have served we are going to see if we can get you to an open prison where you can have a better chance of rehabilitation."

Suspicion and curiosity now gone, David pulled his chair a little closer to the table. He even managed a small painful smile and let the officer speak.
"This is a government initiative and it is not offered to just anyone ... but there are conditions." The smile left David's face, John noticed it and quickly moved on to the next part of his plan. "There has to be some declaration of remorse from the prisoner. Something personal to show that they genuinely wish to make amends."
"Uh-huh"
John pulled his chair closer to the table, picked up the pen and offered it to the prisoner.
"You will have to write a brief statement, I will help you with it."

David looked at the pen and the guard in front of him. All of this seemed to be right out of the ordinary. He felt that he was being watched so he looked over his shoulder toward the door. He half expected to see other guards laughing at his expense. There were none. He turned to face the officer and took the pen.
John felt the suspicion inside the prisoner.

"If we can get a statement of intent showing that you genuinely want to change your ways and become a model citizen, I could have you out of this prison by tomorrow. By the end of this week you will be on your way, I don't know where you will be but it definitely will not be here and I guarantee that you will never have to come back here again."
"What do I say?" David adjusted the pen ready to write.
"Let's start with a statement showing that you have been thinking about what you have done in the past. You have been thinking about your crimes, haven't you?"

David nodded.

"Just write this …. Ever since I was sent to prison, I have been thinking about what I did in the past …." David wrote slowly and John waited for him to catch up.

"I feel that I will never… be able to… pay back… for the crimes I have done."

David looked up. John immediately spoke.

"This means that you feel that while you are in prison here you don't have the opportunity to make amends. If you were in a different place, you could perhaps start to learn a trade or skill that would do the community some good… some pay back."

David seemed reassured.

"Would you like a beer?" John reached down into his bag and brought out a can of beer and offered it to David. Suspicion immediately returned to his face.

"I thought it might make this process a little easier."

It had been a long time since David had alcohol so he gingerly took the can and pulled the ring on the top. He took a long, thirst-quenching drink, from the can. His system was at first a little surprised but then remembered an old friend.

"OK… Let's go on to say …So I am doing this… to make amends."

David never looked up. He took another drink from the can and John sat back in his chair. "I want to go to a better place… where I can be free… from my past."

David took another long drink from the can which emptied it. He put empty can down. John continued to dictate. "I hope everyone will understand why I did this…"

John reached into the bag and pulled out another can. David momentarily looked up from his writing when John pulled the ring and placed the can on the table. David reached for it but John stopped him with a word.

"Wait."

The two men looked at each other for a moment. John held his hand on top of the can.

"You can have this one when we finish your statement. Now, write this… When I have gone… I hope that I… will be able to… leave all of my sins…"

David looked up again. John caught the look.

"I know it sounds a bit religious but they like that sort of thing." He smiled.

David smiled too, and continued to write. John continued to speak.

"… behind me… I have always… been bothered… no, … tormented… by my past… and doing this… might set me free."

John pushed the can towards the prisoner.

David looked at it, finished his writing and took the beer. He took a long drink.

John sat and looked at him. His demeanour had changed but he was still fighting the beast inside. The beast wanted to leap out and trample this animal. He knew that whatever he did wouldn't be enough. It would never be enough.

"Just end with goodbye and sign it. Say goodbye because I can guarantee that you will be out of here by tomorrow."

David eagerly did what he was told. He was in a very good mood. His alcohol starved system had reacted to the drinks and he was a little merry. He took another long drink from the can and sat back in his chair. The men looked at each other for a long and awkward time. John just sitting there and David slouched in his chair on the brink of giggling. It was David who broke the silence.

"What happens now?"

"First you lose the use of your legs."

It was spoken calmly, matter of factly.

David couldn't make any sense of it. It was a statement out of place.

"What?"

"You lose the use of your legs. The drug I placed in your drink should be taking effect now and you first lose the use of your legs and other motor control."

David couldn't move. He couldn't stand up or shift his weight in the chair. He couldn't speak, his lips would not form any words correctly.

"Then you lose the ability to speak."

David watched the guard collect up the papers and the pen and place them in the bag. He watched because that was all that he could do. The guard poured the last of the drink down the sink and wiped the cans with toilet paper.

John went over to the prisoner and hauled him over to the bed, laying him on his back and positioning his head so he could be in view all of the time. He then pulled up a chair to the bed and leaned over the prisoner.

"The drug you now have inside you takes a long time to do its job so I can take my time. There is no return for you. No antidote. Let me tell you a little about myself. My name is John Deverall. Ring a bell? No? Let me remind you then. I had a little girl once."
His voice became rough and the beast inside him was clamouring to be released. It would never be enough.
"She was a sweet little defenceless thing. She was abducted, tortured and murdered. She visits me every time I fall asleep and I try to protect her but I just can't do it there. In the dream I can't do anything. The only place I can do anything is *here*."

David couldn't feel his legs or arms and he was starting to develop a headache. His vision was starting to blur around the edges and there was a low humming sound behind everything in his ears.

"Here in the real world, I can do something. Now, you kept a diary of press cuttings didn't you David. That alone wouldn't make me do this. There are sick bastards out there who do that sort of thing but that isn't proof is it?"
The pain in his head worsened, the tunnel vision increased but he could still see and hear the guard in front of him.
"There was one piece of damning evidence you had, something only the murderer could have had." He reached in his pocket, pulled out the chain and held it directly into David's line of vision.
"This was my daughter's chain and pendant. You took her life from this world and now you pay for it with yours."

The pain was almost physical now but he couldn't move his hands to clutch his head. He could still see the guard standing there, arms at his side with a small sparkling piece of jewellery catching the light. The pain soared, his vision moved further into the tunnel until the light went out.

John Deverall stood there until David Brenner's eyes rolled up into his head and his breathing stopped. He took the first can of beer, pressed David's cold fingers to it and placed it on the table. He took out the pen and written note and placed them on the table. There was nothing else to do so he just left the cell. When the door closed behind him so also did a part of his life.

* * *

She sat there in the sunshine playing with the tufts of grass and the little flowers. The scene was full of colour, warmth and aroma. This was like nothing ever before, it was real. For a moment he believed it, but he knew that if he tried to take too much from it, then it would end. She looked at him and smiled.
"Isn't it a lovely day daddy?"
"Oh yes," he heard himself say, "It is a wonderful day."

There were no clouds, no threats, no stranger on the hill far away.
Helen came close to him and he could see straight into her innocent eyes. Eyes that hadn't learned anything yet. Eyes that never had the chance to widen at the wonders of the world or the scary tales her parents could have told her. Those eyes would never feel the joy of parents love or fill with tears of glee at a birthday party. John could only see what could have been or what was missing and that always made him sad. She always saw that too.
"You are sad again daddy, why?"
"I miss you sweetheart. I miss what I could have done for you, what we could have had." His voice started to fail so she stilled him with her own. "I remember you daddy, all my life was filled with you. You are in my every thought and when I want to be special happy, I think of you. When I see you here, we always get sad. That isn't going to happen anymore. No more sadness anymore."
Helen looked down at his hand and she reached for it.
He pulled back because he wasn't ready to end this moment. She persisted and found his withdrawn hand and held it.

He held his breath.

Her hand was warm and tiny in his. How could her fingers be so small? They both looked at their hands clasped together. He was filled with warmth, her warmth, and strength too, and calmness. All of these feelings were somehow being transferred in this moment.
"Its OK now daddy, I am safe. I can play with the others and every day will be a wonderful day. There is no danger here anymore. Thank you."

John looked at his daughter and somehow felt good. She was in no danger anymore, he needn't worry. She let go of his hand and stood there very close to him and the exhaustion left his body. He heard her voice on the other side of his closed eyes.
"I love you daddy."
"I love you too Helen."
He didn't wake, he was being woken. It was an air stewardess.

"We are coming in to land now, please put your seat in an upright position."
She moved on and he regained his composure. He took stock of his surroundings, sat back and mused.

His early retirement was a surprise to him and even more of a surprise was how quickly it was arranged and the overwhelmingly generous terms he was offered. He sold his flat in record time at a record price. Even the estate agent couldn't believe it.

Brooks had offered him his Spanish property as a place to stay for as long as he liked and with the amount of money he now had in the bank he was going to look for a small property in the sun, near the sea. He craved sunshine and warmth.
While passing through Pablo Picasso Airport in Malaga, every tourist has their picture taken by an optimistic photographer. When you leave you are offered the picture to buy as a memento of your visit.

John Deverall was no exception.

*   *   *   *   *   *

His shoes were made of finest leather and the heels were hard. They made a rich rapping noise on the ancient tiles of the members lobby in the Palace of Westminster. His pace is steady, determined but not rushed. The shoes belong to a man in an expensive Saville Row suit and he looks comfortable in it. He is used to such things.

He looks straight ahead, he knows exactly where he is going. At the end of a hallway he finally ends up at a large wooden door. It is carved, dark and very old. He raps on the door three times. Two quickly then one by itself. From behind the door comes a voice.

"Come."

He pushes the door open to reveal a man sitting behind a desk. The man does not look up, he doesn't need to. He knows exactly who has just entered because of the style of the knock. After closing the door behind him the man speaks.
"Good morning, Minister, I have some news for you."

The Minister looks up from his papers and over the top of his glasses.
"What is it?"
"He has arrived in Spain." The man moves closer to the desk and from a file held under his arm he produces an envelope and places it on the desk. The Minister opens the envelope and looks at pictures of John Deverall walking across the concourse at the airport, hailing a taxi and sitting on the patio of a summer house. He collects all of the photographs and puts them back in the envelope

"Very good, thank you. That will be all."
The man turns to leave the office but the Minister has one last thing to say. Without looking up from the papers he has started to read again, he speaks.
"Leave the file will you?"
The man looks at the file, smiles and says, "Yes, of course Minister."
He leaves, and the sound of his heels can be heard diminishing with distance.

The Minister puts down his papers and looks at the file on his desk. As he stands up, he picks up the file and moves to the other side of the office.

Three selected points on the dial open the safe and he places the file next to the deeds for a flat, a bright yellow police file, a scrap book full of faded newspaper clippings and an envelope which once contained a child's necklace that held a solid silver letter 'H'.

* * *

E N D

Have you enjoyed reading SCREWED?
Please leave a review on Amazon. I read every review
and they help new readers discover my books.
Thanks … Steve